Sign up for our newsletter to hear
about new and upcoming releases.

www.ylva-publishing.com

Other Books by Lee Winter

On the Record series

The Red Files
Under Your Skin

The Superheroine Collection

Shattered

Standalone

Hotel Queens
Changing the Script
Breaking Character
The Brutal Truth
Requiem for Immortals

SLICED ICE

LEE WINTER'S ICONIC ICE QUEENS
DELICIOUS SHORT-STORY SEQUELS

LEE WINTER

Table of Contents

Introduction

When Ylva first suggested the idea of a short story collection, I was over the moon. My short stories have always been scattered to the winds, some tucked away in a clutch of anthologies; others available only to my newsletter subscribers, and one has never appeared anywhere before.

To bring all ten together is so satisfying. I love that, finally, all three of my *Brutal Truth* short stories can rub shoulders in the same place. And, for the first time, I can unveil a short story from the *Hotel Queens* universe, about a certain popular CEO sex fantasies goddess and her most unexpected client.

All these stories were so much fun to write, and I'm delighted to be able to share them with you all.

Five Times Felicity Met Elena

Twenty-three

Felicity Simmons is twenty-three, a junior legal associate, professionally ambitious, personally miserable, and entirely straight, thank you very much.

It's rather odd how vigorously that last fact jumps into her head as she reviews the icy woman opposite her. Elena Bartell. Media mogul. So-called Tiger Shark. Devourer of failing newspapers that get strip-mined for her burgeoning empire.

Today, Bartell is overseeing the takeover of yet another small print masthead. And Felicity's team, led by her boss, is negotiating—disastrously—on behalf of the minnow of a paper to secure a decent deal. Felicity supposes she should be more concerned by how badly they're doing.

Instead, she's staring.

Power exudes from Elena's compact form, making her beautiful in the way of a predatory panther. Short jet-black hair is slicked around her pale face. Elena's piercing blue eyes roam restlessly, dismissing her competition with contempt. Yet for all her unnerving presence, the woman says little, leaving the legal white noise to a phalanx of cloned, gray-suited males on either side of her.

Felicity's never been more impressed in her life. If she wants to make partner, and Felicity *really* does, she should pay attention to impressive women like this.

Much later, when they're back at the office and her boss is chugging antacid like frat party beer, all she can recall clearly of that meeting is the godawful mustard yellow carpet in the newspaper's boardroom…and Bartell's victorious smirk.

For the briefest of moments, it occurs to Felicity she might not be entirely straight after all, when that taunting smile sticks in her mind on a loop. But that is entirely ridiculous. You can admire a woman's power and beauty without wanting to run your fingers down her shapely arms, drop kisses under her proud chin, or take her pink, perfect earlobe into your mouth and run your tongue *all* over it. Obviously.

Twenty-five

The next time Felicity sees Elena, Felicity is a senior legal associate, working on her first ulcer, and keeping herself together with cigarettes, coffee, and willpower.

She's still totally straight, not that anyone's asking, and so busy she can't even remember the last time she went on a date—so it's all rather a moot point.

On that note, her friends think she should try Tinder. "Friends" is a loose term for her regular Starbucks servers—the only people she sees often enough to form any sort of a lasting attachment with. And she is deeply, deeply attached to her Caffè Americano.

She's not going to try Tinder. Well, not before she's made a partner. Her focus on her goals is steely, sharp, and distraction-free—something she picked up from studying a certain someone else.

Elena Bartell's not hard to study these days. Business profiles on her are now appearing regularly in national papers, examining Bartell Corp's transformation, seemingly out of nothing, into a publishing behemoth.

Gone is the surprised undertone about the steepness and suddenness of her brilliant career trajectory. Instead, there is now grudging respect about her acumen and net worth, and the reports are tinged with wonder as to what will follow. Felicity herself has been wondering the same thing rather a lot lately.

Felicity's firm is once again representing a newspaper's interests against the ambitions of the Tiger Shark. This paper's only middle-sized, but it's important. It has a long history, real heritage, and means something to the locals. So it's vital that Felicity's firm pulls off a miracle and gets the newspaper an excellent deal that will keep it running close to its current form. Sometimes Elena allows that—she'll reorganize papers instead of gutting them if she thinks bad management is all that's preventing them from turning a healthy profit.

As Felicity slides into a leather chair in the conference room, she's hopeful for the paper's loyal readers that today's the day her boss earns his six-figure salary and does his damned job.

It isn't to be. Once again, Hank is getting mauled as if someone tossed an antelope into the lion enclosure. This time, though, it's Elena shredding and twisting his arguments with his own verbal intestines. She's not even a lawyer. Her burgeoning confidence and expertise are brilliant to watch—too bright to stare directly at, impossible to look away from.

God, Hank is useless.

Felicity tries to help of course, shoving urgent notes across to her boss to bolster his weak arguments at critical moments.

Each time she does, Elena shoots her a knowing look.

And each time, Hank ignores Felicity's assistance and tosses her an annoyed glance.

Surely the intellectually stunted egotist will be getting his useless ass fired soon? Anyone who nukes an important deal this badly would have to cause a reshuffle. Then Felicity's excellence will be recognized. She should make partner by thirty.

She has it all mapped out. She has everything mapped out now. She's even started diction lessons with Mrs. Allsop to sound the part and scrape any last traces of Pinckney, Michigan, from her lips. Felicity *will* be ready.

The meeting breaks up with a lopsided deal and another triumphant smirk. It's all too easy for Elena apparently, and she can't be bothered hiding it.

Well. The mockery *is* deserved.

Felicity's boss is bowed as he gathers his paperwork and shoots Elena a hateful stare.

She ignores him and clears her throat. "A word, Ms. Simmons?"

Felicity almost drops her own folders and frowns. What could the Tiger Shark possibly want with a lowly associate?

Elena perches on the edge of the boardroom table, her pinstripe skirt riding up just a little, and waits as the room empties out of men in near-identical business suits. Once they're alone, Elena leans in. "Your client might have won today if you'd run that meeting."

Despite being in full agreement, Felicity folds her arms. "We didn't lose. We negotiated a mutually beneficial deal."

"Mutually beneficial?" Elena's voice contains mockery laced with humor. "Sure it was. And if you believe that, you're not the woman I take you for." She slides smoothly to her feet, pivots, and saunters off with a jaunty sway of hips.

Dear God. Felicity makes a mental note to buy a pinstripe skirt suit if that's the effect they have.

Back at their own office, Hank asks what Bartell wanted.

"To gloat," Felicity murmurs. Although, she's not so sure. Her hormones do a delighted little quiver at the reminder of that badass suit.

Totally straight, she reminds herself. Of course she is.

Twenty-eight

Felicity's now older, seasoned—well…jaded—starting to question her partner prospects, and trying to quit stress-smoking. Peering into the mirror of the Ladies Room just off from the Park Hyatt's main ballroom, Felicity wonders whether her fourteen-hour days are starting to show. She prods the darkening skin under her eyes for answers.

A stall door opens, and familiar, taunting eyes lock with hers in the mirror. Their owner glides over to the marble sink and washes her hands.

"Ms. Simmons, we meet again," Elena purrs.

It's a complete mystery to Felicity how this woman is called a shark when she's clearly pure jungle cat, with the lethal, rapier claws to match. She's sleek, sensuous, powerful…

Felicity blinks. Now's hardly the time to reevaluate her sexuality. She has a boyfriend and everything. Tim. No…*Tom.* Christ!

Elena's watching her, waiting for an answer.

"Congratulations on your Businessperson of the Year award tonight." Felicity winces at how stiff she sounds. She reaches for her lipstick and rolls out the crimson. "That's impressive."

"It's meaningless. Bartell Corp is a hundred-foot-high tsunami, impossible to ignore, so they feel obligated to throw awards and other such nonsense at me. I'm more interested in that award you were up for last month. A shame you missed out. You were robbed."

Felicity detests compliments. The awkwardness of having to appear grateful while she works out why they're being offered makes her hyperventilate. She'll be up all night picking over this one. "I'm sure Jason Hampton deserved it more." She grits her teeth.

Like hell he does. The New York Law Journal*'s Rising Star Award? Please. No contest.*

The objective truth is that Felicity has had one hell of a year. Even her boss admitted as much as he turned her down for a promotion.

"You don't seriously believe that he was more deserving?" Elena's eyebrows lift.

Felicity hesitates. Sometimes it's hard being careful not to look too ambitious, too smart, too immodest… She glances around, checking they're alone. "No. I deserved it."

"There now." Elena's eyes glitter. "That wasn't so hard, was it?" She sways into Felicity's space. "Claim your worth, Ms. Simmons. And when you finally give up on waiting to be appreciated, call me. I can make far better use of your talent than your firm." She opens her clutch and flips an embossed pearl business card onto the counter.

Felicity's mouth falls open, but she can't think of a single thing to say.

"Look, I know those men," Elena continues, meeting Felicity's gaze in the mirror. Her expression is intense and knowing but, for once, not mocking. "They'll never let you into their boys' club. You'll never be a partner there. No matter how many hoops you jump through, no matter how impressive your CV, or how you straighten out your Midwest vowels."

She noticed that? Her lessons with Mrs. Allsop have been coming along well, sanitizing any hint of Felicity's unflattering origins, which she prefers not to dwell on. In truth, she borders perilously close to sounding like Julie Andrews these days if she doesn't watch herself. *Spit bloody spot.*

Wait, never be a partner? Her head snaps up.

Elena almost smiles. "Sore point?" She waves at Felicity's fingers as she leaves.

Startled, Felicity looks down. Lipstick has snapped off in her hand—a crime scene of crimson debris spread across skin and sink.

Felicity sighs. She glances over to Elena's card, in two minds about whether to bin it or frame it.

Twenty-nine

The fourth time Felicity sees Elena, she's twenty-nine, still not a partner—a fact which grates constantly given how close she is to her personal deadline—and the jury is out on her sexuality.

She's been having dreams for which she's hard-pressed to find a heterosexual explanation. That's not to say she isn't still interested in men. She is. But she can't tally that up next to muddled, erotic meanderings involving dark hair and blue eyes belonging to high-cheekboned faces that aren't rough in the least.

Could just be the stress.

Probably all it is.

Tonight Felicity's at a glamorous but oddball LA event to launch some blog for Hollywood movers and shakers. A *blog*, for heaven's sake. But due to the powerful, triple A-list guest list, it's been purloined as *the* must-attend networking extravaganza for anyone associated with the print, social media, or entertainment industry. So that includes herself, her boss, and several lawyer colleagues who handle takeovers and mergers for newspapers all over the US.

Hank has dragged his team here tonight in the quest to win over a normally reclusive online news CEO's multi-million-dollar legal business. Even from halfway across the room, Felicity can already tell he's going to crash and burn so badly.

It's a white-themed ball, and the organizers apparently have no qualms about making their guests snow-blind. At least the men in white tuxes look sublime, especially the one who's just sauntered in as though auditioning to play a Hollywood prince. *So much jaw.*

Felicity's dormant-of-late hormones give a little purr of approval. *There. Still firmly heterosexual, thank you very much.* She almost sags in relief.

Tonight Felicity's wearing her favorite gown, a floor-length cream de la Renta that cost her six months' salary and only *just* lets her breathe. It's a good thing she lives on a perpetual carb-free diet. With her pinned-up, long blond hair and teardrop pearl earrings, she's well aware she looks more than acceptable—at least if her useless boss's speculative gazes are any indication.

Her teeth grind. Why the hell is Hank still her boss? She's saved his pitiful ass more times than she can count, and he never acknowledges her aside from empty promises to make it up to her come promotion time.

Every single time he says those words, she tries to believe in him. *Needs to.* Christ, she's like a slot machine addict, too frightened to walk away from the machine she's invested so much in, in case it's about to pay out the jackpot a minute later.

Felicity thinks back to the embossed pearl business card stuck to her fridge back home in her Manhattan apartment. Every now and then, when she's at her lowest, Felicity reminds herself of the time a publishing goddess saw her worth.

She straightens. Well, maybe Hank could shock her completely and do the right thing soon. The company is due to pick a new partner this year. So maybe he'll…

Felicity throws back a gulp of dry martini. *Sure he will.* She's being a fool most likely, but she is committed to seeing her "law partner by thirty" plan through.

She needs air. And a cigarette. Even though she's quit.

The first hotel balcony she comes to involves a jungle's worth of potted trees and a glimpse of two women she can't make out too well in a steamy clinch. Typical for a publishing ball—add alcohol to uptight, stressed-out media types trying too hard to dominate in their field, and they're bound to get smashed and fuck in dark corners.

The next balcony is quieter, only one inhabitant. It's likely a fellow smoker, so Felicity enters and closes the French doors behind her. Her cigarette is lit, and she's halfway to the railing when she realizes who she's joining. She freezes, eyes wide, just as Elena Bartell turns to eye her.

A stunning black organza flowing gown greets Felicity, and it shimmers with the movement. The dress highlights Elena's jet-black hair and brings out shadows under her cheekbones, giving her the look of a classy European model. The deep vee of her cleavage is…well…as hard to miss as it is spectacular.

"Sorry to intrude. I'll go." Felicity's mouth is suddenly dry. She's not sure how she feels about her sexuality jury being out again.

"It's fine, Ms. Simmons. You stay." Elena glances at Felicity's lit cigarette, and her lips press together. "I'll go."

"No." Felicity says quickly. She stubs out her cigarette. "I'm trying to quit anyway. It's a cheater's way to stress relief."

"Hmm." Elena's amused gaze fixes on her. "You need a hobby then, if your job is stressful enough to drive you to an early grave. And by hobby, I mean more than just elocution lessons."

Felicity doesn't bother to deny the lessons. "I'm going to be a partner soon." Does she sound confident? She hopes so. "No time for hobbies."

"*Sure* you are." Elena's voice is pure cynical drawl.

"Well *you* don't have any hobbies," Felicity retorts, irritated at being mocked. It's just a guess of course, but how could Elena fit any in between building up her media empire and smashing any tawdry little rags she deems unworthy?

"Is that so?" Elena cocks her head. "For all you know, I could be the drummer in an indie band."

It takes Felicity a full minute to register the joke for what it is because her brain has just fritzed at the mere idea of Elena Bartell doing something as lowbrow as *that.*

Elena laughs. "Your face." She shakes her head the tiniest amount, then becomes serious. "It's true; empire building doesn't leave me much free time. Especially now."

There's a gleam in her eyes, something there, something she wants to talk about. Felicity can almost smell it. "What are you working on?" she prods.

"Something…special. International. I've been in LA all week talking to a few backers." Pride and excitement light Elena's eyes. "My project is going forward at last."

"Specifically?"

"Why do you want to know?"

Because everything you do is larger than life. You're astonishing. Ruthless. Powerful. I want to be like you. "Curiosity."

"Ah." Elena's eyes cloud over. "An itch to scratch." She seems disappointed in the answer.

Regret floods Felicity, and she wonders what she should have said. Before she can think of something else to say, something better, Elena sighs and glances out over the darkened view.

Felicity stares down too. Not much to see. Headlights and taillights of cars and cabs whizzing by in orange and red trails. Lots of bright, flashy, fluorescent signs and tourist lures.

"I came out here for fresh air," Elena says suddenly. "Well, and to escape the endless sycophants."

"I don't think you'll find much fresh air in LA," Felicity notes.

"No," Elena murmurs in agreement. "A tactical error on my part."

"You don't make many of them." Felicity intends her words to sound dry, but they come out awed. She cringes.

"Didn't I just mention I was trying to escape the sycophants?"

Felicity bristles. "It was an honest observation, not an attempt to curry favor."

"Mm. Perhaps. It's hard for me to tell these days." Elena sighs and gives the view a morose look.

"Tell me about your big project?" Felicity tries again.

"Why?"

"So I can see if I'm right." She smiles. "About you not making many tactical errors. Or whether this is the first." Oh, that's cheeky. She can't believe she even said that. The impudence of her, lowly lawyer Felicity Simmons, daring to judge Elena Bartell's grand schemes. She can't believe her own fucking audacity. Felicity's heart starts thumping faster.

Elena's eyes narrow into slits. "I'm starting an international fashion magazine to rival *CQ* and *Vogue*. It will be extraordinary in scale and content. So, Ms. Simmons, do tell me all about your *extensive* expert knowledge in fashion and magazines that will enable you to determine the success of my new project. I'm all ears."

There's real bite to her tone, and it contains that vicious, mocking sarcasm she sometimes adopts when she's filleting Felicity's boss. She only uses it when someone's dared suggest she's less than excellent at her job.

"You're right," Felicity concedes. "I'm not an expert. But why fashion? Bartell Corp's all about news. It's what you excel at." She can't help the trace of skepticism that leaks at the idea of Elena's corporation dipping its toe into *fashion.*

"You really don't know?"

"Know what?"

"I take it back—you're not a sycophant."

"As I told you…"

"You're worse. You lounge around and poke at sharks, blithely unaware of their natures."

"What does that mean?"

"It means, Ms. Simmons, you should do your research before making a fool of yourself and questioning my expertise." Elena's gaze drifts over Felicity's shoulder to the party beyond. "Ah. I see Richard's deigned to appear," she murmurs almost to herself. "I should mingle. I'll leave you to your…bad habits." She waves at the stubbed-out cigarette still clutched in Felicity's fingers.

Felicity follows Elena's gaze and sees a white-tuxedoed form through the French doors. *Jesus. She's with the perfect-jawed prince?*

Richard's eyes are sharp and interested, devouring Elena's cleavage. As Elena glances down at the handle to open the doors, Richard's gaze slides surreptitiously over to rake Felicity's body too.

Christ. What a catch.

Half an hour later, Felicity is slamming down cocktails, in a proper mood, while her colleague, Larissa, is talking her ear off about environmental law and the caterer's "sublime" cheese canapés.

Felicity's tuned out, having little interest in either topic. No one has accused her of being a fool in her entire life. That barb stings and stings.

Larissa suddenly leans over and curls a loose strand of blonde hair around Felicity's ear. "Want to clear out of here? You, me, and your hotel room?" Her smile is pure mischief.

"I…what?" Felicity's head snaps up. "I'm not…" *What? What aren't I?* "I like men."

"You can like both, you know." Larissa's eyes are laughing. "Bi's an actual thing."

That thought freezes Felicity in surprise, given she's never considered it about herself.

"Don't you like me?" Larissa thrusts her cleavage in Felicity's direction, and Felicity has to admit it is surprisingly appealing. "I always thought you did."

"I rather do." *There.* Felicity flings back the rest of her drink and wonders what's possessing her to be so honest with herself. But it would be rather nice to get Elena out of her head for a little while. Infuriating woman.

An hour later, Felicity is orgasmically sated and *re*-reevaluating her sexuality. This is getting irksome. She's almost thirty. Shouldn't she know basic sexuality stuff about herself by now? Felicity reviews her situation. She's naked, sweaty, postcoital, and rather enjoying Larissa's wandering fingers, which seem to have a sixth sense for all Felicity's erogenous zones.

"Saw you talking to the Tiger Shark earlier tonight," Larissa murmurs. "She's looking fine. Her outfit is perfection. But that figures, doesn't it?"

That gets Felicity's attention. "Why do you say that?"

"Don't you know who she was before she founded Bartell Corp?"

"I…no?"

"She was being lined up to be the youngest editor of *CQ* magazine; hell, she was going to be even bigger than Anna Wintour."

"You're joking."

"Oh no, back in the day, Elena Bartell used to live and breathe nothing but fashion magazines."

The hell? None of the business profiles ever mention that. The finance journalists only ever focus on Bartell Corp and its news-based beginnings. Felicity pauses. The *all-male* finance journalists…who probably think a onetime dalliance in fashion glossies is either too embarrassing to mention or not worthy of the column space.

I'm starting a national fashion magazine.

Elena's words replay in Felicity's mind, along with the way she uttered them. So much pride in her eyes. Her ambitious plan is to go back to her first love, to her fashion roots. And what does Felicity do? Imply she's an out-of-depth rookie trying a risky venture.

Felicity has been foolish indeed. "How do you know all this?"

"Isn't it obvious?" Larissa laughs. "I have the hots for her. She's my celebrity free pass. I do a *lot* of research on her."

"Oh." Felicity's face heats up. She's trying very hard not to think of Elena in such a blatantly sexual way. That would be…impolite.

"Round two?" Larissa suggests. Her brown eyes darken. She rolls over onto Felicity and presses her bare, beautiful tits into Felicity's much smaller ones. "You interested in more fun, beautiful?"

Felicity swallows, then nods. This is the most sex she's had in years, and she's not about to say no. But there's something else hammering away at the back of her brain now. She tries to figure it out as best she can as Larissa slides her sure hand between their bodies and finds Felicity's heat.

Oh God. That feels good.

Larissa is sensual, attentive, and beautiful, with dark, short hair and sparkling eyes. She's someone to fuck through the bed as if there's no tomorrow. Now Larissa's fingers are inside Felicity, and Felicity rocks against them, moaning. Oh, this is so, so good. When has it ever been so good? Larissa's perfect. So lovely.

A shame her eyes aren't blue.

What an odd thought to have.

Felicity comes hard against those thrusting fingers, pressing her mouth into Larissa's, and nips Larissa's bottom lip in playful thanks for a most acceptable orgasm.

Rolling off her, Felicity lies back and languidly trails her fingertips over all that soft, supple skin. Arousal flares again, and she pictures all the ways she'll take Larissa next—when she catches her breath.

A flash of engaging blue eyes darts into mind, and a smirking face to go with them. Felicity's seen these eyes so many times in her fevered dreams.

A clear, perfect picture forms of one Elena Bartell.

Oh. Oh hell.

Thirty

It's time. Time Felicity admits some inconvenient truths. One, she's failed at her plans to be a partner by thirty. Two, she's galled to find Elena knows Felicity's firm better than she does. Three, Elena's sexy as hell, and Felicity can no longer deny it. And four, the big one, Felicity's now honest enough to acknowledge her bisexuality, at least to herself, although she doesn't plan on sharing. Ever. It's no one's damned business.

There've been a few…dalliances…in recent months. Although, lusting for straight women with sharp blue eyes and ebony hair is an absolute no-fly zone. That much Felicity's damned clear on. She's careful to have never made that lapse again.

Still, it doesn't hurt to look. And right now, Felicity's eyes are fixated on the back of Elena's head, where the woman is sitting in the front row at a writer's festival.

Felicity, who's waiting to hear a feminist historical writer she's liked ever since the woman did a guest lecture at Felicity's college, almost face-plants at the sight of Elena. She tunes out the author on stage and wonders why she's so startled to see Elena here. Felicity never expects to see her business hero outside of boardrooms and industry balls. But why wouldn't a woman who is in the business of words go to a writer's festival?

The author on stage is a sandy-haired man with wire glasses and a thoughtful expression. He oozes a sort of rumpled haplessness, like a puppy left out in the rain. He's handsome in a nonthreatening way.

Felicity would gladly ignore him and head for the next tent to fill in time before her preferred writer turns up, but she's too puzzled as to why Elena's interested in this unassuming man to leave.

What possible allure can he have? Elena's dedicated to power and conquest and success. Not only that but she's brilliant at it. Yet here she sits, absorbing the words of a mediocre author of a book about toads as a metaphor for modern politics, which became a surprise hit.

Then, he says it: A media mogul joke. Not even a clever one.

The crowd titters.

He follows it up with a cutting dig about corporate media and those who run it, likening them to Medusa, she of the hissing head of snakes. As he does so, he looks directly at Elena.

What on earth? This whiny, mocking little wastrel unfit to tie Elena's boots clearly means his barbs for her, and he wants everyone watching him to know it. For all Elena's enemies and rivals, not one has ever had the audacity to imply she hasn't deserved her success. Well, not for many years now. And this foppish fool *dares*?

Suddenly, every time Hank has ever dismissed Felicity's intellect or excellence flashes into mind. Every pitiful, mediocre imbecile who's ever put her down, used her work without crediting her, or slithered into the jobs she's earned fills her thoughts. And Felicity's talents aren't even close to the blinding brilliance that is Elena Bartell, international media legend. Yet some snickering, third-rate, man-child gets to make fun of her as if he's even worthy of being in the same universe as her?

Without thinking, Felicity shoots to her feet and strides toward the stage, blasting out a furious diatribe comparing his paltry writing career to that of a go-getting media entrepreneur's. Just a generic entrepreneur, of course. No one specific.

"In conclusion," Felicity finishes, voice rising to a lashing snarl, "two-bit hacks wearing unironic plaid don't get to judge anyone!"

So there.

The crowd's booing now. Yes, well, he's the invited guest; she's a heckler. Fair point.

As a security guard makes his way up the aisle, she makes good her escape. Elbowing her way to the exit amid further boos, her cheeks still burning from her rant, Felicity's unsure whether it's wise to look at Elena.

She sneaks a peek anyway. The briefest flash of surprise is the only emotion on Elena's face before her cool mask swallows it whole.

Outside the writer's tent, Felicity takes a few deep breaths, bums a cigarette from a passing patron, and considers what she's done. She's incredulous. She *never* makes a scene. Certainly not over something that doesn't matter to her one bit. Who cares why mundane writers toss grenades at successful businesswomen?

Felicity suddenly stares at her unlit cigarette in confusion. Hasn't she given up smoking? Apparently not.

"Why, Ms. Simmons, you appear to have offended my husband."

Felicity's head snaps up.

Elena is eying her curiously, arms folded.

"Husband?" But wasn't she on with white-tux man?

"Well, *ex*-husband. Spencer and I were incompatible for a vast number of reasons. I think you nailed quite a few of them." Elena smirks. "To think I was beginning to give up on you. Your potential."

"I…what?"

"Finally speaking your mind? In front of witnesses no less? Standing up for what you believe in? That's something I need from a chief of staff. And you need a new job. It cannot possibly be fulfilling watching junior, less-talented colleagues stealing your promotions."

The careless comment burns like acid. Of course Elena would know about that. Felicity's boss has been offering placating, condescending platitudes to her for weeks since she lost her partnership to an underling while Felicity's blood slowly boils.

She should have known. Hell, Elena knew. She's known for years. "Is this your 'I told you so'?" Felicity asks suspiciously.

"No. It's my job offer."

"I'm a lawyer…not anything else."

"You'd make a better chief of staff. You're smart, organized, and know the law better than most of my suits." Elena cocks her head. "Tell me something: Did you keep my business card? Or rip it up in a fit of misplaced loyalty to your mediocre little firm?"

It's still on Felicity's fridge door. She's been thinking about that card a lot lately, to be honest, wondering whether the opportunity to call Elena is long gone. She'd assumed it was, given how Elena had put her in her place last time they'd met.

Felicity doesn't answer, not willing to let the woman know she matters so much as to have had her card in pride of place on Felicity's fridge all this time.

Elena apparently doesn't require a response. "I'm planning a global media revolution." Her blue eyes are glinting at the prospect. "Want in?"

"Why me?" Felicity croaks in astonishment.

"I see you, Ms. Simmons…*Felicity*. You're ready. It's long overdue, wouldn't you say?"

Thirty-six

Felicity sees Elena Bartell daily. And each day, Elena looks at Felicity, challenges her, and tells her, not in so many words, that she's valuable.

They're taking over the media world together.

Felicity's stress levels haven't improved from her old job, given idiots and incompetence still surround her, but her satisfaction has. Hundreds of lawyers all across the world now have to answer to Felicity if they want to deal with the impenetrable Elena Bartell.

Felicity's old boss is one of them. She takes a perverse delight in taking Hank's calls and explaining in detail just how busy Elena is while they're conquering the world. It's petty, yes, but Elena did tell Felicity she needs a hobby.

Felicity snorts to herself. She probably needs a better hobby. Maybe she should call Larissa back for another hookup. Or even Tim. Or was it Tom?

"Felicity, pull up the contract on *Hudson Metro News*," Elena calls out to her from her glass office. "Time we think big."

That little flea-bitten boot-scraping of a newspaper? How is that thinking big? Curiosity floods Felicity. She's been to its waterlogged, smelly nether reaches near the Hudson River, and there's nothing remotely revolutionary nor interesting about the commuter rag.

But Elena is often mysterious about such things. She rarely explains much, so Felicity never knows what her boss is up to next—her mind whirs far beyond that of mere mortals. Felicity's sure that whatever it is, her plan will be exceptional.

It doesn't matter that Elena doesn't confide in her, she reminds herself. It's just good being this close to the action.

Felicity's thirty-six, has quit smoking, is professionally satisfied, and is thoroughly bisexual, thank you very much.

She never did make partner.

And now she no longer cares.

Want to continue the journey? What happens when the seemingly straight media mogul, Elena Bartell, meets a cute, blunt, slightly eccentric reporter from Australia working at *Hudson Metro News*? Find out in *The Brutal Truth* by Lee Winter.

Aliens of New York

Maddie Grey took a centering breath and tried to suppress her nerves. She could do this. This was just a book launch, right? Just some random collection of the blogs she'd written while homesick and miserable as a graveyard-shift reporter more than two years ago.

She gazed out the window at the New York streets below. In her mind, she was back at her old *Hudson Metro News* office, staring down at the bagel streetcart, suicidal bicycle couriers, and snaking yellow cabs with their winking red taillights.

This was where she'd first tried to make it as a reporter since arriving from Sydney. She was standing on the exact spot she'd failed.

Of course, it was all different now. Her struggling commuter rag had been gobbled up by Bartell Corporation, then knocked down and turned into the Hudson Shard—1,200 feet of vast, gleaming office space, a building as sleek and beautiful as the woman behind it.

On the ground floor sat a bookstore/café that, in a matter of minutes now, would be the site of the launch of Maddie's first book. She still had to pinch herself to believe that a major publishing house had asked for the rights to her whimsical collection of blogs on life, loneliness, and drowning in a city everyone else seemed to love.

Book boxes stamped *Aliens of New York* surrounded her, along with stacks of other novels the bookstore had no space for downstairs. The smell of freshly printed ink wasn't that far removed from that of her old paper, where she'd hunched over her desk turning late-breaking stories, obits, and crime stats into something interesting for the next day's commuter crowd.

Her publishing house's publicist, Alicia Keen, had blown in fifteen minutes ago, deposited Maddie in this storage room with a foldout chair and a view, told her to relax, and announced that a crowd was building in the bookstore, one that included several influential book reviewers.

Maddie still didn't quite understand why her blogs had captivated the online attention they had, let alone earned a buzz when the book deal had been announced.

Alicia reappeared, eyes gleaming with excitement. She blew out a breath. "Almost ready for you. I must say, there are a *lot* of finance reporters downstairs."

"What? Why? My blogs were about emotions, not business."

"Yes, well, darling, there's this absurd rumor that's spread like wildfire that a VIP would be making an appearance." Alicia rolled her eyes. "I mean, it's silly. Why would a media mogul and fashion-editing icon of Elena Bartell's international standing bother with a..." She faded out, realizing her mistake.

"A weird set of blogs like mine?" Maddie replied dryly.

"I was going to say a small, esoteric book of blogs, darling."

Maddie grinned. "Nice save."

"Well." Alicia looked flummoxed. "I didn't mean anything by it. Your book is *fabulous*; of course it is. I loved it!"

Uh-huh.

"But Ms. Bartell is *insanely* busy," Alicia rushed on. "She spends most of her time in Sydney these days. It's likely that she's not even in town!"

Maddie grinned. "I heard she was." And she'd *seen* her, *felt* her, *kissed* her, and a few other things that would doubtlessly scandalize Alicia Keen and the greater population of New York if they knew.

Maddie's secret relationship with Elena had led to some awkward moments at times, especially lately when it came to Maddie's book. There had been much confusion from her publishing house when Bartell Corp had, out of the blue, offered to host the launch of the *Aliens of New York* blog collection at its popular Hudson Shard Bookstore. Then there had been utter bewilderment when the media corporation had told Maddie's publisher it would be promoting *Aliens of New York* in all its newspapers and magazines globally.

Privately, between kisses and mumbles about nepotism, Maddie had protested Elena's decision, only to be cut off by Elena's fierce declaration that it was a business decision.

"Excellence deserves to be celebrated, Madeleine," Elena had said, her breath hot against Maddie's ear. "And I won't debate this. It's done."

It might have been *done,* but no one at the publishing house could make sense of it.

Alicia shook her head, causing a dramatic bounce of hoop earrings. "Look, just don't expect to see Ms. Bartell today. I know you once worked for her, and that's probably what's fueling the rumors, but you were her assistant for barely five minutes; am I right, darling?"

"Yep." Maddie hid her smile.

"Exactly! Would she even be able to pick you out of a lineup given how many assistants she goes through? Pfft. It would be lovely of course, if she did drop by. What a boost that would be! But, I mean, really, why would she? Trust me: I deal with *that* type a lot. The Tiger Shark and her sharp little teeth wouldn't be caught dead in here."

Alicia leaned over and tucked the tag down in the back of Maddie's blouse. "There, all set." She patted Maddie's shoulder. "I'm glad you went with *this*. So much better than that grunge T-shirt you threatened to wear. You weren't serious, were you, darling? No, don't answer that. Now, I'll just head back downstairs and make sure everything's shipshape. I'll come and get you when we're due to start."

At the door, she hesitated. "And just in case the rumor *is* true, could I please ask that you don't act so…*Australian*? You can be a bit overfamiliar at times. Very… *down-to-earth*. Oh, it's refreshing—I mean that in a good way—but I doubt a woman of Elena Bartell's reputation and status would appreciate someone who…" Alicia paused. "Well, *you know*."

"Right." Maddie bit the inside of her cheek. "I'll do my best."

"Lovely." Alicia beamed. "Okay, I must finalize things. Back soon, darling." She disappeared in a rustle of skirts and a clinking homage to seventies jewelry.

Maddie finally released the laugh she'd been desperately holding in. Oh, the Tiger Shark was indeed the possessor of a fine set of teeth. They'd gently nibbled along Maddie's thigh at five this morning to take her mind off her nerves about today. By the end of it, Maddie couldn't even remember her own name, let alone that of her book.

"Madeleine?" The door clicked open and shut behind Maddie before a familiar warmth pressed itself into her back. "It's only me."

Funny how she said that. There was no "only" about Elena Bartell.

Maddie leaned back against Elena, inhaling the scent that was distinctly her. "Do you recognize where we are?" Maddie asked after a few moments of basking in Elena's presence.

Elena peered over Maddie's shoulder into the street below. "Should I? Beyond being in the same location where your old newspaper used to be?"

"Remember when you moved into *Hudson Metro*'s office for a month? *This* was your view from your window. I should know; I gazed into your office often enough. For reasons." Maddie gave a small laugh.

"Ah. You know, I don't think I ever looked outside even once. My attention was fixed on my redesign plans…and, occasionally, on this maddening junior crime reporter who sat outside my office at crazy hours."

"Oh, *her*." It still surprised Maddie that Elena had noticed her at all in those days.

Threading her arms tighter around Maddie's waist, Elena asked, "So what do you see out there?"

"Memories. How alone I felt. Me failing in a city everyone dreams of being in. It was hard, feeling too far from home and being unable to make friends when I worked crazy late hours. I craved connection."

"Feeling isolated in a city of millions?" Elena murmured. "Mm. I think that's why I loved your blog, why I was drawn to you. Your words resonated."

"Plus I bribed you with treats so you'd talk to me." Maddie grinned.

"Ah, now all those late-night food drops make sense." Elena's voice became amused. "So I was just…*there*? A warm body to talk to and take your mind off things?"

"Oh, no. You were also all kinds of fascinating."

"You didn't always think so." Elena's voice was a soft purr. "Once you called me a calculating, icy, money-hungry bitch of a shark."

"For good reason!" Maddie frowned.

Elena's tone turned cautious. "The decisions I made were necessary, Madeleine."

"I know. I get it. *Hudson Metro* was a crappy newspaper parked on prime real estate. What you did made business sense. It just…" Maddie breathed in. "It was hard being in the middle of it, feeling so…disposable. And it's odd feeling those emotions all rushing back again. I can't help it." She pointed at the window. "Because it looks *exactly* the same."

"I suppose it does."

Maddie turned from the view and met Elena's gaze. "You've created an iconic building out of those old bones of a paper, Elena. We could argue for days about the value of keeping or killing old newspapers, but from an architectural point of view, it's beautiful."

"Well, I *do* appreciate beautiful things, Madeleine." Elena's blue eyes darkened as her gaze slid over Maddie's form.

Her breath caught. To the whole world, Elena Bartell was someone icy, dangerous, and ruthless. But waking up each day to Elena's softness always blew that persona out of the water.

Elena might not speak of her love often, but she didn't have to. And while few people knew what they meant to each other, the sense of belonging Maddie felt was enough for now. Even if Elena's presence in Maddie's world often confused the hell out of everyone…like her publishing house.

Thinking back on Alicia's certainty Elena would never show at some insignificant little book launch, Maddie laughed.

"Care to share?" Elena asked.

"Last week, my publisher, Mr. Mandell, started running theories past me as to why Bartell Corp was bothering to help out my book."

"Oh?" Elena's eyes twinkled.

"Was it because I was a Bartell Corp reporter once? Loyalty to one of the company's own? I pointed out I only worked for a short period under Bartell Corp's reign."

"True."

"Then was it because I was your assistant perhaps? I explained that my assistant stint was even briefer—and that you fired my ass…*twice*."

Elena's eyebrows lifted in protest. "In my defense, I did try and reinstate you."

"Mmm. Didn't try very hard," Maddie said with a grin. "So then he wondered if maybe you'd read my blog."

"Perish the thought."

Maddie laughed. "But Mr. Mandell decided that was ridiculous, because what busy media goddess such as yourself would have the time or interest in 'scribblings about whimsy, loneliness, and dissecting the human condition'?"

"He has me all figured out. That doesn't sound like the Tiger Shark at all."

"Exactly. Anyway, the poor man gave up, declaring it a mystery. Then, not five minutes ago, my publicist was in here, breathless over some ridiculous rumor going around that *the* Elena Bartell might appear at my book launch today."

Elena snorted. "Me? I'm a *very* busy woman."

"That's what she said. Anyway, Alicia suggested that if that crazy rumor proved true, could I try not to be *so Australian*? I suspect she thought I might embarrass myself or her in front of your greatness."

"A wise precaution. You can be blunt. What *would* I make of someone like you?"

"Anything you want, love." Maddie ran her fingers down Elena's silken black vest, then placed them over her heart. "Thanks for wearing my favorite outfit… and for turning up today when we both know you've only got two weeks to prep for Bartell Corp's AGM. You've been amazing about all of this."

"Hardly. I was in the neighborhood."

"Next you'll deny that you're why there's a roomful of finance journalists downstairs, hopeful for a glimpse or a chat with a notoriously camera-shy global media mogul."

Elena's lips quirked. "Well. Felicity *may* have spread a rumor I might be here. I do appreciate how proactive she can be at times. She's earned her promotion. And if that rumor or my presence sells more of your books, who am I to argue?"

"I owe Felicity. Maybe I'll buy her a beer or two next time we catch up."

"Maybe not. She doesn't react well to carbs, alcohol, or random acts of kindness."

"Good point. Hey?"

"Mm?"

"I love you."

Elena's hand tangled with Maddie's against her breast. "Now there's a coincidence."

Alicia stuck her head in. "We're ready, Ms. Grey. I have to…" The words died in her throat as she took in Maddie and Elena's intimate pose. "M-Ms. Bartell. What a surprise!" Her eyes widened.

Alicia's lips parted, and a deep red bloom spread across her cheeks and neck. She blinked in disbelief, then waved at the door. "I'll just…downstairs. Me. Goodness! *You two?* I had no idea. Oh, Ms. Grey, you must think I'm such… Sorry, I'll go now. Um. See you soon." She flung herself back outside, shutting the door after her with a firm clunk.

"Oh dear. She really is quite tightly wound," Elena said dryly. "I thought she was going to pass out."

"Yeah. Poor thing." Maddie chuckled. "I'll calm her down after the launch. Don't worry; I know her. She'll be discreet. Besides, she'd be frightened you'd crush her like a bug if she blabs."

Elena chuckled, low and soft. "I wasn't particularly worried. She doesn't hide her terror well."

Maddie laughed. "No. She really doesn't." She took one last look around the room. "Know what's crazy? Last time I was here, I wrote blog after blog about feeling lonely and lost. And now, on the day I'm launching a book of those blogs, I've never felt more safe and at home."

"The universe has a wicked sense of humor." Elena brushed her lips against Maddie's mouth, then paused to press her lips properly against them.

Maddie responded enthusiastically, loving that heady, excited thrill she always felt whenever Elena kissed her.

Elena pulled away, giving Maddie an affectionate look. "So…ready?"

Am I?

She glanced back out the window. The view was identical, that was true, and yet… "Same on the outside," Maddie murmured. "So different on the inside."

"The building?"

"Me." She met Elena's gaze with a smile. "You're here with me. Of course I'm ready."

The story of when Aussie reporter Maddie met media mogul Elena is in *The Brutal Truth* by Lee Winter. Maddie's blog posts from that book appear below.

Extract from ALIENS OF NEW YORK: A Book of Blogs by Maddie Grey

OLD EYES

Today, there was an old woman sitting on a garbage can outside my Williamsburg apartment building, next to the auto repair shop. She sang softly to her bags of junk, a chaotic pile of blankets, clothes, newspapers, and food wrappings. Off-key and missing some teeth, she swayed gently to the rhythm. A scraggly white dandelion dancing in the wind, hairless in a few places but undaunted nonetheless.

The upturned hat in front of her gleamed inside with a few coins. As I passed her, I realised one of the bags was actually a small child.

The girl, maybe aged ten or so, had old, old eyes. She didn't smile at me or the woman beside her. She stared into the distance.

I swayed along with the song for a few moments before dropping a few notes into the hat. That earned a wide, toothless grin.

Look after her, *I thought. As I walked away, I wasn't sure which of them I'd meant.*

~ ~ ~

BROKEN PROMISES

They promised to visit. They haven't. The reasons pile up like unpaid bills. I get it. They're busy. Life gets crazy. But I long for the wash of home and wish I could afford a ticket back.
I want to hear, hidden in their broad accents, the hum of cicadas in summer and the gentle tik-tik-tik of backyard sprinklers.
I want the smell of them to be a reminder of the salty air of Bondi Beach, mixed with the tang of vinegar from fish and chips spread on butcher's paper across the sand.
I want the whiff of cut grass and eucalyptus trees and the faint disinfectant on the train to Bondi Junction, which always signalled the start of the weekend.
I want the taste of them. In the hello-again kiss, brushing tanned cheeks, I want to find the unique, almost dusty, taste of the air back home.
When they promised to visit, was it a lie told knowingly? Do they think having my best friend here means I don't need them?
Even if we didn't work the wrong shifts, my housemate has absorbed New York into his skin. He's become the city I recoil from.
I miss them.

~ ~ ~

EXPECTATIONS

Expectations are one of life's most powerful, invisible forces. They crush our throats tighter than any necktie. We chafe at them, deny they exist, pretend we don't care about them, yet we can't get enough of them.
Expectations alter our world. They can win or cost us a job, a lover, a lawsuit, a life. We are addicted to expectations.

Me, I'm the expectations junkie. Check me out, living the life I'm expected to. I could be failing happily back home. Instead, I'm succeeding miserably here.

I know focusing on expectations is a pointless waste of mental resources. They aren't real. They're entirely in our own minds. And yet I'm always going back for another hit. Why?

~ ~ ~

MASKS

Someone once said: "Be yourself; everyone else is taken."

Surely this is the hardest advice ever offered. We all wear masks. We're all practiced liars, neatly curating ourselves for the benefit of others. It's only natural, isn't it?

We don't want strangers to know we're secretly nervous or shy or intimidated or cowardly. That we're not brave enough or smart enough or well-off enough or that we're barely coping. So we fake the ease and perfection of our lives.

I'm the first one to admit I've posted my own grinning selfie at Times Square with #lifegoals in the caption. I'm a fraud. But writing #drowningslowly or #lostandembarrassed doesn't have the catchiest ring.

You never truly know what's under anyone's mask until you take one corner and start to peel. It awes me that anyone would allow another human to do this to them. To willingly say, "Hey, this is me. Do you still like me?"

The advice might be right—but by God, it's asking a lot of us.

~ ~ ~

SMILING

I remember the time I learned to ride a bike. I pushed off from the curb at my old house on Mitchell St, South Penrith. I was wobbling like crazy. My older brother was holding his sides from laughing and calling out names, and my mother was telling him to be quiet and offering me encouragement.

I fell off. It hurt. I got back on. I fell off. It hurt some more. I got back on. When people say something's like riding a bike, I think maybe they mean it will hurt sometimes, but it will get better.

Today, I remembered how to smile. I wonder whether it will hurt later.

~ ~ ~

CHANGING THE WORLD

Bruno, the mechanic who runs a car repair shop next to my apartment building, once told me, "When the world gets too overwhelming and things feel too big for us to fix, just change your little corner of it."

I tried to do that. I held a tearful young man's hand at one in the morning and made him a life-changing promise. I went home and wrote his story. In another day, it will belong to the world. What will the world make of it? Will it fix what's wrong or make a liar of me?

Bruno also says we should change our engine oil more often. Make of that what you will.

~ ~ ~

RIDING THE SUBWAY

The loneliest place on earth, I think, is the New York subway after midnight. Not just for people like me, finishing their late shifts, who stare with tired, empty eyes out the window, drawing into themselves, tighter and tighter. It's the others. The people who have nowhere else to be. They are there for the warmth or the escape.

See, once you get off a train, you have to have a purpose. A destination. But on a train, you can just sit and contemplate with no pressure to do anything at all.

Sometimes I think I've spent too long just sitting, watching the shadows flash by at light speed, not excited to get off and be wherever I'm supposed to be. It's easy to be a passenger. Life is about purpose, not sitting still. It's a shock to realise I've allowed my whole existence to become something to be watched from a worn-out train seat.

I started really noticing the colours outside last week. When had they become brighter? And today, I woke up and couldn't wait to get on with my day. I had a story I was proud of in print, an idea for a follow-up that could make a difference, and someone fascinating who I'm looking forward to seeing again.

I examined myself in the bathroom mirror and didn't recognise who looked back. I think I've been riding the rails for too long, watching the world through windows. High time to get off the train.

What are you doing to me, New York? Playing with my affections like this? I may even start liking you if you keep this up.

~ ~ ~

GOODBYE, NEW YORK

Goodbye, New York. Sorry I never understood you, as hard as I tried. We had our moments, didn't we?

Remember that laughing old woman outside Saks Fifth Avenue, who tried to hug everyone she passed and called them Sally?

I've often wondered who Sally was. A lost daughter? An absent lover? It doesn't matter; we all got to be Sally and have a hug that smelled of wet wool cardigan and nutmeg.

I think that old woman's life must be a delight, because everywhere she turns she finds exactly what she's looking for.

I wish that had been the case for me. I came to New York hoping for the Dream. I leave now, having lost a little of myself, found a little of myself, and learned some harsh truths about the mistake in assuming that everyone sees the world, and friendship, as I do.

But no tears, New York. It's not you; it's me. I'll pretend we were the best of friends, if anyone ever asks. And they will.

The Brutal Lie

Power and intimidation oozed from the New York penthouse office of Bartell Corp's international headquarters, with its sleek round floors, chrome, and tinted glass.

Maddie Grey padded along the thick carpeted floor, one hand tight around a bottle of champagne, in search of the fashion-editing world's newest conqueror.

The first time she'd been here, almost two and a half years ago, Maddie had felt like a boot scraping, out of place and lost. Tonight, wearing a blue T-shirt, leather jacket, and worn jeans, Maddie wasn't a much better fit, but she was no longer awed. This space was now as familiar to her as the imposing woman who ruled it. Elena Bartell: Media mogul and the founder, President, and Chief Operating Officer of Bartell Corporation.

Elena didn't stalk the corridors of this building often anymore, having divested the day-to-day running of her company to her deputy. Her heart and focus had shifted, as had her home base. These days she was engaged in a furious magazine war against iconic fashion bible, *Catwalk Queen*. Elena had been in the trenches, from Sydney to London, trying to make her fashion magazine, *Style International*, the world's number one.

Eighteen months later, it was official. The latest circulation figures had landed a few hours ago while Elena had been holding Bartell Corp's annual general meeting. *Style* hadn't just beaten its rival, it'd ground it under heel.

This was definitely cause for celebration.

Maddie found Elena scribbling notes at her desk, still wearing a cocktail dress from the party after the AGM, as if she'd been distracted and forgotten to change. Maddie leaned against the door, appreciating her lover's dress—a scarlet second skin with a plunging neckline that hinted at the delights within.

Dear God. Elena did wear red well. It reminded her of a particularly sinful garnet dress that had undone Maddie once. She'd been a junior night-shift crime reporter and had made a total fool of herself, face-planting in front of her then-boss. And Elena had seemed…amused.

"Hey, sexy. When you didn't come home, I brought the party to you." Maddie placed the champagne on Elena's glass, designer desk.

Elena's head lifted in surprise. Regret darted into her eyes as she glanced at the clock. "I'm sorry. I didn't intend to be so long."

"Time flies when you're vanquishing your mortal enemies."

"Now there's a pleasant thought." Elena's eyes lit up. She tapped a sheet of numbers. "Almost as pleasant as my figures."

"Well, I do like one of your figures in particular." Maddie's gaze lingered. "God, *that* dress. It reminds me of a certain other creation."

"You remember that?"

"Is that a trick question? I'm astonished I could still walk after the first time I saw you in it."

"If I recall, you spent more time on your face than walking." Elena rose, smoothing the dress down her hips and thighs. "I also recall you watching me in the reflection of the window." Moving toward it, her hips gave a languid sway. "I was standing right here, staring outside."

Maddie came up behind her, close enough to feel Elena's warmth. "Gazing at me in the glass you mean."

Elena's eyes twinkled at her in the reflection. "I distinctly remember the impressive New York City skyline."

"Uh-uh." Maddie pressed herself into her lover's back. "Fess up: What *were* you thinking that night?"

"Truthfully?" Elena's expression in the reflection became distant. "I was transfixed by how hungry your eyes seemed. You surprised me."

"And me. I had an epiphany that night."

"Oh?"

"Mmm. How hot my boss was. How I wanted my hot boss. And a few other unspeakable things."

"Unspeakable?" Elena's voice dropped a register lower.

"Mm-hmm. You know…" Maddie licked her lips. "We could re-create that night. I may have suggested to Tony on the front desk not to interrupt you except for emergencies."

"That seems somewhat presumptuous." Elena's voice warmed.

"It's late. Barely anyone's left in the building." Maddie paused and added slyly, "I mean…unless you have other plans?"

Elena pretended to consider that. "Well, I am rather busy. One doesn't destroy *CQ*'s circulation in a day. It must be ongoing. There's planning."

Maddie dropped a kiss at the base of Elena's neck, then another under her ear. "True, but today you're a golden goddess who can ignore her work and accept her glorious reward."

"What form does this reward take?" Elena's voice was low and interested.

Maddie slid her hands down that sleek dress, and then reversed course, bringing the hem up with her. Her fingers slid to between Elena's thighs. "Well, the usual accolades and tributes. Plus sexual favours, naturally." She rubbed Elena's thong pointedly.

Elena's mouth parted slightly. Her eyes became half-lidded, and there was no mistaking the arousal in her expression.

Fingers dancing and teasing, Maddie listened to the shift in Elena's breathing. Oh, how she loved this bit, where Elena wouldn't ask for more, not yet; because she enjoyed the games and foreplay as much as the sex. Elena's jaw clenched, biting back a gasped moan, and her eyes pleaded for things Elena's lips would never ask for.

Maddie played with her lover for long minutes, soaking in the naked want on the beautiful face in the window: high cheekbones, pale skin, jet-black, sculpted short hair, and arching eyebrows that always seemed mocking. But there was nothing but desire in those hooded eyes tonight. All for her.

She loved seeing Elena in a way no one else did. Emotionally naked and vulnerable. *Mine.*

"Take this off for me." Maddie tapped Elena's soaked thong.

Sometimes Maddie ordered Elena to do intimate things just to watch her wordlessly obey. That was arousing. Telling the woman who controlled almost a billion-dollar empire what she *had* to do.

Elena always seemed to know what that meant for Maddie. That this was where Maddie had power too. After a delicious pause, Elena reached under her dress and slid her lace thong down. She met Maddie's eye and her need was clear.

"Madeleine." She drew out the word until it sounded French and naughty, becoming a demand. Elena's way of saying, *enough playing.*

Smiling at her impatience, Maddie reached for her soft thigh. She trailed higher. Without a barrier, Maddie's fingers moved easily across swollen skin.

"Tell me something," Elena said, voice breathless. Her eyes became far too knowing.

A shiver skittered down Maddie's spine at that taunting, devilish gaze. *Uh-oh.* Elena did love to fight back, to try to wrestle the power away from Maddie when she felt her own control slipping too fast.

"What did you wish you could have done that night two years ago?" Elena asked. "When you watched me in this window?"

Maddie parted Elena's folds and slid her fingers through wet flesh. "That night, I wished you'd kissed me. Pushed me against a wall and kissed me senseless." Her nipples tightened at the reminder. *God, that night.*

"Is that *all* you wanted?" Elena rolled her hips forward, pressing harder into Maddie's fingers. She quivered and bucked into Maddie and seemed to struggle to keep her arousal in check as she finished the deliberate words designed to crack Maddie's restraint.

If only Elena knew how pitifully close Maddie already was.

"You just wanted a kiss from me that night?" Elena's hands landed on the window, bracing herself. Her fingers shifted a little, leaving steamy, smeared imprints on the glass.

"Well, maybe my fantasies included you flinging me on your desk, tearing off my jeans, and—"

"On my desk?" Elena's eyebrows lifted to cocky heights. "My desk is only for work, Madeleine."

Jesus. The soft, playful timbre of her voice would kill her yet.

"You know that," Elena finished, adding a soft growl as Maddie pressed harder.

She *did* know that. It's why it was so fun to tweak her about desk sex. Maddie smirked, then dipped inside her. "God, Elena, you're so wet. So needy."

Elena bucked into Maddie's hand and muttered: "I am *not* needy."

Sure she wasn't. Maddie lifted her other hand up the dress, tracing heated skin within the deep vee. She slipped her hand under the silken material and lifted Elena's bare breast outside the dress. They gazed at the sight in the window.

Maddie's breath hitched. It seemed so naughty, so daring, that pale, soft breast lying against a blood-red dress, an erect nipple crinkling in the air. *Jesus.* Maddie rubbed the tight nub while moving her other hand through coarse, trimmed hairs, to Elena's clit, circling it. She shifted her legs trying to alleviate the rising heat between her own thighs. One touch, hell, one pointed look from Elena, and she'd fly apart.

Elena moaned.

"Not needy? Are you sure?" Maddie tongued the salty skin of Elena's neck until the other woman shivered. Then she drove her fingers deep inside her, curling them up, at the same time pinching her nipple hard.

Elena choked out a gasp, pushed a hand between her legs, and rubbed herself frantically. She shuddered, trembled, and slumped her forehead into the glass with a pained groan. "Oh God. That was… Oh, Madeleine, I had to. Couldn't wait."

Maddie would never get used to this arousing sight, no matter how many times they'd made love. Elena unable to stop herself. Elena lost. Whimpering. Finally, irrevocably undone. She smiled. "I love it when you do that. Lose control so completely you can't help yourself."

Maddie withdrew her fingers, pausing to spread the wetness around Elena's most intimate flesh until she twitched again.

Turning Elena around to face her, Maddie kissed her deeply. The response was hungry, heated, and arousing.

When they parted, Elena's mussed hair, smudged lipstick, and bare breast pushed Maddie right to the edge. Her swallow was shaky.

Elena's smile was cocksure. She trailed a fingertip down Maddie's neck. "Now then. What to do with you?"

"The desk?" Maddie croaked hopefully, already knowing the answer, as she unbuttoned her jeans.

"Absolutely not." Elena's cool gaze raked Maddie's form as if deciding exactly how to devour her. "How would I ever be able to work if all I could picture was me debauching you all over it?" Pushing a hand inside Maddie's jeans, she cupped her heat through the boy shorts. "Well, well. Speaking of needy."

"It's not like you work a lot on *that* desk, though," Maddie protested weakly, as Elena rubbed with determination. Her underwear was soaked through. She was helpless whenever Elena's fingers got anywhere near her. Maddie couldn't get enough, and her moans were soon filling the room. Just her touch, combined with the thought that Elena might consider flinging her down on her desk, where she ruled her empire… *Gah.* "*Style Sydney*'s desk gets most of your attention these days," Maddie gasped out. "We could just…"

Elena pressed against her clit with unerring accuracy, and oh God, Maddie was about to…

The desk phone started ringing.

Both women froze.

Maddie frowned. She'd been clear to Security about no interruptions.

Elena yanked her hand out of Maddie's jeans, adjusted her breast back into her dress, and stalked to the desk, irritation sharp in her stride. Wiping her fingers on a tissue, she then stabbed the speaker button. "Yes?"

"Ms Bartell, sorry to bother you, I have Perry Marks here to see you. He says he has urgent business. Shall I send him up?"

"One moment." Elena stabbed the Hold button. She glanced over at Maddie. A speculative, dangerous look crossed her face. Elena perched on the edge of the desk and leaned back, which pushed her ample breasts hard against red silk. "I suppose I *could* take you on the desk," she said as though considering it. "Spread you out, strip you bare. Splay you before me. Then I'd roll up to you in my chair, lick my way up those delightful thighs, and feast on you. Would you like that? *Madeleine*?"

Oh fuck. Arousal surged through Maddie. Elena loved to do this to her, describe in detail her erotic plans. She searched Elena's daring expression and came closer. "Y-you mean now? B-but—"

Elena gave her an imperious look. "Well?" She moved in front of her and rubbed the seam of Maddie's jeans, hard, between her legs. "*Would* you like that, Madeleine?"

The pressure and positioning were perfect—as Elena well knew given the look in her eyes.

With a sharp, startled cry, Maddie came on the spot. Her knees and thighs trembled as warmth spread through her nerve endings. "You'd actually agree to that?" Maddie gasped out. "Next time, I mean?"

Elena's smile was equal parts triumph, amusement, and delight. "Of course not. My desk is for work purposes only."

Maddie groaned. God damn it. Elena could play her like a fiddle. She used her power so perfectly in their sex life, with such precision, it should be a crime. Maddie both hated and loved how well Elena knew her weaknesses and every turn-on. It was arousing, thrilling, and probably a little pathetic if she bothered to care, which she absolutely didn't. Maddie was, quite simply, putty in Elena's hands, and they both knew it.

Heat flooded her, and only part of it was to do with that magnificent orgasm.

Elena smirked, dropped a kiss on Maddie's cheek, and then stabbed her phone. Her voice was stern and dry: "Send my global art director up."

Elena made it into her chair with seconds to spare when the elevator dinged announcing Perry's arrival. Madeleine—teasing, intoxicating Madeleine—had insisted on distracting her with further passionate kisses, leaving barely any time to fix her appearance. Elena squirmed in her chair, self-conscious about what was missing, and darted an appalled look toward where a tangle of thong still lay. She hadn't had time to reclaim it. Still, those kisses had been quite something. She prayed Perry wouldn't notice what lay at the foot of her office window.

Madeleine followed her gaze and mouthed "sorry", just as Perry swished into the office in an elegant, lilac, Brioni suit.

He stood in front of Elena and ran a hand over his dark-skinned bald pate. "What *did* you say to Tony for him to give me the third degree about sending me up?" He almost pouted.

"A better question is what has you in here so late? And what constitutes enough of an emergency for him to override a Do Not Disturb?" Elena drawled. "Especially after Bartell Corp's dividend that'll see half its shareholders off to Aspen, and a certain fashion mag's destruction." She leaned forward. "Do *not* tell me you're here to ruin my famously good mood with bad news."

He snorted at that characterization of her mood. "Yes, well, it's *CQ* I'm here about." He sagged a little. "Emmanuelle Lecoq specifically."

Elena's pulse kicked up at the mention of the rival magazine's editor. "What's she done now?"

He opened his mouth, then caught sight of the visitor's sofa. "Sorry, Maddie, didn't see you there. Hello."

"Hey, Perry. Great to see you again." Madeleine grinned, and her genuine affection for the man was infused in her voice.

Then again, her warm, affectionate lover seemed to like pretty much everyone. Elena could not relate to that in the least. She folded her arms. "Perhaps if you just spat it out."

"Fine." Perry reached into his briefcase. "You know I have contacts everywhere. This is out tomorrow." A newspaper hit her desk.

Madeleine joined Elena to read over her shoulder.

'NO PASSING FADS FOR ME!' LECOQ DISHES DIRT

Elena scoured the page. Just a shallow profile about the *CQ* editor's style, beauty, leadership, and, *Christ*, genius. The puff-piece was designed, no doubt, to take the heat off her circulation figures.

Perry tapped a paragraph. "Here's where the bile begins."

Unlike some, I'm not into fickle fads. You won't see me having a desperate, midlife-crisis Sapphic fling with my empty-headed assistant-turned-reporter to feel young or relevant. I also don't need the obscene trappings of success to prove I'm powerful. What would I want with a round, monolithic office and a helipad, any more than I need some ambitious, gold-digger lesbian lover? I'm as classic as my Jimmy Choos. I've been around longer than any other fashion magazine editor, and I will endure long after certain others get bored and move on to their next toy.

Elena stiffened. *Of all the nasty, underhanded…*

Madeleine hissed in an outraged breath. "She stuck a neon arrow on your head with all those clues. Round office? Helipad?"

Elena didn't answer. She stared at the insults. *Empty-headed assistant-turned-reporter. Ambitious gold-digger.* How *dare* she? Madeleine was one of the most clever, insightful people Elena had ever met. She cared about people more than money. She was kind, decent, and loved with her whole heart. "I'll kill her," Elena hissed. "How dare she say this about you? I'll sue her into the ground. Get me Felicity!"

Madeleine's hand came out to latch onto Elena's forearm. "Hey? Take a breath for a sec? Look, I know she crossed a line. But let's not do some knee-jerk thing. Let's talk first."

"She called you *empty headed*." Rage filled Elena. "A gold-digger. My mid-life crisis fling! I'm apparently desperate?"

Perry's cheeks darkened, and he looked like he'd rather be anywhere but in the middle of this.

"Fuck it," Elena snarled, "I don't care what people say about me. God knows I collect insulting nicknames. But she attacked *you*."

"Um, I'm not sure you've focused on the big thing here," Madeleine cut in. "She also outed *you*."

Elena paused. *Oh.* Her brain had skated right over that. Well, hell. She and Madeleine had never addressed their relationship. It was obvious to her valued staff members, such as Perry. But they'd never discussed officially coming out. "She outed you too," Elena murmured.

"I'm just some Australian freelance reporter. But you're…*you*. Emmanuelle was obviously hoping shareholders would choke on their cornflakes and see you as a lightweight flake having some scandalous fling."

Elena glowered. "Nothing she said is true." God, why had she never properly discussed any of this with Madeleine before? It had been so easy to hide themselves away at the ends of the earth in Sydney and forget their private life was newsworthy. "You are no fling," Elena said heatedly. "I'm…a lesbian. This isn't some experiment. What she said has no truth."

Madeleine wrapped an arm around her shoulder. "I know." She glanced at Perry. "We know."

"We do," he said kindly. "Most people will see through what she wrote as the bitter, petty revenge it is. The problem is that 'most' people isn't 'all'. This could be harmful if left to fester."

"But if we sue," Madeleine said, "it looks like we're saying we think our relationship is shameful or wrong."

Elena ground her teeth. "I can't believe this. Lecoq loses the circulation wars, so she shreds me personally? Defames us as air-headed and desperate?"

"She did much worse than that." Perry said thoughtfully. "She outed you. I don't mean she outed *you,* which is bad enough. She's *outed* you. It can be seen as homophobic violence given how dangerous outing can be for some. So a woman heading a magazine about fashion—the gayest industry on earth—just committed homophobia because she was pissy she'd been beaten professionally. Now how do you think that'll play in our world?"

Madeleine gave a slow smile. "Oh…dear. That's true. Perry? Could you give Elena and me five minutes?"

"Sure." He disappeared.

"What has crossed that furtive mind of yours?" Elena asked.

"That depends. How would you feel about being outed in a big way?"

"I thought I already was." Elena folded her arms.

"Please, *The New York Daily Commute*'s readership barely gets above a hundred and fifty thousand on a good day, and only then because it's given away on street corners. Do you think even ten percent of people will read that Lecoq crap on their subway ride? They'll flick through news and sport, if that. What I'm asking is how you'd feel if you woke up tomorrow, and *everyone* knew."

"I…" Elena hesitated as she turned that over. Her conservative Polish-American parents had likely worked her out years ago but were sticking to "don't ask-don't tell". Not that she was close to them. Her most intimate friends, well, friend—Perry—already knew. So…that just left herself. Being talked about and criticised were nothing new given her job. But none of it had ever been so personal. "What of you?" Elena dodged. "Won't people wonder if you got ahead thanks to dating me? Lecoq's mud could stick."

Madeleine snorted. "You mightn't have noticed, but I made a point of never writing for any of your mastheads. As me for personally? Everyone in my life knows and is cool. Mum thinks you're adorable by the way. That's hilarious."

"Adorable? Me?" Elena stared in astonishment.

"Yup." Madeleine snickered.

"Does she know my reputation? The names I'm called? They're not unfounded."

"She knows. She still thinks you're adorable—has done so ever since you got me that birthday cupcake."

Elena sagged. "You're both as mad as each other. I never *could* intimidate you even the slightest."

"Nope." Madeleine grinned. "Don't know why you even bothered. So in answer to your question, I'd be honoured to be outed as yours." She added softly, "Now stop stalling and tell me: *Is* this a big deal for you?"

"Professionally? Once, I might have thought it was a disaster. But after today's figures? Hell, they're lucky to have me."

"Damn straight." Madeleine chuckled. "Sooo....did you just convince yourself? Or do you still have doubts?"

Elena sighed. "I always have doubts. But that's me. I always ensure I've thought of all angles. It's what makes me so successful. I live with doubts."

"And personally?"

"I've loved having you all to myself. It's been wonderful not having to share you with the world, our secret. But I'm not ashamed of us."

Madeleine nodded. "All right. So, I do have a plan. It's a subtle way to point out the error of Emmanuelle's ways and possibly spark a grovelling apology—while you stay above it all."

"Oh?" Elena liked the sound of that a great deal.

"Let's get Perry in here to run it past him too."

A moment later, the art director returned with a pensive look on his face. His gaze scraped the whole room, as though fearing there might be blood on the walls. He paused at the champagne bottle on the desk, shifted his gaze, and then squinted at something by the windows.

Elena followed his eye. *Oh.* Yes, well, he hadn't given her much time, had he? Or, rather, Madeleine hadn't.

"Is that…?" He pointed at Elena's crumpled thong.

"You'd be well advised not to finish that thought." Elena glowered at him, willing a blush not to rise on her face.

Perry snorted. "Celebrating earlier, were we?"

Elena tossed him a death glare.

Madeleine laughed hard.

And the planning began.

Four days later, Maddie nervously eyed the Features Editor for the esteemed *US Review* magazine she was sitting opposite. The woman was in her sixties, with a sharp face and a weary expression.

"To recap," Dorothy Follows said, "you wish to change that brilliant pitch you emailed last month and instead write something on…" she consulted her notes, "…the ethics of outing gay people?"

"More than that." Maddie leaned in. "I'll talk to people who've been outed and how that affected their life. Some celebrities, political figures, maybe a coach on a high school team, an ethicist. I'll ask where we draw the line in a nation that prides itself on free speech."

Fallows regarded her. "An interesting concept, but no."

Maddie's heart sank. "But it's so wrong."

"It is. It'd be like running a story on the ethical question of racism. Why would we, when the answer's obvious?"

"It's, um, topical?" Maddie said weakly.

"How so? Who's been outed?"

Maddie fidgeted and wondered if she should be honest or…

"You know you could have just pitched me an exclusive on you and Bartell if you wanted to tackle Emmanuelle Lecoq's outing you."

Maddie blinked, stunned.

"Glossy mags are a small world, Ms Grey." Fallows looked amused. "We're well aware, for instance, of who always goes to media events together. And then you coming in with this pitch, right after Lecoq's story, well…"

Oh. Maddie's cheeks burned.

"So I can offer a cover for you and Bartell's…" she twirled her finger "grand romance."

Maddie shifted uncomfortably. "That's not what I had in mind."

"Oh, I'm well aware. You intended to embarrass Lecoq with your evils-of-outing story, without getting any mud on you or your lover. Right?" She arched an eyebrow.

"I just think she should understand what she's done."

"So don't go soft. Own it. Get out in front of the story; spin it your way so that the vacuum won't get filled with someone else's lies and innuendo. Yes, you'll have to put yourselves out there, get muddy, but it's a better result: *You* set the message."

"Elena's private. She'd never—"

"Even if she says no, I'm still offering *you* the chance to tell your story."

"But I'm a no one."

"You really think the woman who turned the head of the world's most mysterious and ruthless media baron is a no one? Look, Lecoq's rumours are now out there. They'll keep swirling until they're addressed."

"Paparazzi have been staking out our home and Elena's office," Maddie conceded with a huff. "Since the day that damned story hit."

"Shocking," Fallows said dryly. "Can you do it by the thirty-first? I'll need it that soon if I'm to capitalize on Lecoq's stunning idiocy."

"I haven't agreed yet."

"So think about it and get back to me ASAP."

Maddie nodded. "I'll let you know."

Elena was in a foul mood, having dodged more intrusive reporters on her way into her office building. Damn them. It would only get worse when Madeleine's story came out. Elena had dearly wanted to say no, but she'd been helpless in the face of her lover's pleading look.

She wouldn't be involved herself, of course. The very idea of explaining herself to strangers who had no right to her life made her shudder. But Madeleinc would make it work.

"Tell the truth for both of us," Elena had told her. "Just remember, if you make me sound even the slightest bit soft…" She'd pursed her lips in a veiled threat that only made Madeleine laugh.

Elena wished it were over already. Instead, each day the rumours intensified.

The word from Perry was that *CQ*'s staff were in near open revolt about Lecoq's article.

"I can see why Véronique calls the media *cafards*," Felicity Simmons hissed, as she stalked up to Elena's desk. "Your stalkers might be few, but they are persistent as scuttling roaches."

Elena glanced up at her Deputy Chief Operations Officer. While the highly strung former lawyer had lost some of her skittishness in the past year since her promotion, she still reminded Elena of a well-bred dressage horse—all tight ribbons, flounce, and attitude. "So, what calamity brings you to my floor? I thought you were organizing Hudson Shard's first anniversary party."

"I'm multi-tasking." Felicity slapped a newspaper page down. "And you'll want to see this."

A full-page advertisement from *The New York Time*s stared back.

We, the following fashion designers, photographers, advertisers, artists, and models declare a boycott against CQ Magazine while Emmanuelle Lecoq remains editor. As proud allies or members of the LGBT+ community, we feel outing a rival editor reveals a serious lack of character and judgment. Further, outing anyone who has never harmed the queer community is an act of violence and hate. It is irresponsible, dangerous, and something we cannot support. Our services to CQ are withdrawn effective immediately.

Signed…

A list of names ran down the page, some famous. At the end were social media hashtags: #FireLecoq and #boycottCQ.

"Eighty-seven names," Felicity nodded with satisfaction. "Plus dozens more boycotting unofficially."

Elena couldn't believe it. "*CQ* made half of those careers. To boycott the hand that feeds them is astonishing. I had no idea outing was this despised."

"Elena, it's not just the principle. They admire your work, respect *Style*, and are disgusted at how Lecoq treated you. They're fuming." Felicity's expression darkened. "My God, I'd happily poke her eyeballs out myself if I could reach that high."

Elena smiled at the thought of her deputy squaring off against the towering Lecoq. "Whose idea was the boycott? Yours?"

With a spectacular eye-roll, Felicity said: "It may astonish you to know I'm actually rather busy running Bartell Corporation for you. I don't have time to manage campaigns. Although I must say it's good someone's finally standing up to that ego-puffed cow. She's been untouchable for far too long."

Turning her gaze back to the ad, Elena said: "If not you, then who? Madeleine?"

"Oh, please. We both know your Australian is far too nice."

Elena's lips twitched. "Yes, well. I'm not denying Madeleine's mystifying eternal niceness."

Felicity snickered softly. "It was your favourite designers. The Duchamps. Apparently it amused Véronique to put the 'noxious *cafard*' in her place. Natalii supplied the hashtags, including a few ruder ones not fit for print. They're trending like crazy. I hear Lecoq's sweating hard now advertisers are pulling out."

"Cockroaches do have a habit of surviving the apocalypse, though."

"Or not." Felicity called up a page on her iPad. "*US Review* just tweeted a story about the *CQ* boycott. They have nine million followers. *Vanity Fair* followed suit. Another five million."

"Oh. Dear." Elena trusted her smile was as evil as it felt.

"Right? Check out *CQ*'s share price today on the back of the boycotts, low circulation, negative publicity, and advertiser withdrawals." She held up her tablet again.

Elena stared at the plunging arrow. "Seriously?" That really was low. A daring plan suddenly hit. Her fingers tingled. "Can you get me Tom Withers? I might need to make a large outlay soon."

Felicity's eyes narrowed. "You wouldn't." Her voice was almost a whisper. "Would you?"

"Wouldn't I?" A hint of mischief laced Elena's tone. "Tell no one. Speed is of the essence."

Felicity's expression was awestruck. "Yes, Elena." Her voice came out a dry gasp.

Maddie was beside herself the day her article was out in the *US Review*. She'd barely slept the previous night, wondering if Elena would hate it. A few hours spent staring at the long, fluttering lashes and quiet intake of breath of the woman asleep beside her hadn't answered the question. Her lover had refused to read it first, saying only that she trusted Maddie.

The hardest thing had been balancing Elena's need to be seen as fierce and tough with all the ways Maddie knew she could be generous and kind.

So Maddie had written the truth: How they'd met. Late-night chats in an empty newspaper office. How they'd come to understand each other, two watchful souls connecting, despite being worlds apart. And that gut-wrenching day Elena chose business over Maddie.

Clutching the glossy magazine, Maddie stared at the cover in confusion.

Elena was pictured with the headline: *Elena Bartell on love, life, and power: 'It would be a grave error to take me on'.*

What? Maddie hadn't quoted Elena saying that. She flipped to the story and then gasped. Two first-person articles were sitting beside each other.

The Mogul.

The Journalist.

Elena had written something after all? Since when?

Elena's piece was a dry, humorous recounting of meeting a "style-deficient reporter from Sydney" and finding her manner to be "blunt to the point of interesting" and her company to be "acceptable despite her refusal to do anything I demanded".

It was funny. God, Elena so rarely showed this side to the world. The piece also made it crystal clear they'd never been involved while Maddie worked for Elena.

The article also explained how Elena had married because she was expected to. And then she'd found love where she hadn't expected to. It finished with an explanation.

"I write this piece solely to correct the record. To suggest Madeleine Grey is brainless or a fling is disgusting. Madeleine is an exceptional, award-winning journalist. She is kind, honest, amusing, and beautiful. Madeleine is a remarkable woman whom I love and wish to have in my life forever. That's all there is to say. The end."

Holy shit. Maddie grabbed her phone, dialled Elena, and croaked out one word. "Why?"

"Ah, you've seen it."

"You didn't say a word! And what happened to you not commenting?"

"I didn't tell you because you might talk me out of it. And I did it because it occurred to me that whatever you'd write would all be about making *me* sound good. It wouldn't enter your head to correct the record on you, would it? Having read your piece, I was right."

"I…oh."

"So I decided to correct the error." Elena's amusement was evident. "Meanwhile, my board issued a statement this morning backing me, condemning Lecoq's smears, and pointing out Bartell Corp's stellar success."

"How does that feel?" Maddie asked quietly. She knew this was what Elena secretly feared: Making a mistake that could see her empire ripped from her. It made sense, since it had happened before, decades ago. Lecoq had stolen Elena's promised editorship when they'd both worked at *CQ*. Overnight, Elena's short career had ended.

"It feels…acceptable." Background voices murmured and then Elena spoke again. "I was in a meeting with Perry and Felicity when you rang. They're being very complimentary about your article." She sighed. "Really Madeleine, did you have to make me sound nice?"

"You *are* nice!"

"Many would dispute that."

More disjointed talking. "Felicity has asked me to convey to you that your article was accurate, nuanced, beautiful, and you should stop being smug."

"What makes her think I'm being—"

"She is quite sure you are." Elena chuckled. "I've shooed them out now. Madeleine, I want to say that Felicity wasn't wrong. What you wrote was beautiful. I'm constantly amazed you see me that way."

"Elena, it's the truth."

"To you."

"Is there any other kind? And you can talk! You told the whole world you want me in your life forever."

"I was merely being accurate." Elena sniffed for effect. "I'm a big believer in truth in publishing."

Maddie laughed. "Forever's a long time. You should probably put a ring on it."

There was a silence as they both digested Maddie's startling comment.

"Oh…" Maddie faded out. *Fuck*. "I mean…"

"*Did* you mean that?" Elena asked softly. "You'd be amenable to…you wish to be proposed to?"

Oh, hell yes. "Yeah?" Maddie groaned at herself. "Only, can we not do this over the phone? Because I've seriously just made this the worst proposal hint ever."

"Understood." Elena sounded delighted. "We will…table this discussion."

Only Elena could make a future wedding proposal sound like an agenda item.

Maddie laughed. "Sure, yep, table that sucker." Her phone pinged. "Ooh, someone's sent me a link to Lecoq's statement about our *US Review* article." She fell silent as she read. "She says she was taken out of context and didn't out anyone. That's such bull. You're the only media mogul with a round office and a helipad."

"Don't forget the only media mogul with a hot, young lesbian lover." Elena chuckled.

"You're in a weirdly good mood," Maddie said. "I thought you'd be skittish today with everyone knowing your business. What's up?"

"Well, aside from being almost proposed to…" Elena's voice dripped with amusement.

Geez. Maddie would never live this down.

"…the *CQ* drama hasn't quite finished. Give it another, hmm, nine or so weeks. It depends on how competent Felicity and Tom are."

"Elena Bartell, what *are* you up to?"

"You'll see." Her voice was all purr.

Elena strode into *CQ*'s gleaming office like she owned it. Of course now that that was actually true—as of an hour ago—it did make the saying all the more delicious.

Bartell Corp had snapped up the freefalling shares at *CQ*. Her management team had done some fast footwork with key *CQ* board members to smooth takeover proceedings. And, now, here she stood, with a fifty-one percent stake in *CQ Magazine*.

Heads snapped around as she passed, curiosity burning. Staff had no clue yet. The news would break within the hour.

The managing director playing escort pointed out a corner office. "That's Ms Lecoq's. As per your instructions, she has not been, er, kept in the loop about any of this. I'll gather the staff for your meeting afterwards." He strode off.

Elena entered the office filled with shiny trinkets, pop art, framed covers, and appalling yellow and blue decor.

Lecoq's head shot up, suspicion coating her features. "What the hell? You can't just barge in here."

Ignoring her, Elena strolled around the room.

"Look, about the article," Lecoq said cautiously, "I may have…misspoke. It was a throwaway line. Suddenly there're boycotts and irate shareholders? Maybe you could spread the word that we've sorted this out between us?"

"Why would I do that?" Elena moved to the window and stared outside. "You want me to clean up your mess? You've just realized how offensive what you did was after staff, investors, and Twitter all pointed it out?"

"It was a flippant remark." Lecoq actually sounded flustered. "Come on, Ellie…"

"Your commentary on my life isn't why I'm here." Elena turned. "You're in my chair."

"Excuse me? This isn't—"

"Bartell Corporation is the reason *CQ*'s shares are no longer plummeting. We bought them; you're welcome. *CQ* is now my company. And that's *my* chair. You're fired."

Horror flitted across Lecoq's features. "B-but…"

Elena felt little sympathy. This woman had ridiculed Madeleine and told the world she was nothing. *How fucking dare she?* "Effective immediately. Security will pack up your things."

"All this…because I suggested you're gay?" Lecoq gaped at her.

Elena's eyes narrowed. "Don't be so asinine. I'm not ashamed of who I am. You're the one who made it seem tawdry."

"Revenge then? For…losing your job to me years ago?"

"I run a Fortune 500 company now," Bartell drawled. "I'm fine."

"So it's because I hurt the feelings of your piece of fluff?" Malice flitted into her eyes. "You're all protective because I suggested you screwed your little assistant? How precious!"

Elena inhaled sharply and leaned into Lecoq's personal space. "You know, you're nothing to me," she snapped. "If you'd just kept your mouth shut, none of this would have happened. But you're not that smart."

"I'm—"

"No. You're not. Do you know the only thing more foolish than spreading lies about the woman I love? Spreading lies about who your *new publisher* loves. And since I don't allow fools in my employ, don't bother seeking a job at any Bartell company. Not that I need to blacklist you. No one in fashion will work with you now. You're toxic. And you did it to yourself." She straightened. "We're done."

With a cold, satisfied smile, Elena swept out of the room.

Elena signed off on the documents she was reviewing. It was late but she was finally done. She stretched.

A throat cleared.

She glanced up to find Madeleine leaning against her office door frame. She blinked at the sight of her, in a grunge band T-shirt, tight black jeans, and boots. "This is a familiar look. Weren't you wearing this the first time we met?"

Madeleine sauntered over. "It seemed fitting given what I heard today."

"Oh?"

"There's this insane rumour that my beautiful corporate warrior woman defended my honour. She bought out *CQ*, fired its nasty editor, and then gave the staff a speech. Something about how she's giving them all a month to prove themselves. And she's going to base herself there for that time to see what they're capable of." She laughed. "Now isn't that where we came in?"

"Except I don't recall some garage-band extra getting in the elevator with me today and insulting me." Elena smirked.

"Argh! I didn't insult you! As you *well* know." Madeleine shook her head. "So tell me, why the stay of execution? You told me this morning that if you hadn't bought out *CQ* it'd be bankrupt in a year. Shouldn't you be holding the last rites?"

"Truthfully?" Elena said. "I just wanted to edit one issue of *CQ*. Tick it off my bucket list and move on."

"And *then* you're firing them? Is it fair to give staff false hope?"

"It's not false. They're being reviewed. I've decided to merge *CQ* and *Style*. *CQ* has some excellent writers and designers. The management's the cancer. Besides, a merger will send a rocket up *Style* that they can't be complacent. I can clean house on two magazines." Her eyes glittered. "Just because I made *Style* doesn't give it a free pass."

Madeleine shook her head. "God, that's so you."

She shrugged. It was.

"So," Madeleine grinned. "You actually did it. Beat *CQ*."

"I did." Satisfaction warmed Elena.

"And all it took was Lecoq outing you."

"All it took was her coming after you. I have my limits—a fact I pointed out to that diseased raccoon. I fired her for stupidity."

"You fired her for being mean to me. You're such a romantic." Madeleine stole a kiss.

"Lies!" Elena snorted. "My God, though, Lecoq has zero taste. You should have seen her office. I might have to get a flame thrower in before I take over." There was a thought.

Madeleine slid her arms around her. "I'm really happy for you."

"I couldn't have done it without you. Or the Duchamps and their boycott. I might have to send them flowers. A whole houseful." Her lips curled up.

"That'd go down about as well as last time." Madeleine laughed.

"Honestly, I never thought I'd ever get back my first dream."

"And you did. You got the girl, too."

Elena licked her lips and darted a nervous look at Maddie. "You know, I've been thinking. About the proposal you made?" She was pleased how flippant she sounded. She swallowed. *Now or never.*

"What proposal?"

Elena gave her desk a testing rap.

"Oh!" Madeleine's eyes widened. "Are you serious? And don't you dare tease me like last time. That was so cruel promising desk sex and not delivering."

"About as cruel as you leaving me to attempt a serious conversation with Perry while my thong stared at me from across the room."

"Okay, that was a little evil of me."

"So it *was* on purpose? Distracting me from retrieving it?"

"You deserved it. Torturing me with impossible fantasies." Madeleine looked unrepentant.

"Hmm." Elena's lips twitched. "Perhaps it was a *little* cruel. I'm prepared to make amends."

Madeleine's face lit up. "Are you seriously talking desk sex after all this time?"

"Don't be ridiculous. It's something else." She knocked the desk again, above the drawer. "Open it."

Madeleine slid open the desk drawer. A velvet box sat inside.

"I promised to 'table' something last time," Elena said. "This counts as a table, does it not?" She held her breath, placed the box between them, and opened it to Madeleine.

Her lover stared at the diamond ring for so long that Elena wondered if she'd made a terrible mistake. Elena had spent an eternity trying to find the right one, even enlisting the services of Perry, who was officially insufferable now. "Don't you like it?" she asked pensively.

"Are you kidding?" Madeleine's eyes shone. "I love it. But you know…a beautiful ring like that usually comes with a question."

"Is that so?"

Madeleine nodded. "Spoiler alert, I'm going to say yes. And then I'm going to kiss you. And then we're going to have hot fiancée desk sex."

"Well, now I'm conflicted." Elena laughed. She held the ring out, and said seriously, "Madeleine Grey, I knew the day we met that you were trouble. How right I was—and how much I needed it. Needed *you*. I love you. Will you…"

"Yes!" Madeleine slid the ring on and kissed her breathlessly.

"You do realize I didn't actually ask you anything," Elena pointed out. Her heart was thundering, her mouth dry, and she couldn't seem to control her grinning mouth. She'd never felt anything like this before. She was pretty sure it was a sign of true love—or a heart attack.

"Asked and answered." Madeleine laughed. "Now then, I'm certain promises were made." She patted the desk, a gleam in her eye.

"I'm quite sure I didn't agree to that," Elena protested, although truthfully, it was the reason she'd proposed in her office: To give Madeleine her fantasy.

Maddie's T-shirt was already half off her head. "Uh-huh," came the muffled sound.

With a sigh to hide her mounting excitement, Elena sat back, unbuttoning her silk blouse. She watched appreciatively as Maddie tried to haul her skinny jeans down her legs. "You're so beautiful," Elena noted quietly.

Kicking her jeans away, Madeleine grinned. "I love it when you get mushy."

Elena slid off her blouse and gave an imperious look. "It's not mush. It's accuracy. And the truth is you *are* beautiful." She lowered her voice. "I love you more than is sane, Madeleine."

"I love you too." Madeleine smiled. "And who knew you were so romantic?"

Elena sighed at the frankly preposterous comment and kissed the lie straight off those lips.

If you enjoyed this short story, check out *The Brutal Truth* by Lee Winter, the novel in which Elena and Maddie met and fell in love.

Skye Storm's Invite Absolutely Everyone Ultimate Pool Party

Skye Storm was not one to boast, but her end-of-year pool parties were pretty much the talk of LA. It wasn't just the who's who guest list that put her all-day event on the map. Oh no, it was the *how*. Indeed, creating the how was Skye's second-favorite thing in the world involving her parties.

This year's theme was *At The Movies,* and guests who were so inclined would be able to kick back on giant floating pink flamingos in the pool while classic films were projected on one wall. *His Girl Friday,* starring Cary Grant and Rosalind Russell, was playing at the moment. Waiters in jaunty togas that Skye had designed herself, all wearing name tags that read *Spartacus*, would wade in at regular intervals and keep the food and drinks flowing. The Something About Bloody Marys were proving the surprise hit of this year's party.

Skye had learned years ago that the more intricate she made her events, the more attention to detail, the more her guests felt appreciated and the happier they were.

Oh, how she loved making people happy.

Besides, injecting a little color and absurdism into the universe was expected of her. Eccentric, they called her. As if that was a bad thing? *Please*. Being larger than life took about the same effort as being smaller than life, so why not go big?

Adding a spritz of homemade lilac perfume behind each ear (she'd vlogged two months ago on how to make it using only homegrown ingredients), she nodded to herself. *There. Ready.*

Skye wondered where her errant live-in lover of three decades had gotten himself to. Brock was probably still doing a "perimeter sweep" as he called it, prodding the bushes, looking for paparazzi. They often staked out these parties for a glimpse of A-listers arriving. He'd get distracted sooner or later. Probably when Elizabeth Thornton made an appearance.

Skye inhaled at the reminder of Brock's perpetual scowl on the topic of their youngest daughter's partner. When Summer had first brought the austere Elizabeth home to meet them both, Brock hadn't been able to disguise his incredulity that they were together. Oh, they weren't *together-together* back then, but even so. As a couple, Summer and Elizabeth were…unusual. Sunshine meet ice. Brightness, optimism, and openness meet walls of wariness, British reserve, and caution.

Now that they'd dated two years and lived together for more than half that, Brock was having an even harder time understanding Summer's affection for the gifted, introverted actress that she'd adored since she was a teenager.

But just because Brock couldn't see it didn't mean it wasn't meant to be. Sometimes combinations went together in unexpected ways, didn't they? As an artistic soul, Skye knew all about that.

"Hey, Mom?" Summer's voice wafted up the stairs, getting louder. "Your Head Spartacus says we're getting low on Death Star Daiquiris and that someone's elbow went into the Cheeses of Nazareth platter. I'm not sure if it was a religious protest or an accident, but we've had to toss it out. Also, two of Dad's stuntmen friends are apparently wrestling out front, and no one can work out if they're for real or not. Can you…" She entered the room and froze, her mouth dropping slightly open.

Oh, that. "Like my ears?" Skye preened a little at the reaction.

Summer leaned forward and prodded them. "Whoa, they're amazing. You wear Yoda well."

"I like to think so." Skye tweaked her green foam ears that she'd molded herself. She'd stuck them to a headband that also kept her wild, curly, gray-blonde hair from escaping. "Or is it, *Think so I like*?"

Summer groaned. "Anyway, about Dad's friends…"

"Oh, I saw them before. They're helping your father on his little security patrol." Brock did take his guests' privacy very seriously. "They've probably found themselves another photographer in the bushes and are helping the gentleman understand it's rude to spy on our guests."

"Um… I hope it doesn't go to court. Again." Summer shot Skye a worried look.

"No, no. Your father knows where the line is. He invokes a little psychological terror rather than the physical kind. I'm sure he and his friends will have simply given any intruder a good shake, without damaging the equipment. And, really, breaking that paparazzo's camera was the main reason your father got into trouble last time." *More or less.*

Summer frowned. "I guess?"

"Anyway, as for the other issue, please ask Head Spartacus to top up the Lord of the Onion Rings platter to make up for the Cheeses of Nazareth loss. Now then, enough party business. Darling, how long do you have to wait? Is Elizabeth's plane arriving soon?"

Summer beamed. "She's already landed and is on her way over. She's coming straight from the airport."

"Well now, that sounds enthusiastic. Reminds me of someone else I could name." Skye gave Summer a knowing look. "You've been climbing the walls for weeks. What will you two get up to tonight, I wonder?"

Summer's jaw dropped for a second time. "Oh God. Seriously?"

Cupping Summer's cheek, Skye forced herself to look earnest. "You know I have a Princess Leia outfit somewhere around here that I almost wore today. If you want to spice things up later? Your father always loves me in that."

"Mom!" Summer gasped, her eyes darting to the exit.

"All right, fine. I'll stop teasing." Skye laughed. "You're so easy, though."

"You know this isn't normal, right?" Summer's finger twirled to and fro between them. "Parents telling kids about their role-playing sexy times?"

"Normal's just an arbitrary societal construct designed to keep us all in our little boxes. I know I taught you to be less 'normal' and more yourself." Skye patted down the front of her Yoda robes. "Now then, time to go we must."

"Ha-ha." Summer sneaked a furtive glance at her phone.

"So impatient. Elizabeth's definitely going to get her bun buttered tonight." At the appalled look on Summer's face, Skye lifted her eyebrows, "What? Was that in any way inaccurate?"

"Ugh, I can't. You're impossible."

"Thank you, darling. I do try. You'd complain soon enough if I was just like every other mother."

"I don't know about that," Summer grumbled.

"What's that, dear?"

"Nothing." She sighed. "I'll go talk to Spartacus. And try to bleach my brain of this conversation."

Pulling along her wheeled luggage, Elizabeth Thornton picked her way up the path to Skye and Brock's bright yellow Granada Hills home. After so long on set in the middle of nowhere, she couldn't wait to see Summer again, even if it was here—at a crowded party in an eccentric house with Summer's even more eccentric parents. Well, one parent in particular. Elizabeth had learned long ago to expect nothing less than the unexpected from Skye Storm.

A wide, tall shadow fell over her, freezing her midstride at the front door. From it came a low rumble. "Elizabeth."

She looked up and up into probing, powerful, pale blue eyes that could probably cause a charging rhino to quail. "Brock."

"Nice you're in town again. Been awhile." Brock's lips didn't quite complete their trajectory into a smile, and his eyes remained flinty.

"It has. Glad to be back. Less…humidity." Right, sure, it was the weather she'd missed.

He grunted. Folding his bulging, muscled arms across his wide barrel chest, Brock looked her up and down. "Welp. I guess that's true."

Silence fell, as they'd clearly exhausted the topic at hand. *Okay then.*

Elizabeth glanced around. Boisterous laughter, along with tinkling conversation, and the clink of glasses drifted to her ears. And, if her love of the classics was reliable, matinee idol Rosalind Russell's unmistakable rat-a-tat delivery was machine-gunning a co-star from somewhere near the rear of the property.

Elizabeth slid her gaze back to the street just as a short man who looked like a muscled, mustache-less Yosemite Sam sprinted past out of nowhere. With a predatory gleam in his eyes, he suddenly leaped into the air, landing in bushes with a gleeful shout. The shrubbery let out a startled "oomph," and an expensive-looking camera tumbled out.

She blinked and pointed. "Um… What—"

"Summer's dyin' to see you," Brock cut in, apparently unmoved by the drama unfolding just behind him. "Been talking about it all week." Somehow he made it sound like an accusation. As if it was Elizabeth's fault her filming location had been out of state?

"It's mutual." Elizabeth was craving Summer after six long weeks away in Louisiana.

"Good."

Good? As if there was any doubt? Wait, maybe there was? The way Brock weighed Elizabeth up, as if he didn't quite think she was committed to his daughter… Was that what this was about?

"I love her," she said quietly, pushing the words out past her teeth, resenting a little bit her need to justify herself to Summer's father. But that's what fathers were for, she supposed. Even though her own was spectacularly uninterested in involving himself in Elizabeth's love life. Too embarrassing. Might lead to an awkward conversation. He'd sooner chop off an arm.

"Good," Brock said again, but this time those blue chips softened. "Me too."

Oh-kayyy. This was now officially the most he'd ever said to her.

"Don't let her down," Brock finished, his thick graying brows knitting into a small forest.

"I won't. I wouldn't do that."

"You already have." He turned to go, his voice edged with finality. "But I get it. Just don't leave her hanging too long while you get your shit together is all I'm saying. Got it? Enjoy the party."

What the hell? And what was she supposed to *get?* She squinted up at him in confusion.

Before Brock could expand on his withering verdict regarding Elizabeth's apparent relationship failings, another guest arrived. Distracted, Brock headed over to greet him. It was a producer, a very famous one at that.

Elizabeth left the men to it, including the pair wrestling in the bushes. The owner of the camera suddenly staggered to his feet, dusted himself down, snarled some indelicate comments about Yosemite Sam's parentage, grabbed his photographic equipment, and bolted down the street. The other man loped after him, making no effort to catch him, cackling with laughter.

How…random.

She shook her head. Elizabeth needed to get a Summer fix and a stiff drink. *Now.*

After dropping her luggage out of the way upstairs, Elizabeth headed out to the pool area that was brimming with about sixty guests, each as famous as the next.

Seeing them relaxing among friends, family, and lovers startled her a bit. Somehow Skye did that: Gave people, including incredibly private and powerful people, a safe oasis to be themselves. Elizabeth's gaze roamed restlessly. Where was Summer?

"Impressive names here, aren't there?"

She turned to find her manager giving her an amused look.

"I suppose," Elizabeth conceded. "If you enjoy rubbernecking at famous people."

"Which you were doing, darling," Delvine said with a chuckle. "Don't you dare deny it."

Elizabeth rolled her eyes. "It's hard not to notice the existence of people hyped bigger than God who are paid more than the GDP of small countries."

"You do realize you're in that bracket now? Maybe not *quite* at their pay grade but recognition-wise certainly. Sometimes I think you forget you're famous too."

"I never forget—that's the problem," Elizabeth muttered, folding her arms. "I'm not…ungrateful for the success and opportunities my career affords. It's just complicated having a life lived in the public eye."

"Mmm. Trouble in paradise, darling?"

Elizabeth peered around to buy herself some time before answering. An action star was showing off his Pomeranian dressed as an Ewok. *Well. That's different.* A starlet was getting a massage from a masseuse in a small hot pink tent with two canvas sides designed to look like a harem, with colorful silk cushions tossed all over the padded floor mat.

After Elizabeth's bumpy flight, she wouldn't mind being next in line to get her kinks worked out.

A young man with slicked-back hair was talking fast with his mouth and even faster with his hands to the producer she'd seen being greeted earlier. She caught some of the young man's impromptu pitch: "…Not zombie-zombie, though, more like, um, high-functioning ghouls. Female ghouls, mainly. Not entirely *fully* dressed… The disease may have rotted their clothing…"

She snorted. *High art then.*

"Darling?"

Oh. Delvine was still waiting for an answer. "Not…trouble. Beyond my usual issues with the fishbowl. The fakeness of it all. And my place within it."

"Is this about your film shoot? How's it going?"

"It's fine. We're almost finished. I have discovered a loathing for Louisiana's mosquitoes, though. They're bigger than most pet dogs. They see my delicate English skin and rub their evil little legs together with glee. I've spent weeks wafting around in a toxic sheen of bug spray. Our makeup artist told me there's sixty-eight varieties in Louisiana alone." She shuddered.

Delvine laughed and plucked a small plate from a passing waiter. "Have you tried these Silence of the Lamb Cutlets?" She didn't wait for an answer. "Superb. Almost as good as the Jurassic Pork. Okay, so insect life aside, if it's not your film irritating you, are you just having general existential issues regarding Hollywood? Just more of the same?"

"Probably." Was that it? Ever since Elizabeth and Summer had spent half a year in England, they'd both come back much more acutely aware of the differences between the two acting worlds. The Brits didn't tolerate divas or celebrities shouting at the top of their lungs about who they were. Talking yourself up was considered bad form. And the theater scene Summer had been immersed in had been incredibly gay-friendly, warm, and accepting, not just with her fellow actors but among "theater luvvies" who made up a lot of audiences. So accepting was that world that it had become increasingly difficult for Summer to keep the truth of who she loved a secret.

Their London sabbatical had been both the perfect tonic to Hollywood and the worst reminder of its downfalls. They'd returned to a place bursting, as always, with selfie-snapping fame-whores, power-hungry executives, and wannabe starlets, not to mention the constant swirl of secrets and lies…including their own.

It was impossible not to notice how Hollywood was a huge sucking vortex of superficiality that corrupted everyone with the belief that any serious players must feign perfection and heterosexuality. All to maintain that shiny fantasy veneer.

This created an insidious little trap. While Elizabeth hated Hollywood's fakeness, image control, and the lies of omission she told, she also couldn't relate to Summer's desire to be out about her sexuality. And it was something Summer wanted a great deal now she was no longer chasing girl-next-door roles.

Wanting to be out was a hard thing for Elizabeth to understand. Even though she rankled at the masks she was expected to wear, she'd spent so long preventing the world from seeing who she was that she wasn't sure she even *could* be honest now. She wondered how Summer related to her at all some days. On this they were so different.

"So fill me in," Delvine said. "What brings on this latest round of introspection? Or has the lovely Summer Hayes been rubbing off on you? Well, more than just literally."

Elizabeth snickered softly. "Have you been saving that one up?"

"Possibly." Delvine's eyes twinkled.

"I doubt you'd want Summer's viewpoint to rub off on me on certain… sensitive… issues," Elizabeth noted, her eyes suddenly widening as she caught sight of an A-lister canoodling with another actress. Both women had fiercely heterosexual reputations.

"Ah. You might be surprised. It depends on a great many things." Delvine followed her gaze but didn't seem the least bit surprised by the sight. "I take the view that anyone with prodigious talent, as you have, rarely suffers much long-term damage from minor controversy. And, in my experience, miserable clients aren't nearly as easy to work with as fulfilled ones. So I'm open to discussing the options if you really are seriously considering weighing up…certain things. I'm not your skittish, risk-averse agent, after all. Your happiness does matter to me."

"Thank you."

"So, darling, are you considering a change in…image direction?" Delvine probed.

Am I? What a ghastly thought. Being singled out, labeled, talked about, and… "No," Elizabeth said adamantly.

Delvine looked faintly surprised. "I see."

A drinks waiter drifted by, so Elizabeth stopped him, realizing how parched she was. His name tag said Spartacus. "So *you're* Spartacus," she said with a slight smile.

"The one and only, ma'am." His drawl told her he'd been getting this joke all day. He bent forward with a flourish, holding out a tray. "Clockwork Orange Juice? War of the Rosés? C3Pellegrino?"

She took the Pellegrino water and glanced back at Delvine's curious expression as Spartacus moved away. "I mean, who wants all the scrutiny, trolling, special interest groups' expectations, and loss of privacy?" Elizabeth finished.

"I'm guessing Summer?"

God. Elizabeth sagged. A sliver of guilt went through her. She was well aware, though she and Summer tiptoed all around discussing it, that the only thing now stopping Summer from outing herself was the scrutiny it would bring on Elizabeth, since they were so often out and about together.

Delvine patted Elizabeth's hand. "Love is a bitch, isn't it?"

Elizabeth exhaled, then drew in a large gulp of water.

"It's also worth a great many sacrifices when you find it," Delvine continued.

"What are you suggesting?" Elizabeth's gaze shot up to meet Delvine's.

"Relax. Nothing. But when the time is right, you won't need to wonder about any of this. You'll just know." Delvine smiled ruefully. "And while, as a general rule, making certain things public may be terrible for business, know that I will always be your friend first. Albeit one with a fabulously acerbic commentary to put things into perspective. I might remind you, for instance, that there are far worse things in life than to have the world know you're madly in love or…" She lowered her voice. "…to have someone look at you the way Summer Hayes does." Delvine paused and squinted toward the pool, shading her eyes. "Speak of the adorable devil, isn't that your lovely woman over there?"

Elizabeth's attention snapped across the water and fell into the dizzying sight of Summer in a red bikini, a sun hat with some festive green tinsel looped around it, and flip-flops. "There's a sight," she murmured.

She could have done without Delvine's knowing chuckle.

Summer swirled her Yoda Soda as she milled around, poolside. Her drink was supposed to be green-dyed Diet Coke, but it only looked the same fizzy black while inadvertently dyeing everyone's tongues greenish-brown. Summer had a deep aversion to green dye. For reasons.

"Miss me?" Elizabeth's rich, warm tone sounded next to Summer's ear, sending shivers cascading through her.

"You're here!" Summer spun to face her, her eyes widening at Elizabeth's outfit. Her mouth went dry. "Oh God. Wow, Bess! You're *so* here…"

Summer's eyes roamed the delicious ass-hugging, tan, designer linen pants emphasizing Elizabeth's long legs, and the crisp, figure-hugging cream vest, with only the faintest hint of white bikini under it, exposing a deep vee of cleavage and toned, bare arms. Italian leather sandals and a broad-brimmed hat finished the chic picture. *Gah. Stunning, sexy, with an edgy dash of soft butch. Lesbian Indiana Jones.* "Um. Hi." Summer's gaze did a free fall down that glorious, teasing vest. "Tell me you didn't wear that on the plane? There'd be riots."

"Hi, yourself. And I changed upstairs when I arrived." Elizabeth studied Summer with amusement but made absolutely no movement toward her.

Tease.

Summer was dying to throw herself at Elizabeth and kiss her senseless. Instead, she slid herself into Elizabeth's arms for a nice, innocent(*ish*) hug. Okay, maybe she snuck in a little squeeze a *little* lower than was socially acceptable. Elizabeth's chuckle against her ear told her she was totally sprung. "Mercy," she whispered into Elizabeth's rich brown hair. "You're lethal."

"You say the sweetest things." Elizabeth offered a hint of a smile. She regarded Summer for a moment, then gave a quizzical frown, "Darling, did you know your tongue's…well, green?"

The party was going exactly as predicted. Skye was most pleased, given the number one thing she loved about her parties: the *why*.

She threw parties to bring people together. To help people come out of their shells. To give joy to those who felt miserable, which was a lot of people in Hollywood, even though everyone faked the opposite. (Skye knew the truth). And her parties gave permission. Freedom for all the guests to get out of choking suits and sleek, "perfect" dresses and just be themselves.

Autumn, her eldest daughter, who was more tightly wound than a racing greyhound, wandered by in a white jumpsuit that looked repurposed from the ABBA party Skye had hosted six months ago. Although far be it for Skye Storm to offer wardrobe advice to any daughter who didn't want to hear it. Autumn was far too sensitive about helpful suggestions on any part of her life, even her love life. Which, frankly, was a shame since Skye knew at least half a dozen eligible bachelors who would be perfect for her, if only Autumn…

"Mom? No."

"No what?"

"Your scheming 'get Autumn a date' face isn't a mystery to me." Autumn peered at her. "I'm happy doing a long-distance thing with Andrew again. I know he's miles away in London, but still. I need you to respect that."

"But of course." Skye offered a contrite expression. Why, the very idea she didn't respect either of her girls' space. "He's lovely."

"He is." Autumn's jaw firmed. "On those rare occasions I get to see him."

Touchy topic then. "Have you tried sexting? Strip Skyping? That always spices things up for lovelorn couples. Trust me."

Autumn's eyes narrowed. "Mom! Shit. Don't joke about that. I got the visuals."

"I am quite serious, though. Why, your father and I once…"

"Do *not* finish that sentence." She held up one hand in a stop motion. "Look, I came to see if you've got any more Rocky Road to Perdition. George and Ron were asking."

"In the fridge. I'm so glad they came."

"So are they." Autumn's crooked smirk surfaced. "They're proving popular with the B-list starlets."

Skye rejoiced at the sight of Autumn's rare smile. *So highly strung*, she tsked to herself. "Well, that's excellent. Everyone seems to be having a good time."

"Sure." Autumn extracted the dessert slice she'd come for, laid it on the counter, and slid onto a barstool. "Especially Summer. Elizabeth's just turned up. She's strutting about in some vest-and-pants thing, looking so Indiana Jones cool that I think Summer's about to throw her down and take her under a deck chair."

"Is that so?" Skye laughed. "Well, she has been deprived. My poor girl doesn't hide it well either."

"That's one word for it. Seriously, Summer has been hard to manage lately. Shoot me if I ever get that needy for my other half."

"Don't make fun of your sister. It's been hard for her since she got back from England. You know why."

"Yeah." Autumn frowned. "I keep waiting for her to out herself in some huge accidental blurt that I'll have to rush in and manage. The subconscious is weird like that. The longer she keeps her secret, the twitchier she's getting."

"I wish they would both be honest, though," Skye said. "It's easier on the soul. Truth first. I understand why they're being cautious, of course. It's hard to avoid the fear over careers stalling and the rest of the nonsense that passes as logic in Hollywood. But Summer's ready now. I want you to support your sister whenever and however she comes out. No matter how…ridiculous." Because Autumn wasn't wrong—Summer could do ridiculous like the best of them.

"Of course I will. Assuming Elizabeth doesn't kill her first."

"Why would she?" Skye cocked her head. "Elizabeth would support pretty much anything Summer does."

"It's *Elizabeth Thornton,*" Autumn said, as though that explained everything. "And she won't support her on this. No way. She's terrified of being out…or outed by proxy by her girlfriend."

"Elizabeth's simply reserved and hates being gossiped about. Big difference."

"I don't think you know her as well as you think, Mom."

"Actually, I think you're reading far too much into her aloof image. Once you really get to know her, you'll find she's more sensitive than people give her credit for. She enjoys being left alone by the world in most things. Especially this."

Autumn gave her a doubtful look. "Well, either way, if she and Summer keep burning sexual-tension holes into each other whenever they're near, it won't be much of a secret for long."

Batting the Rocky Road to Perdition tray around for a moment, she cleared her throat. "So, to change the subject, Delvine's offered me a job in her firm. A mentorship and a whole career path in talent management. I'd still get to manage Summer, at least for the first few years. It's a huge opportunity."

"That's wonderful!" Pride filled Skye. Delvine was such a well-respected manager in LA.

"It's…unexpected."

Skye said nothing for a moment, aware her taciturn oldest daughter processed her emotions in a much different way to Summer, or herself for that matter. "It's a sign Delvine thinks highly of you."

"I get that. But it's a lot to take in. And it means I'd be tied to LA. If I wanted to move to London to be with Andrew, I couldn't if I took this job."

"Or Andrew could move back here." Skye wondered why Autumn always assumed it was down to her to fix everything herself. She did that with Summer too. "There are more options than people usually notice. You just have to look for them."

"Well, I'm considering the offer. If Summer's okay with me working for her girlfriend's manager." Autumn paused, watching as Skye set out some ingredients in front of herself. "What are you doing?"

Skye smiled. "Inventing a new drink. You're just in time to help. I need some lemon rind grated and…hmm…olives."

Autumn squinted at her. "You're inventing drinks now? Mid-party?"

"Yes, because it's just come to me. Follow your muse, honey. And it'll either be fabulous or awful. But who cares? It's the journey that counts. Through example, I teach everyone it's okay to experiment and try new things. It's okay to fail too."

"Riiight."

"Normally, Summer would help, but it sounds as if she's absorbed in something tall, beautiful, and British right now."

"No kidding. I'm surprised Elizabeth's still wearing any of her lez-catnip outfit given the way Summer keeps looking at her."

"Well, far be it for me to get between that fevered reunion." Skye offered a satisfied sigh. "I'm just delighted my children have healthy sex lives. That's so important. How many times did I explain that to you both, growing up?"

"Ew. Far, far too many times."

"What is it with you millennials? So prudish." Skye bent down and rummaged around in a counter cabinet before emerging with a plastic lemon juicer that she held aloft like Rafiki showing off Simba.

Oh! That gave her an idea for her new drink's name…

"Sure, Mom, *we're* the problem."

Summer leaned against the upstairs lilac bathroom door, careful to avoid the seashell trim, and groaned. "It's not fair."

"Mmm?" Elizabeth feathered kisses against her ear, curling her blonde hair out of the way as she continued her path. "What isn't?"

"You and me, finally in the same location, and instead of alone time, we have to be at Mom's party."

"But when I suggested going straight home from the airport and reuniting properly, didn't you tell me Skye Storm's Invite Absolutely Everyone In Her Phone,

Ultimate Must-Attend Christmas Pool Party was THE event of the year?" Elizabeth smiled against the ridges of Summer's ear. "I'm fairly sure those were your exact words."

Summer slumped against her. "Doesn't mean I have to like it." Okay, so she sounded petulant. But, seriously universe, it had been six weeks apart.

"Oh? You mean you're not having fun catching up with your family again? What about meeting all those industry A-listers? Or the beautiful actresses swanning around? I'm sure at least one caught your eye."

"One did," Summer agreed readily. "And I can't have her the way I'd like to for hours. Which is driving me crazy because it's been ages since we've been together… and look at you." She slapped the enticing tailored vest before her. "Insisting on parading around in *that!* My God, every queer woman here has been swallowing her tongue over you."

"This old thing?" Elizabeth murmured, amusement lacing her tone. She dropped a kiss on Summer's neck, causing her to whimper. "Actually, I bribed the bored costume designer on set to make it exactly the way I thought you'd like it."

"Oh? And how's that?" Summer's eyes became half-lidded.

"Hmm, a deep vee here," Elizabeth suggested, drifting her hands to her cleavage that showed her pale, smooth skin. "Tight here." Her fingers slid to her bust, then down to the curve of her ass, where her designer pants hugged it. "I trust you appreciate the full effect."

Appreciate wasn't even the half of it. "I do," Summer croaked.

"Excellent." Elizabeth's hand wandered south, mapping the contours of Summer's flat stomach, and teasing the waistband of her red bikini bottom.

Summer groaned. "Why can't we just stay in here and fuck like bunnies till it's time to go home?"

"I'm sure Skye would notice your absence eventually. And I suspect someone might have to use the bathroom sometime."

"That's why I hauled your ass into the upstairs one no one can ever find." Summer leaned into Elizabeth. "Please?"

Elizabeth's eyes darkened. "I know this lacks decorum or…or something. But you are impossible to resist." She gently thudded Summer against the door, the sound echoing around the room. Crushing their hips together, Elizabeth's thigh insinuated itself between Summer's legs. "At least you didn't suggest taking this to your mother's bed."

"Ugh. She'd have been fine with it, which made it too off-putting to consider. You know when other kids were sneaking off to have sex? My mother was explaining how I should only have enriching sexual experiences and gave me *permission.* Nothing makes sex less exciting than having your mother give you the thumbs-up and a pat on the head. So I sneaked off to see plays instead."

"My little rebel." Elizabeth smiled. "Although you're making up for lost time in adulthood."

"Well, of course. I discovered how fun lesbians are to play with. And more recently, I discovered how tasty *your* lips are. How excited your nipples get when I tweak them like so." She demonstrated through Elizabeth's clothing.

Elizabeth shifted, offering a strained moan that was pure aphrodisiac.

Tugging at the buttons on Elizabeth's vest, Summer pushed the two halves aside and then stared. "No bra? It's just a *tiny* bikini top under here."

"It would have ruined the effect. And possibly impaired access."

Summer eyebrows shot up. "So you planned this?"

"Hoped, maybe." Elizabeth slid their bodies closer together. "I've missed you a great deal. There I was, stuck filming on a remote Louisiana bayou, stuffed into a rigid costume for months on end, needing you so badly."

"Please, your murder mystery is set in modern day, indoors, and you wore a business suit the whole time. And it was six weeks, not months." Summer slapped Elizabeth's chest lightly at Elizabeth's outrageous rearranging of the facts. Then, enjoying the heated skin she'd found, kept sliding. She pulled apart the bikini top, dropping it to the floor.

"Semantics," Elizabeth conceded with a breathy gasp and leaned into Summer's soft touch.

Summer gathered a naked, pale breast, weighing it reverently, running a thumb over Elizabeth's pebbling dark pink nipple. She pinched it and smoothed it over and over.

"I love that," Elizabeth said with a blissed-out sigh. "I missed you. It's never the same when you're too far away."

"How *much* did you miss me?" Summer's eyebrow lifted. "Did you think of me at night? All those long, long nights out of cell phone range, with just you…and your imagination."

"You want to know if I touched myself and thought of you?" Elizabeth's voice was dry, amused, but contained a hint of roughness that did all sorts of things to Summer's insides.

"Did you?" Summer's cheeks heated at how breathy her words came out.

"Hmm. What a question. You want to know if my hand rucked up my shirt and pushed down my bed shorts, and I pretended it was yours? You want to know if it was your fingers I imagined sliding across my skin, making my back arch, as I cried out your name? You think the mere idea of you can do that to me?"

Summer's mouth was bone-dry as those taunting, teasing words fell from Elizabeth's curling lips.

Elizabeth's voice dropped to a throaty purr. "Would it please you to know that you can?" Her intense eyes regarded Summer. "That you do make me come apart in my thoughts when I can't have you in reality, in my bed, under me, touching me. Do you know I took you so many times, over so many nights, until even just picturing you spread out naked for me made me start to shudder."

"Oh God."

"So what I'd like to know is, what you plan to do about this?" Elizabeth's eyebrow lifted in challenge. "I mean, since you've left me in quite a state for so long."

Summer's entire lower body clenched at the haughty, teasing tone. Her nipples hardened into painful knots. Elizabeth's words stroked her without laying a finger on her.

In answer, Summer bent her head to Elizabeth's closest nipple and laved it with her rough tongue, invoking small moans from her lover. One hand tugged at the button at Elizabeth's waist, yanking it undone, then slid the fly down in a soft clicking noise that seemed magnified in the silence.

Summer's fingers slipped inside Bess's briefs, finding coarse whorls of hair, followed by a source of heat and copious liquid. "A little deprived?" Summer suggested.

"You already know the answer." Elizabeth sounded both miffed and needy. "Definitely deprived. My fingers can only do so much on their own. It's you I need. So stop playing and start…getting to business."

Her lack of pretense over what she needed was so unexpected that Summer obeyed instantly. She slid a finger inside Elizabeth, then drew the moisture she discovered back up to rub her clit.

Elizabeth stiffened. "Yes," she hissed. "Oh, right there, God, Summer, yes."

After rubbing and teasing for a few moments, Summer circled Bess's most sensitive spot with two slippery fingers, until Elizabeth thudded her head back against the door, eyes glassy, voice breathless.

Extracting her hand, while ignoring the startled "nngh?" of complaint from Elizabeth, Summer dropped suddenly to her knees. She curled her fingers slowly over the waistband of Elizabeth's undone pants, testing the material under her fingertips, before wrenching them and her panties down without warning.

Elizabeth gasped as the cool air hit her aroused center.

Their eyes met, and it felt as if fire were arcing between them, scorching and powerful. Summer's underwear was drenched. Even the thought of Bess touching her intimately made her tremble. It was intoxicating to know it hadn't just been Summer who'd felt their absence so keenly. The proof was before her. She could smell Elizabeth's interest, see it glistening.

Summer leaned in and breathed against those folds. "Just so you know, I'm going to go slow and savor you the way you deserve, until all you remember is my mouth, my lips, my heat on you. Then, when you've barely recovered, I'm going to make you come again. Fast and frenzied, until you can't even remember how you got here or what day it is."

Elizabeth shuddered. "Yes."

"You look so gorgeous today, Bess. But you knew that, didn't you?" Summer drew her hands up and down Elizabeth's naked legs, kneading her around the muscles of her taut thighs. "You knew I'd be a puddle when you strutted in here like a wet dream, with that sharp vest and that tantalizing hint of boobs and your toned arms. You just love fucking with your icy, classy, don't-touch image, don't you? You're so fucking hot that everyone wanted you; their eyes were all over you. But it's me who gets you like this. Bare and wanting. I get to melt you." Summer inhaled at that prospect, trembling. "And I will."

Summer sliced her tongue up and down Elizabeth's folds, retracing the pathways to bliss her fingers had found earlier, reveling in the faint tremors she was drawing out of Elizabeth. "God, Bess," she murmured. "You had me so on edge the moment I saw you today. If you'd accidentally brushed your fingers against me down there, I'd have shattered."

Elizabeth's lips curled into a smile as her fingers found the top of Summer's head, tangling in her hair. "I knew that. Your eyes don't hide much. It made me feel powerful."

"That's how I feel now." Summer stroked her tongue hard against Elizabeth's clit, pressing into the slippery bundle of flesh that dipped and danced under her lips. Then she slipped a finger inside Elizabeth and curled it up.

Elizabeth's hands tightened painfully on Summer's her hair. "*Ohhh.*" Her breasts swayed as she curled over, as though protecting herself from the onslaught of her body's response, biting down on a low moan. The rush of her release washed Summer's lips, and the sensation sparked quivers in the pit of Summer's stomach.

"So beautiful," Summer murmured against her, licking away the slickness between Elizabeth's wet thighs. "Delicious. I could have you all day. In fact, wear this more often, and that could be a reality."

Elizabeth sagged against the door. "I don't think I paid the costume designer enough. Clearly she did an outstanding job."

"Mmmm. And how." Summer began sliding her tongue over Elizabeth's folds once more. "Now, I believe I promised you something fast and furious."

Elizabeth's breath hitched. "I don't think I have two in me right now."

"Don't sell yourself short," Summer teased.

Elizabeth's eyes fluttered closed as her protests died.

Summer renewed her efforts, sliding her fingers where her tongue had been, and was soon richly rewarded.

A banging on the bathroom door made them both jump. Elizabeth panicked for a moment before remembering the door was locked, so no one was about to find her in a tangled, sweaty mess with her naked girlfriend on the plush pile purple bath mat.

"Summer?" a female voice called impatiently.

Summer mouthed, *Autumn.*

"I know you're in there. Process of elimination. So get your hands out of each other's pants and check your phones."

Groaning, Summer called back, "What the hell is so important?"

"HGZ is trying to out you again. I've sent you both the link. Oh and, um, hi, Elizabeth," Autumn called, apparently realizing belatedly it was rude to ignore her.

"Autumn, hello." Elizabeth reached for her clothing and began dressing. "What's going on?"

"It's stupid. Some paparazzo asshole hiding in the bushes got a snap of Elizabeth getting out of a taxi here a few hours ago."

So *that's* what the nonsense in the bushes had been about? Elizabeth scowled.

"Why's that worth a story?" Summer frowned, pulling her bikini back on.

"She was hauling her bags, and it looks a bit weird going to another actress's parents' place with luggage, so they made up some whole story about how it's proof you're more than just friends. And Elizabeth's apparently been heartbroken without you, so she rushed from her film set to be with you, and they've rehashed all those earlier rumors about you both. Oh, and they didn't even mention Mom's party, so it looks even more intimate somehow."

"This again, huh?" Summer muttered. "Shit. They love recycling this stuff."

"Yes," Autumn's disembodied voice agreed, "they do. Not that it's your fault. But still."

Elizabeth gritted her teeth as she looked up the story on her phone. "There are quotes here from sources about me apparently looking *withdrawn and upset.* Some people around here, maybe your neighbors, have big mouths and a bigger imagination."

"What?" Autumn asked. "No. Our neighbors are nice. They tipped Dad off about seeing photographers in the bushes. They're always great like that. Besides, our parties aren't exactly a secret to the paparazzi. They're always stalking around out front, hoping to snap an A-lister. It's not the neighbors."

That didn't exactly prove the party guests were innocent of supplying unflattering quotes, though. Elizabeth had found out firsthand on *Choosing Hope* that her own colleagues had been the worst at gossiping and media leaks.

"Fine," Elizabeth said skeptically, buttoning up her vest. "The neighbors are saints. And I'm guessing you also believe that no one here in this piranha pool decided to invent lies about me either?"

"They wouldn't. It's a condition of being invited. Didn't Summer tell you? If you come to one of Mom's parties, you can't take photos, you can't post on social media about it, and what happens at White Oak Avenue stays at White Oak Avenue, or you'll never be invited back. Since that is networking suicide, they all follow the rules. Elizabeth, I promise these are just made-up quotes by the bored media. No one here would have said a single word to HGZ. No way."

Elizabeth finished dressing and checked Summer also had her basics covered. She flung open the door, unable to believe Autumn's complete trust in her guests. "It's *Hollywood*," she ground out. "Everyone here would sell their own grandmothers to get ahead. I've seen it. People I trusted who…"

She faded out at the reminder of her acting mentor who had turned out to be the worst example of the corruption of this shallow, empty town. Grace had flung aside a seventeen-year friendship with Elizabeth as if it meant nothing. That had clearly been a lie too. "Anyway, this place is just a cesspit of deception and fakeness, filled with the narcissistic and fame-hungry."

Beside her, she felt Summer stiffen.

"You're wrong." Autumn's eyes flashed. "So fucking wrong. There are good people here too. And a lot of them are *right here*!"

"Really?" Elizabeth drawled. "And the Easter Bunny is real."

Hurt spread across Autumn's face. "May I remind you that your girlfriend's family, *my* whole family, is made up of people who are all natives of LA? Hollywood is our livelihood, our friendship network, and our world. You're spitting on us when you spit on Hollywood." Her expression became frosty. "So maybe you could shove aside all your self-righteous, stuck-up, judgmental crap for a minute and think about this rationally?"

"Autumn! Stop it," Summer cried out. "And Bess, for heaven's sake. You can stop winding my sister up as well."

Anger churned in Elizabeth's belly at Autumn's insults. Her jaw worked, but she couldn't bring herself to look at Summer. Her gaze remained fixed on Autumn.

She'd been called stuck-up all her life, although most frequently since coming to America where her personality was often misunderstood. She hated those two words. People who didn't know her called her that. However, Autumn had made one valid point. Summer was as Hollywood as you could get. And yet she was a decent, warm person anyway. Elizabeth's fury faltered.

"Look," Autumn said with a bit less venom, "can you just calm down, have another drink or another fuck, and relax, for God's sake? I only told you about the gossip story so you don't get photographed leaving together and stoke it any further. Don't shoot the damned messenger." She threw her hands up and stormed off.

Elizabeth exhaled in frustration, then turned and sat on the closed lid of the toilet, still not meeting Summer's eyes. Her pulse slowly dropped from frantic to galloping. Finally, she looked over at Summer.

Summer's expression said it all.

"I'm being an ass, aren't I?"

"No argument from me." Summer's eyes radiated hurt. "I had no idea you hated our life here so much. That you thought so little of everyone we know."

"I don't!" *Do I? No. Of course not.* "It's just that this is where we came in," Elizabeth said with a sigh. "Those photos, leaving the studio that day? When you tripped and I caught you? They were innocent. Me coming here today with my luggage, it was…well, it should have been innocent." Her lips twitched in acknowledgment it hadn't exactly stayed that way. "It feels as if everything I do gets poked at, watched, and mocked. I feel as if I'm in this damned fishbowl, unable to live any kind of life without scrutiny. I hate that. So, so much."

"I know."

"I don't know what to do," Elizabeth finally admitted.

Summer was silent for a moment. "I know that too."

"I don't really think *everyone* in Hollywood is a bunch of selfish jerks or worse."

"That's a relief." Summer's tone was light, but the pain remained in her expression.

"I think I've let this go on too long," Elizabeth said quietly.

Summer stiffened.

"No." Elizabeth leaned over and kissed her swiftly. "Whatever you're thinking, not that. We're great together. But we don't ever talk about it, do we? My not wanting to come out and you wanting to so badly."

"I just didn't want to raise a topic you're clearly uncomfortable with." Summer studied Elizabeth pensively. "It's true we don't talk about it often, but your reaction to just another stupid rumor tells me you're not even close to ready to come out. Even further away than I'd realized. And, yes, that makes me sad. I think I'd make a great role model for young people who are struggling with their sexuality. I'm proud of who I am. But I also know people would put two and two together regarding you if I came out. Since I don't want to do that to you, it's not happening anytime soon, is it? So what's the point of raking the whole topic over the coals?"

"Maybe it's time we did rake some things around." Elizabeth said slowly. "I'm sorry for how I reacted just now. I…panicked. I had visions of half of Hollywood at this party outing us or worse. I pictured them all sitting around laughing, gossiping, sharing photos of us together to all those websites that love to torment me." Even the thought made her sick.

"Autumn explained why that won't happen. Mom wouldn't stand for it. She'd know in three seconds and root them out. Everyone knows that about her parties. I thought you did too."

Elizabeth considered that. "Maybe that's not the issue. Not really. It's the symptom. Because the main thing is there's still us on opposite sides of this coming out debate."

"I guess."

"My position on this is it's who I am. Deep down, I'm not ready. I'm protective of myself, my personal life, and that's not about to change anytime soon. And I know coming out matters to you. I'm trying to think of a solution. It's just a lot for me to overcome. You know I hate being talked about. I hate being trolled by the public and being the center of attention."

"So you became an actress," Summer deadpanned, "neatly avoiding all those things."

"I know I'm not making much sense. I don't make much sense as a person, come to think of it. I'm a work in progress."

Summer leaned against her. "I get that this is hard for you. Outside of our inner circle, I know how very private you are. But I love you. In or out of the closet, I love you."

"And I, you." Elizabeth kissed her. "One day, I'll be better at this," she promised.

Summer looked as if she was trying not to draw too much hope from Elizabeth's words.

Elizabeth hated herself for that. "Let's go back to the party," she suggested. "I hear the Lawrence of Arabica coffee will make a convert out of me. Make me forget all about tea for eternity."

"That I'd like to see." Summer's troubled expression faded a little. "Sure."

Elizabeth's gaze raked the party for her quarry before finally spying her. Autumn was sitting on the edge of the now-empty massage tent area, peering up at a Hitchcock classic, *North by Northwest,* projected on the back wall. The sun was starting to set, and most of the guests were lazing around in deck chairs, murmuring to each other, or had assumed positions in the pool on the floating flamingos.

"Here." Elizabeth handed Autumn an obnoxiously pink drink. "I asked around and apparently 'Cosmoblancans' are what are all the cool kids are drinking."

Autumn's eyebrow lifted as she took it. "I'm not sure where you got the crazy idea I'm cool." She prodded her white jumpsuit as proof. "And I gave up hours ago explaining my clever homage to Captain Lance from *Legends of Tomorrow.*"

Elizabeth hmmed, having no clue who that was. "Well, how about Cosmoblancans are also established by a great many sources to be an excellent apology drink?"

"Sources?" Autumn's crooked smile appeared. "How many?"

"Okay, admittedly the sample size was one. I asked Skye for a drink you'd like. She says this is her newest and absolute best creation and we should be grateful I'm not offering you her Lemon King cocktail she invented earlier. She called that one a 'fabulous learning experience.' I didn't ask what was learnt."

"You know Mom's just using me as a test dummy," Autumn drawled. Nonetheless, she took a sip. Her face compressed into itself for a second, almost turning concave, and her eyes watered. "Ugh! Tart." But then she took another slurp. "Grows on you, though."

"Good to hear." Elizabeth lowered herself to sit beside her on a silk cushion. Wrapping her arms around her bent knees, Elizabeth's gaze drifted to the projected movie. "I'm sorry about earlier. I was angry and flung around a lot of insulting nonsense. You're right: there *are* good people here. I've been dealing with some issues and tarred the whole town with the same brush."

Autumn eyed her. "Are they dealt with now? Your issues?"

"No." Elizabeth gazed up at the big shimmering image. Cary Grant was in a suit, trying to run from a crop duster. As if *that* would be effective. "But I am working on them."

"Okay." Autumn nodded. "And, um, sorry I called you stuck-up. I actually knew that was close to a nerve for you. I hit it anyway. I can be a bit of a bitch sometimes."

"At least it's not your nickname," Elizabeth countered.

"Lucky me."

"You're not much like your sister, are you?" Elizabeth gave Autumn a considering look. "Personality-wise."

"No. But then neither are you." Autumn jutted out her chin, then took another sip of her drink.

"You have me there." Elizabeth wondered what that meant. Or if it meant anything at all? Would their differences be something that might come between her and Summer one day? How far apart they were on some things? The depth of pain Elizabeth felt at that thought surprised her.

Elizabeth slid her gaze back to Autumn. Summer was close to her sister, though, despite their obvious differences. So having differences didn't always have to mean anything, did it? You just had to figure out a way of crossing the divide. That's all. It was all about communication.

"I hope the crop duster gets him," Autumn said out of the blue, staring at Cary Grant. "I really hate his smug chin."

Elizabeth laughed. "Harsh. Well, on that note, I'll leave you to your in-depth critiquing." She rose, and looked around, wondering whether Summer was still catching up with their former director, Jean-Claude Badour. The enthusiastic Frenchman had kissed both Summer's cheeks and launched into an effusive monologue that looked as if it might take a while to finish.

"Anytime," Autumn said. "And hey? Thanks for the apology. I know that was hard for you." She tilted the pink fizz Elizabeth's way in a salute. "And cheers for the drink. Tell Mom not to give up her day job just yet."

"I think I'll let you break that to Skye." Elizabeth gave a small smile. "Until next time."

"Yep. See you around, Bess." Autumn was already back to glowering at Cary Grant's chin.

As Elizabeth walked away, she realized it was the first time Autumn had ever called her by her nickname. Her smile widened. Just a little.

Skye Storm rinsed the assorted cocktail glasses, slid them into the dishwasher, and set it to clean. As the machine hummed softly, she gazed thoughtfully out the kitchen window.

Autumn and Brock were making a rowdy game of folding and stacking away the chairs, doing the same speed contest they'd indulged in after every party for years.

It was, of course, much funnier tonight when they were both a little drunk and a lot older. Brock's skilled reflexes meant he was always going to win. And he was always going to take a perfectly staged pratfall at the last gasp so Autumn could claim victory.

Skye smiled to herself as she heard the inevitable crash, then Brock's entirely unconvincing yelp—bless him, he'd never be an actor—followed by Autumn's laughter and cries of "Beat you!"

It was one of the few times she ever saw Autumn let down her hair. So tightly wound. Autumn was certainly nothing like Summer. The great goddess obviously had a sense of humor about these things.

Skye began covering and putting away the leftovers while deciding which of her less palatable food experiments would go straight in the bin.

Oh, Summer had always been sweet and gentle, a free spirit who floated on the breeze like a dandelion. Autumn was more a hardy groundcover plant, constantly prepared for and expecting to withstand anything.

Skye had always worried more about Summer and that open heart of hers. She needed someone as strong and loyal as Brock to stand in her corner and protect her, fierce as a lion. And tonight Skye had seen it.

To think that Summer's special someone would turn out to be an introverted English actress as tightly knotted as a fist. But seeing Summer and Elizabeth together tonight, Skye now had no fears for her youngest daughter. That was love. The protectiveness, the adoration. If you knew what to look for, oh, it was so clear. Elizabeth Thornton would do anything to keep Summer safe. She'd love her too, with passion and care. That was all a person needed in life.

Satisfied that Summer was all settled, Skye turned her speculative gaze to Autumn. Her smile turned impish. Well now. *One down, one to go.* Maybe she'd work out a way to get Andrew back here so Autumn would finally stop pining.

Perhaps she'd have another party. Her mind began to whir at the prospect. All she needed was a theme.

"I thought we'd never get home," Summer said, trailing her fingers down Elizabeth's bare arm as they lay in bed. "You are so beautiful. I've been dreaming of having my wicked way with you again and again."

Elizabeth regarded Summer with a tiny grin. It faded as she remembered what had been on her mind for the rest of the party. "I've been thinking about my knee-jerk response earlier. I know I reacted badly." She shook her head. "And I made a lot of unfair assumptions about your family's friends. Autumn was right to call me out on it. I'm not saying Hollywood isn't a dumpster fire on occasion, but still, I was being a judgmental ass."

Summer's eyes crinkled at the edges.

"No disagreement then?" Elizabeth's eyebrows lifted.

"No."

She snorted. "By the way, I admit I've checked the gossip sites, and there's not a hint about us from the party beyond that first story. Autumn was right about that. It wasn't the guests feeding HGZ."

"Mom chooses her friends well. She's selective."

"I think you're right." Elizabeth exhaled. "I'm sorry, Summer."

"What for?"

"I've been avoiding even talking to you about your need to come out. Out of sight, out of mind. That's not fair. We need a way forward. A plan."

"Maybe we should just do something bold then," Summer teased. "Like ripping the Band-Aid off. Put it on a billboard. Huge letters: *Summer Hayes and Bess Thornton are QAF.*"

"Well, that would certainly be one approach," Elizabeth said dryly. "Although it's a little shouty."

"And you're not the shouty kind."

"I can be shouty. It depends where your hands are." Elizabeth's lips twitched. "In fact, not too long ago you had me close to screaming."

"Yes, I did enjoy that." Summer grinned. "I was pretty proud of myself."

"You should be." Elizabeth smiled and drew a lock of hair away from Summer's eyes with a whisk of fingertips. "You're the only one who's ever done that to me.

Made me lose control so much. Although I remember returning the favor and having my way with you against a bathroom door. And a sink. And on the floor. It started to blur in the end. Like your gasps."

"Sounds about right." Summer smirked. "You have a lot of talent."

"Except on the biggest thing. Being bold. Fearless."

"There's no rush. One day, we'll come out in style. Even if the big shouty billboard is out." Summer rolled over, pinning Elizabeth to the mattress.

Elizabeth's fingers tangled with Summer's hands. The gesture was so intimate. "No billboards, true. Maybe something tasteful. Like skywriting."

"That works too," Summer said with a snort. "I could even leave you out of it. Something simple: *Summer loves the ladies*."

"Plural?" Elizabeth drawled. "I have competition?"

Summer laughed. "Please. You own my ovaries. I'm helpless to resist you. As I proved by dragging you into a bathroom for smoking-hot sex today."

Elizabeth studied Summer's face, the desire clear in those bewitching eyes. "If you keep looking at me like that, we won't need a skywriter or a billboard."

"Yeah, well, we're alone. Who cares? No one to see how much I want you except you." It seemed as if Summer was trying so hard to hide the sadness in her voice, but Elizabeth picked up on the faintest trace of it.

Elizabeth frowned, regret filling her. No, this wouldn't do. Exhaling, Elizabeth made a decision. "I've been debating this all afternoon. Summer, I don't think I'll ever be ready to come out or be comfortable with the world knowing my personal business."

"Oh." Summer sagged. "Okay, that's, um… Damn."

"Wait." Elizabeth took a steadying breath. "Having people know might make me all kinds of uncomfortable, but I think, now, maybe it's a discomfort I can live with. As bad as my fears can be at times, I also keep coming back to the truth. What matters to me is your happiness, far more than some nebulous idea about me coming out when the time is right, which, honestly, will likely be never."

Summer's brows knitted together. "I don't follow."

"Look, it's simple when you do the maths. Yes, I believe I'd be unhappy being out. But equally, I've never been fine with the lies to stay closeted, so either way, I can't win. So it makes sense to at least give one of us her happiness if I'm going to be unhappy either way. At least you can come out and be all you've ever wanted to be. Besides, you being happy makes me happy, so maybe…we'll both win after all?"

Elizabeth wasn't convinced that was true, but it sounded good in theory. Maybe the universe could shock her.

"What?" Summer sat up, straddling Elizabeth's thighs. "Are you saying what I think you are?"

Elizabeth nodded. It was time. Overdue, in fact. She reached for her phone. "Every time we're together in public, it feels as if there's a large flashing neon sign that we're so obvious. That's why stories like HGZ's make me so twitchy now. It feels as if they're stripping us naked. But now I wonder, if we're that obvious, why not just stop pretending and get this over and done with?"

"Bess?" Summer's eyes flew wide open.

"I may be about to do something totally out of character and impulsive," Elizabeth murmured, her pulse thudding. "Stop me now if you don't think I should."

Instead, Summer pressed her lips tightly together, as though any twitch would be taken as an objection.

Elizabeth would have laughed if this wasn't so serious. "Right then." She took a deep breath, logged into her Twitter account, and tapped out a message. They were words she'd felt for a long time. How surreal to say something so private "out loud" for once. Heart now beating almost out of her chest, Elizabeth slowly turned the phone around to show Summer, thumb hovering over *Post.*

Relaxing at home with the woman I love. Yes, love-love. Like that. Summer Hayes is my world.

At Summer's slight, incredulous nod, Elizabeth brought her thumb down.

The post hurtled into the feed. Out into the world for everyone to see.

"Bess…" Tears filled Summer's eyes.

Uncertainty rushed into Elizabeth. "You wanted this, didn't you?"

"Yes. These are happy tears."

"Oh. Good."

"Oh my God." Summer slid fully across Elizabeth and clung to her. "Bess… I think I just fell for you more."

Well then. That couldn't ever be a bad thing. Right?

Elizabeth's phone was ringing. Again. It had been, on and off, for the past hour. The tweet had gone insane, with retweets, surprisingly supportive comments, and their old show's #Hunter fans demanding confirmation…which Summer had duly delivered with a retweet of her own and a heart emoji.

Fans were now posting swooning and CPR memes. Cute.

Elizabeth contemplated answering this call. "It's Delvine." She finally conceded defeat and hit the *Answer* button. After listening to her animated manager for several minutes, she made appropriate noises, laughed, then hung up.

"Delvine said it's a beautiful tweet," Elizabeth murmured, "and she knew we'd do something stupid soon. Direct quote. I think she's genuinely happy for us. Also, she says my agent is having a heart attack, a metaphoric one I assume, given Rachel wants to talk to me tomorrow. That should be as cuddly and sweet as Roller Derby."

Summer snickered before her own phone launched into life. "Ugh. Autumn." After answering, she had to yank her phone away from her ear as the volume of Autumn's voice assailed the room. "Um, yeah, okay. I'll tell her," Summer said when she could squeeze a word in. "Can we deal with the rest of your hyperventilation tomorrow? Yeah. Okay. Love you too. Bye."

She tossed the phone down. "Apparently my sister thinks the universe is upside down because you were supposed to be the sane one not prone to random outbursts of truthy blurting."

"Ah."

"And she says not to worry; she'll figure out a strategy soon. Although she added a lot of swear words and didn't use euphemisms."

Elizabeth smiled. "Maybe she and Rachel can compare panic attacks."

Summer's phone beeped with a burst of incoming texts. She studied the list. "Right. So we have a tweet from Mom. She's thrilled. She's also claiming credit, convinced it has something to do with her party. Hmm," Summer continued, "something from Dad…. *Well done.* And he adds *Glad E. finally got it*, whatever that means…"

Oh. So that's what Brock had been bitching about? Me being closeted? Could Brock have been more vague if he'd tried?

Summer resumed scrolling, spotting a message from her best friend. "Chloe's texted from the set of her granola ad: *About bloody time!* Plus there's a bunch of dead emojis and smiley faces. And…huh. Oh, hello, a text from Tori. Remember my drinking buddy from *Choosing Hope*? She couldn't imagine the scary horrors I had to face having to kiss you for the show?"

With a smirk, Elizabeth said, "I remember."

Summer opened that message with an eager tap. "All it says is *you go girl, hahahaha, fuck me dead, I have no gaydar at all do I?!*"

Elizabeth couldn't disagree. She worked her way through her own texts. "I have hearty congratulations from Rowan and Brian, Amrit and Chris, and Zara, a snide comment from Grace that *I didn't think you had it in you* and…" Elizabeth stopped and digested that little dig. It didn't hurt even a little. Huh. It seemed as though she'd well and truly moved on from caring what her former mentor thought. That was telling.

"And?" Summer prompted, lips pursing at the mention of Grace, although she made no further comment.

"And a promise from Alex that we'll process this really soon via many colorful alcoholic beverages. *That* sounds good for my liver. Plus a few media requests for interviews. I'll let Delvine figure those out." Elizabeth sucked in a breath. "Okay. That's it."

Her heart was still thundering at her impulsiveness, but it was more than that. She still couldn't believe how her worst fears hadn't materialized. All she felt was gut-churning, thrilling, overwhelming relief. She hoped Summer felt the same. "Are you pleased, Summer?" Elizabeth asked gently, meeting her gaze. "Is this what you wanted?"

"God, so much. Thank you."

They regarded each other. "Huh." Elizabeth huffed out an incredulous breath as the full import of what she'd done hit her. "I guess I've done it now. But I don't feel as if the world's about to end, so that's new."

"Well, that's good." Summer smiled and ran her fingers up Elizabeth's arm. "So how *do* you feel then?"

"Like a newly outed woman involved with the most adorable person in Hollywood."

"I feel exactly the same."

"Except I'm not the most adorable person," Elizabeth amended. "I'm not even slightly adorable, remember?"

"That's such bullshit, and we both know it. You were never your reputation. Not even once." Summer dragged her gaze over Elizabeth's body. "But, Bess, honey? Now that you're *officially* into me and apparently available to show how much you love me whenever you want, do you think you actually would?"

Elizabeth's eyebrows shot up. "Oh?"

"We have some serious time to make up for. Kiss me, you crazy woman."

"Oh!" Elizabeth smiled genuinely, delighted to comply. "Of course." And then she let her lips melt into Summer's.

Read all about co-stars Elizabeth and Summer falling in love in Lee Winter's *Breaking Character.*

The Friend

Number nine Maxwell Brown Drive, Southport, Queensland was, unfortunately, exactly how Dani Sullivan remembered it.

She turned off the ignition to her beat-up mustard Datsun 120Y and stared up at the two-storey building in front of her. Developers had been trying to get her eighty-four-year-old great-aunt to sell it for years as it was a five-minute drive from one of the best beaches on the Gold Coast. But like most things related to the formidable Jean Thirkhill, the answer was a firm no.

"This is it, huh?" Ro asked. "Hon, it doesn't look *that* scary. Yeah, it could use something to bring it out of the seventies, but still…"

Dani eyed the yawning concrete drive and, to the right, a pool of white, jagged pebbles that caught the glare of sun every afternoon. Not a tree, bush, or skerrick of life was allowed to flourish. Jean didn't lean towards warm, soft, or living things.

Perspiration slicked Dani's palms at the reminder of two years of her childhood spent inside this precisely ordered house. She'd never called it home. Her sister had.

Ground floor had a pair of brown garage doors at the left of it; a line of curtained windows to the right. The floor above was lined with large, square windows. No curtains there. All the better to size up interlopers from. Above that, at the top right, sat a box-shaped room with a tall aerial on it. The ham-radio operator's nest that Fred, Jean's husband, inhabited.

Each storey was delineated by a fat strip of brown paint, like a layer of fig jam on a double sponge cake.

Ro nudged her. "Shake a leg. We can't sit here forever."

"But it *is* tempting." Dani shot her girlfriend a pained glance.

Today marked her first Christmas with Ro—the first of many, she hoped. Dani prayed her oddball family wouldn't scare off her girlfriend too much, but then Ro Tapu was tougher than most. You didn't go from a sprawling family of Samoan immigrants in a poor outer suburb to captaining the elite national netball squad without a lot of stern stuff shooting around your bloodstream.

Ro's light-brown skin glowed from her lean athlete's diet. Her pixie-cut black hair was sculpted around her high cheek bones and ended in wisps at the back of her sensuous neck.

Dani sighed. They could be seeing in Christmas in the cosy Brisbane townhouse they'd shared for five months, and teasing each other while wearing nothing but Santa hats. Instead, they were here, where even Santa would fear to tread.

A squawk of chickens echoed from somewhere nearby. A car honked a few streets away. The anxious pattering of Dani's racing heart almost drowned it all out.

I can do this. I can.

Ro placed a comforting hand on her thigh. "Come on, hon, stop freaking out. It'll be fine. So you brought a friend for Christmas for the first time. No big deal. Jean's what, mid-eighties? And her husband? Ninety-something? They won't know what it means."

"No, I know." Dani fidgeted. "Although younger-me was convinced she was a mind reader."

Ro laughed.

With an aggrieved sigh, Dani slid out, locked up, and peered over the expanse of mustard-yellow metal. Ro parked a round food container on the roof as she gathered their bags.

Dani had spent half the night trying to make the perfect trifle. This one was her third effort. She knew her dessert choice was about as cool as a purple mohair sweater, but for some reason Jean enjoyed the concoction of jelly, custard, and sponge all soaked in sherry.

Dani had balanced the alcohol content as best she could to meet her great-aunt's exacting standards—more than enough to daze a koala, not enough to sink a croc. So…'tipsy lizard' for the win. Not that she held any delusions the gift would be appreciated. But at least she could tell herself she'd tried.

Collecting the trifle box from where Ro had placed it, Dani inhaled deeply, and looked back up at the house. "Right. We're going in. I'm sorry in advance."

"It'll be fine. I have a hundred percent track record on meeting parents, in-laws, and outlaws. It's universally accepted I'm awesome." She gave her eyebrows a teasing waggle.

"So you keep reminding me," Dani said. "But you're not the issue. It's me they don't love."

"Now I know you're exaggerating. You're so adorable and sweet. Who could hate you?"

"Fine. It's mainly Jean. She looks at me like I'm beneath her. She's been like that since I was twelve and lacked all my sister's lady-like decorum. I loved running, jumping, climbing trees, being loud. She called me an undisciplined wild child. It was death by a thousand nit-picks living here."

"Well, to be fair, you are kind of wild."

At Dani's huff, Ro added hastily, "But I love that about you." She waved their bags of wine and gifts. "Now, stop stalling, and let's crush this Christmas lunch."

*

Dani nudged the outer white door with her elbow, trifle carefully balanced in her hands, and it swung open. She led the way up the inside polished wooden stairs, dodging two freckled blurs of nephews playing tag amidst a mountain of boxes of wools and fabrics. These teetering cardboard piles were leftovers from Jean's former life running her beloved haberdashery shop.

There was a solemn bass beat coming from above. "Little Drummer Boy," a staple of Jean's Christmas mix tape. Her battered, old-style cassette came with a faded name from a felt-tip pen. If you held it just so, you could almost make out "Xmas 1998" on it.

They reached the second level and stepped onto a flecked white carpet. Dani turned to explain that her aunt loved everything hospital-grade clean, so spill something on that carpet at her peril, when she noticed Ro was frozen, looking transfixed.

Ah. *That.* Down the left wall was an enormous glass display case that contained thousands of little glass and crystal animal figurines. Tiny dogs, cats, mice, and birds were neatly corralled inside.

As a child, Dani had longed to be able to take them out and inspect them, name them, befriend them, give them little stories, but Jean's bony fingers held the key to the cabinet. She'd been very clear: pretty things were for looking at, not touching with clumsy children's hands.

A white-haired Fred roamed by, in his trademark singlet, blue shorts, white knee-length socks, and leather sandals, clearly on a mission of some sort. He'd obviously shucked his shirt, most likely despite Jean's best hopes. When her husband wasn't in the mood to stay fully dressed, Jean had never successfully kept him that way.

Dani called out a greeting, but the old man's focus was complete.

Fred was always like this. He spent most of his life upstairs in his hidey-hole talking to ham-radio friends. His constant companion was a Huntsman spider the size of a tea plate. The terrifying arachnid kept the mice away, he told everyone. It also kept Jean away, and Dani had long suspected that's what he enjoyed most about it.

Fred and his wife of sixty years had little in common beyond their marriage. Jean was an imposing woman, held together by sinew, subtle sneers, and plumes of hairspray on her stiff, coiled grey bun.

Fred, by contrast, was fuelled by a childlike fascination for anyone on the other side of the world. Or just anyone not in the room. The pair didn't share beds, conversations, or philosophies. Dani had never seen them even touch in her entire life.

It was a little sad, now she thought about it. Apparently, Jean's rules for figurines also applied to husbands. Both were for display purposes only.

"That was Fred," she murmured, as he reappeared, crossing their path again, now bearing a glass jar.

"Hey, Fred," Dani called out.

He ignored her, but then his hearing wasn't the best.

"What on earth is he holding?" Ro whispered as he disappeared again.

"Curds?" Dani shrugged. "Or it could be whey. I forget which he prefers from week to week. So does he. On that note, don't be alarmed if he calls me Edith. It's his best friend's late wife. They were all really close mates."

"He's senile?"

"Shh! We do not speculate on that around here no matter what."

"Doesn't Jean notice?"

"We think she's in denial. But this is not a safe topic. Okay?"

Ro nodded, for the first time looking a little less confident at winning over Dani's family.

Dani glanced around the small front room. There were wide windows on opposite walls, an arched doorway in front, and against one wall, facing an ancient TV, were a pair of green armchairs with faded crocheted armrest protectors. Nothing had changed in the three decades she'd been coming here each Christmas.

From outside came a loud, indignant squawk. Ro's face lit up, and she rushed to the windows facing the backyard. "Chickens! We had a chook pen when I was a girl." Ro squinted down and tapped the window. "Whoa. Those chooks look like they've put their claws in a power socket."

"Because they are not *chooks*." The angular, whippet-thin form of Jean Thirkhill swept in and stepped up beside Ro at the window. A maroon knit-dress clung to her lean body.

Dani blanched. Damn, Jean was still fast and silent. A greyhound came to mind. She wished she could warn Ro to change topics, because no one dissed Jean's fancy-pants chickens and lived.

"Well, they sure cluck like chooks!" Ro grinned, heedless to the danger.

Jean's expression became pure disdain. "Young lady, you are looking at prize-winning *show* chickens."

"People put chooks on show?" Ro blinked. "Seriously? What type are they?"

"Bantam frizzled Cochin. Less accurately dubbed *frizzles*."

"Frizzles?" Ro gave her a sceptical look.

"It denotes the outward curl of the feather." Jean tapped the window with her clear-lacquered nail, pointing at one. Her tone warmed slightly to her pet topic. "I also keep Plymouth Rocks and Silkies. Silkies are sometimes called sizzles."

"Okay, now I know you're pulling my leg." Ro laughed.

Dani groaned inwardly. At least Ro hadn't nudged Jean in the ribs, too.

"I'm entirely serious. See that white one? That's Leonora. She won the Grand Champion Soft Feather Fowl of the Queensland Royal Show last year. She also won Grand Champion Fowl of the show, and would have won Supreme Grand Champion if not for some skulduggery on the part of Mrs Rutledge."

"Ooh, a show scandal?" Ro's eyebrows shot up. "What'd evil Mrs Rutledge do?"

"*She* knows." Jean huffed. She turned and sized up Ro. "So, I take it you are the *friend* Danielle was so intent on inviting to our *family* Christmas?"

Her voice was cool and polite, but her emphasis was damn rude, as if Ro was some interloper they'd allowed in.

"Yep. I'm the friend." Ro ignored the subtext and gave her a cheerful smile. "And you must be Dani's Great-Aunty Jean. I'm Ro Tapu."

"How nice for you." Not a hint of warmth flickered across Jean's features. "I trust you play netball better than you identify chickens?"

Ro laughed and shrugged. "Well, you gotta admit that wouldn't be hard."

Astounding. Dani stared at her girlfriend in amazement. It was like the barbs just bounced off her. Yet they'd always stuck to Danni like bindii prickles to her bare feet.

Jean glanced to Dani and the box in her hands. "And what have you there?"

"Trifle," Dani said. "I, ah, tried to make it the way you like it."

Ro darted her a curious look.

Dani didn't blame her. She sounded all kinds of pathetic.

"We may not have room for trifle as I've prepared pavlova as well as fruit mince pies." Jean waved at the archway. "Put it in the kitchen. Mind Harriet. She's attempting to become one with the kitchen rug today. I've lost count of how many times I've shooed her out and she's ignored instruction."

Dani, smarting at the trifle dismissal, turned to Ro. "Harriet's the cat."

"I'm sure even your *sporty friend* could have worked that out," Jean said.

Wow. Only Jean could make "sporty" sound like an insult. Dani reddened. What must Ro think of her family?

There was a bellow of laughter down the hall—one of her uncles—then a giggle that was far higher and louder. Aunt Rhoda. Sloshed already. Dani glanced at the antique wooden wall clock. Barely eleven.

Jean's eyes narrowed, and without another word, she ghosted down the hallway towards Rhoda, with a look that did not bode well for Dani's merry aunt.

"You lived with her for two years?" Ro whispered.

Dani nodded. "My parents were out of work, and she let us all move in downstairs while they looked for jobs. Problem is it took them ages."

Of course, there was way more mess, stress, and anger to it than that. Jean had used the situation as an excuse to slowly dissect Dani's awkward pre-teenage existence and dismantle her budding self-esteem.

Her sister Sally's beauty and deportment had been held up as an example. But Dani just didn't have that gene. She'd felt like a bull in a china shop most days as she grew into her broad shoulders, five-foot-ten height, and tangle of solid, strong limbs.

The day Dani's mother had finally noticed Jean's sly, usually subtle, ridicule was the day Dani's parents packed up and moved to live in a tiny, mouldy-smelling, second-hand caravan in the middle of nowhere. As bad as living on the outer reaches of Hell had been, it still beat enduring a clipped daily diatribe listing Dani's many failings.

Not everyone agreed. Sally had forever resented that their living conditions had been downgraded just to spare Dani from Jean's cruel tongue. They hadn't been close since.

Ro leaned against the window, watching the frizzles peck at grain. "I've never heard someone make my athleticism sound like I must be stupid." She sounded awed. "I'm sorry, hon. It musta been hell living here."

Dani grunted in agreement, not wanting to get into it. Her stomach was churning enough. "Come on. Let's drop the food in the kitchen so we can do the round of rellies. Mum and Sally are much friendlier. Which wouldn't be hard. Don't be alarmed if Mum doesn't say much—she's shy—and Sally's a bit of a snob. On the plus side, there's Rhoda's rum balls if you need a pick-me-up. Just don't operate heavy machinery after them."

"No probs." Ro looked back on solid footing.

The saying that a table was groaning with food was clearly invented for Great-Aunt Jean. At the centre, atop the white linen tablecloth, was an enormous roast chicken, its orange-brown skin sticky from marinade. Beside that sat a roast lamb beneath an aromatic crown of rosemary, lemon, and garlic. Next to that were fat turkey slices, the skin studded with peppercorns.

Little pots of gravy, mint sauce, and cranberry sauce were dotted up and down the table, along with giant blue-and-white bowls of potato, green-leaf, and tomato salads, freshly cooked prawns, and mounded platters of roast vegetables. The smell was incredible. And so was the heat generated by all the dishes.

As if the day wasn't hot enough. The days of slavishly paying tribute to Australia's English roots had been fading for decades across the country, in favour of cold dishes and barbecues or picnics at the beach. Not here, though. Jean always opted for the full, glorious hot English spread because that's what she'd had as a girl.

The matriarch in question was seated at one end of the long table that was bursting with uncles, aunts, and random cousins, facing Fred. Three along from her, Dani and Ro were positioned under Jean's watchful eye. Dani's mother sat opposite them both, nibbling on finger foods, sipping wine, and saying little.

Ro's eyes were wide as garbage can lids. "There's so much." She patted her stomach. "Thank God it's the off-season."

Dani laughed. She lowered her voice. "Please, with your metabolism, you'd burn all this off in one training session. Well, unless you have the plum pud with brandy sauce—that's ten sessions easy. So maybe skip that."

"I can't have *any* dessert," Ro whispered. "I'll be full just on this. And I haven't had processed sugar since I made the national squad."

"You have to," Dani said with a worried gulp. "The pavlova and fruit mince pies are Jean's pride and joy. If you skip either one, it's like spitting in her eye."

"Oh hell." Ro swallowed. She stared at her plate. "Um, I better pace myself."

"Thanks." Dani glanced at her great-aunt and saw her immersed in conversation. "It'd be impossible to claw your way back into her good graces if you turned that down."

Ro laughed and leaned into her ear. "Wait, she has good graces?"

Biting back a snort of laughter, Dani refocused on the rest of the table.

Her uncle Stephen, at her left elbow, was watching them both curiously.

Dani braced herself for awkward questions. Her sexuality was firmly in the "don't ask-don't tell" category with her extended family. Bringing Ro today meant some of her more aware relatives might join the dots.

"You two," Stephen began, waggling his finger to and fro between them.

Dani tensed.

"Any interest in real estate? Have I told you about my new business?"

Ugh. No. He always had some get-rich scheme underway.

"See, it's all about leveraging. Negative gearing. Right?"

Right. Dani glanced across the table to find her mother's gentle smile.

Jean glanced at her, too, and cleared her throat. "Clarice, where is your husband? Why would he drive that truck on Christmas day?"

Her mother's smile faltered. "He volunteered. He's transporting toys this run. For the January sales."

"Consumerism. How lovely." Jean lifted her wine glass and tapped on it, quietening the room.

"Before we continue…" She paused and eyed Rhoda sharply until she put down her utensils with a clatter. "…a few words. We come together as one to share these bountiful gifts from God."

Dani's eyebrows shot up. This was new. Her great-aunt was not a religious woman. Probably couldn't stand the thought anyone was higher up than she was.

"That means we're grateful not only for what we have in our lives, but whom."

Ro's warm hand snuck under the table and found Dani's fingers, giving them a squeeze of agreement.

Dani sighed with contentment.

"We celebrate the people we have known and the ones we have lost."

She sounded so sad. Frowning, Dani sifted through the family gossip from the year. Who had Jean lost? Her eyes followed her aunt's gaze and landed on Fred who was humming softly to himself. Oh. So they *were* going to mention it?

"Never forget the privilege you all have. You enjoy lives of opportunity previous generations never had. You are lucky. Spoilt even." Her eyes settled on Dani.

The hell? Was that how Jean saw her? Some lazy wild child swanning around?

Her mother's brow knotted together in confusion.

Dani clenched her paper napkin into a ball.

"You should appreciate what you have, as others have considerably less." Jean's lips bared.

What might be an uplifting sentiment was now sounding a lot like a threat.

"Come on, Jean," Dani's oldest uncle whined. "Lunch is getting cold."

Rhoda took that as the go-ahead and reached for the potato salad. Everyone else swallowed their drinks, called a polite "Cheers," and it was a free-for-all.

Jean sat back with a discontented sigh at the unceremonious end to her speech. "Decorum is dead," she muttered.

Dani smirked at how aggrieved her great-aunt sounded at the mutiny. It fell away when Jean's cool gaze fixed on her.

Every. Time. That damn woman could sour a plate of milk with that look. Dani was suddenly beyond grateful that Jean obviously didn't know the true nature of her relationship with Ro. There's no way she'd have missed the chance to toss something vicious into her speech to embarrass them both.

"So, girls," Uncle Stephen continued as he forked some lamb and dragged it through a gravy puddle on his plate. "Have you two thought about what I was saying? Negative gearing? I could help."

The Christmas mix tape had been flipped three more times and was back to "Little Drummer Boy." Dani had by now sat through numerous anecdotes about how perfect, accomplished, and smart her sister's kids were. She'd tuned out at the trombone classes.

"And Ted is doing so well at learning Polish."

That woke her up. Dani glanced at her sister. "*Polish*? Who's he going to talk to in Polish around here?"

Sally shot her a condescending look. "Knowledge for the sake of it is never a bad thing."

"Quite right," Jean said. "Not everyone has aspirations to sell shoes at Athlete's Kit. I'm sure my great-grand-nephew will go on to tremendous things with that fine mind of his."

"Hey, I don't sell stuff at Athlete's Kit." Dani put down her knife and fork.

"Well, you did." Acid dripped from Jean's tongue. "I recall how excited you were. You felt the need to share with everyone."

"When I was twenty. Now I'm the assistant manager."

"In a *sports shoe* store. How…impressive."

Right. Like selling haberdashery was such a step up to greatness. Dani tried to keep a mutinous glare off her face.

"Well," Ro said, spearing a prawn and eying it for a moment before looking around at the faces watching her, "I'm glad she works at Athlete's Kit. I met her there. We bonded over sneakers for people with narrow feet."

Dani had a sudden flash of memory of how Ro had flirted with her so shamelessly that she'd been a wreck. She hoped her blush would be blamed on the room's rising temperature.

"So is that your crowning career achievement?" Jean asked Dani, eyebrow sky high. "Befriending a sports star?"

Sally laughed. "Probably."

Fury slashed through her.

The table fell silent, as if expecting more of the fireworks that had punctuated their teen years. Even Jean's eye took on a vague gleam of interest.

Dani inhaled sharply. The carols tape started a cheery version of Dean Martin's "Let It Snow." The ceiling fan was making lazy *whumpf, whumpf* noises as it circulated the stifling air.

Out of nowhere, a chipper voice from the end of the table shattered the icy silence. "I remembered to flush today."

All eyes turned.

Fred. Looking so damned proud.

"What was that, Fred?" Rhoda asked, looking confused.

Jean blanched. "Who'd like seconds?" she asked loudly. "If anyone..."

"I remembered to flush today," Fred repeated helpfully. "The toilet. After a poo."

Several of Dani's smaller nephews and nieces at the children's table nearby tittered. Teddy, Sally's Polish-mastering, trombone genius son, didn't. He was too busy putting a pea up his nose.

Jean's lips thinned. "Yes, well, thank you for that update, Fred, but that's not appropriate for the table."

His enthusiasm seemed undimmed. "I don't always remember," he explained to everyone. Spying a piece of tinsel on the Christmas tree behind him, he reached for it, yanking hard. Baubles and fake snow sprayed off it.

Fred beamed at his prize and wrapped it around his head like a bandana. The excess tinsel hung down one ear like a possum's tail.

"Very cool, Uncle F." Dani shot him a thumbs up. "Could spark a whole new trend."

He beamed back at her and chuckled. "Zactly."

Jean hissed at her under her breath, "Don't you dare mock him. I will not tolerate that."

Dani's jaw clenched. "I would *never* do that."

"Soooo," Rhoda called from Fred's end of the table, "if we're talking embarrassing stuff, I have news. Got a *vicious* urinary tract infection. Like, Jesus H. Christ, the itchiness. You got no idea. But don't worry, not catching."

"What's a yinary track affection?" Teddy piped up. A pea popped out of his nose.

Ro laughed, and Jean shot her and the boy an appalled look.

Rhoda picked up her glass and waved it about. "It's as fun as pissing staples, young man, thanks for asking. Thank Christ I got it fixed. The doc says I have to remember to stay hydrated. So, on that note, cheers!" She skulled her wine, finishing it with a satisfied smack of lips.

"Really?" Fred sounded intrigued. "That's good to know." He reached for a glass in front of him.

Dani squinted. Definitely whey. She shuddered. He really loved his health kicks.

Unfortunately, Fred's bid for rehydration failed as he missed his mouth by a wide margin and wound up with an expanding yellow stain on his shirt. He blinked at it in confusion. "What?" His look was heartbreaking. He glanced around the table, as if seeking answers.

You could have heard a pin drop. Even the music fell silent between songs. The fan continued its slow whumping sound. Nobody met Fred's eye.

Dani gave her plate her fullest attention.

Jean was out of her seat in an instant, striding to her husband's end of the table. "You must be more careful, Fred." She hauled him to his feet by his elbow. "We're getting cleaned up," she added, with a look so fierce it dared anyone to mention what had just happened. Then she frogmarched her husband out of the room and down the hall.

The moment she was gone, the table broke into chatter.

"Oh boy," Uncle Stephen said. "I thought we were finally going to discuss the elephant in the room."

"Not likely," Sally snorted. "He'd have forgotten his own name and Jean still wouldn't notice."

"I'd have thought my UTI would merit some support," Rhoda called out. "More important than genius Teddy updates. Jesus, Sally, does your kid suck at *anything*?"

"You're just jealous, Rhoda," Sally snapped. "I have a wonderful family and you have a series of failed AA meetings."

Dani winced. "Shit, Sally, lay off."

"What do you care?" Sally's blonde hair swirled as she spun back to glare at her. "Look at your life, little sister."

"What's wrong with it?"

"Where to start? The pathetic job or inability to find a boyfriend."

Seriously? She still hasn't worked it out?

Ro snorted.

"Girls," their mother cut in. "Please don't start."

"Does no one want to talk about property investments?" Uncle Stephen asked no one in particular.

"Ha!" Rhoda cackled. "Get Genius Ted to sell it to me, since he's perfect at everything. Including peas up noses."

"Not really good at *everything*," Mike, Sally's husband, inserted. His tone was placating. "I mean, he's only had two lessons in Polish. On YouTube."

"I hate Powish! Powish sucks!" Teddy called out.

Rhoda cackled. "Now it all comes out."

"Michael!" Sally looked askance. "Would it be too much for you to support me?"

Her husband shrugged and reached for the roast vegetable serving spoon.

Dani cast a glance at Ro, wondering if she'd ever be forgiven for bringing her into this madhouse. Would explaining they weren't ordinarily like this be believable?

Ro merely shot her a grin. "Hey, have you tried those garlic prawns? They're wicked."

Shaking her head, Dani rose. "I need a loo break. Will you be okay alone with the rabble?" She leaned closer and whispered in Ro's ear, "You have my permission to poke my sister in the eye with the salad spoon if she badmouths either you, me, or the high-octane world of sneakers sales."

"Leave 'em to me," Ro said. "No spoons of doom will be required."

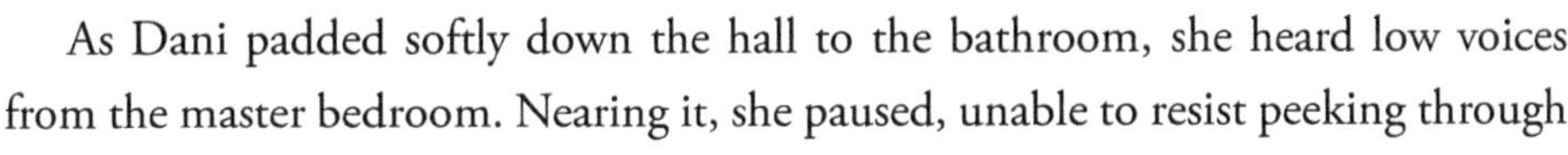

As Dani padded softly down the hall to the bathroom, she heard low voices from the master bedroom. Nearing it, she paused, unable to resist peeking through the ajar door.

Fred was sitting on the bed, his bared chest on display, which was covered in liver-spots and white-hair.

Jean bent over him, using a flannel to wipe his torso of splashes of liquid, and murmuring to him softly. Her face was no longer disapproving or austere. She looked…sad.

"Silly duffer," she said with a voice so tender that shock flooded Dani. "Always making a mess and a fuss." She drew the cloth with gentle slowness across his skin. "What am I going to do with you? Hmm?"

"Anything you want, love," he said with the roguishness of a man who still believes himself young…or young enough.

"Incorrigible, too," she said with a fond tsk. She slipped a clean shirt over his head and straightened it, tugging the hem and collar into place. Jean smiled. Her thumb whisked over his cheek. "There now, good as new."

There was so much love in that statement. So much ache and despair, too. Like she was saying good-bye to the man she loved, with the dusting of her fingertips, memorizing his skin.

Jean's head turned slightly, just enough for Dani to see the gleam of a tear in her eye. She inhaled in surprise.

Jean's head snapped around.

Dani held her breath as suddenly cold, fierce eyes met hers in challenge.

Twisting around past his wife, Fred turned to see what had her attention. His face broke into a wide grin. "Why hello, Edith." He waved. "It's been such a long time. I'm so happy you came."

Jean strode towards Dani in four sharp steps and glowered at her. "Spying on me?" she asked, her voice a low snarl. "To what end? Will you mock Fred? Share what you saw with the rest of them? Laugh to your friend about your confused uncle who needs help to get cleaned and dressed? Are you so cruel?"

Dani sucked in a startled breath. "No! I was just…" She jerked her thumb behind her. "I needed the loo."

"Then why are you standing here, pressing your ear to my door? It's sly and rude." Her eyes flashed. "Leave!"

With enormous restraint, Dani only just avoided slamming shut the door of the bathroom behind her. Slumping against it, she took stock of how angry and embarrassed she felt. She was tired of being treated like the idiot toddler. Her irritation soon began to ebb as she processed what she'd seen. Jean's aching sadness began to settle around her.

As she finished and washed up, Dani mused on how strange it felt to discover Jean cared deeply about anyone—even if she hid it behind layers of disapproval as thick as winter clothes.

How must it feel to be losing a loved one, piece by piece, as their brain slowly forgot itself?

And Jean hadn't been oblivious after all, instead carefully hiding his secret to protect Fred's dignity. How long had this been going on? Months? Years? Longer?

The sticky air hit her the moment she arrived back at the dining room. Sweat was prickling down the back of her shirt. She glanced at the clock. It wasn't even the hottest part of the day. Was it forty degrees yet? At times like these, she wished Australia used the American scale. A hundred and four sounded much closer to the furnace this was.

Ro was telling her famous netball grand final story about their glorious come-from-behind victory against England that had her family agog. Even Rhoda had forgotten to drink.

Holy shit. Ro really was the in-laws whisperer.

Dessert usually signalled the beginning of the end.

They had survived Rhoda's additional proclamations about her medical issues, which had been brought to an abrupt end after Jean pointedly turned up "Little Drummer Boy" when it came around again.

Fred settled back into his seat with a fresh shirt on and was popping rum balls like grapes.

They all pulled the paper crackers and read out the terrible jokes and squeezed on paper hats.

"I like my joke," Dani said, examining the white rectangle of paper. *"Why did the hedgehog cross the road? To see his flat mate."*

Ro pouted adorably. "Nooo. You gotta feel so bad for the little guy. His mourning is for our amusement."

"Oh damn, now how can I unsee that?" Dani smirked.

Jean shot Dani an icy look. "If you're quite finished talking nonsense, it's time for dessert." Her mood had become progressively worse since Dani had caught her with Fred.

A burble of approval went around the table. It was impossible not to salivate at the thought of Jean's gooey pavlova and crispy fruit mince pies.

Jean headed towards the kitchen, waving off any offers to help.

"Right," Dani stood the moment she was gone. "I'm gonna make sure my trifle is at least on the menu." Making that concoction had taken half the night after all.

"I love trifle!" Fred called from the far end of the table. He beamed. "Thank you, Edith."

In the kitchen, Dani found Jean pulling the tray of fruit mince pies out of the oven with thick oven mitts. Her pavlova was already on the counter, artfully drizzled with passionfruit. It looked as though a food stylist had slaved over it for hours.

Dani stepped over the ginger cat curled in the centre of the room and flipped the lid on the trifle box.

"There's no room for that," Jean snapped. "Don't bother plating it up."

Up all night. She reminded herself. *Up all night.* She ignored her and reached for a large plate from the shelf.

"Did you not hear?"

"I heard. But I spent ages on this. Uncle Fred seemed keen."

"He prefers my pavlova. And this is my kitchen, in my home. Even though you apparently feel you have the right to invade any space you wish."

"I'm sorry I upset you before. And I'm bringing it out anyway." Dani bit her lip, heart thudding at her uncharacteristic show of defiance, and slid her fingers into the container to carefully remove her trifle.

"Absolutely not. I—" The rest of Jean's sentence turned into a startled half shriek.

Dani spun around to see Harriet darting through Jean's legs and the tray of mini fruit pies flying across the kitchen. Jean was falling. Her arms flailed as she sought her balance, her left arm catching the edge of the pavlova. It flew off the counter.

Time slowed for Dani as she saw her choices. Save Jean, save the nearby pavlova, or fling herself at that airborne tray hurtling toward the door.

Her hand shot out to catch the dropping pavlova from underneath as she slid her other arm around her great-aunt's waist, controlling her fall to the floor. She lay the pavlova beside Jean just as a loud grunt sounded at the door.

Dani's head snapped up.

Ro, at full stretch, had somehow managed to catch the tray of fruit tarts. It was a spectacular save—well, until her fingers closed fully around the scalding metal.

Her agonised yelp was sickening.

Ro tossed the tray on the oven top with a hiss. The little tarts played dodgem cars but somehow stayed on the metal. Tears streamed down Ro's cheeks.

"Ro!" Dani jumped up and ran to her side, grabbing her wrists. Two parallel lines of angry red welts ran across her fingers. "Oh my God! Your hands!"

"I'll live," Ro ground out. "Ow, ow, ow. Really glad it's off-season now though. Shit."

"Get OUT!" Jean bellowed.

Dani saw red. She whipped around, a sharp barb on her tongue to unleash at her ungrateful aunt. It was one thing for her to belittle Dani her whole life, but that gave her no rights to insult her girlfriend.

Jean, however, was flapping at the sulking cat, whose ginger fur was on its end like a toilet brush.

Harriet bolted.

Jean gingerly rose, and returned the battered but saved pavlova to the counter.

"Are you okay?" Ro asked, her voice a rasp.

"You're asking me that?" Jean's lips were white and her hands seemed than less steady as she wiped them on a dish towel.

"Yeah." Ro flapped her hands as if to get a breeze on them. "I mean, people don't bounce so well when they get older. Y'know?"

Dani winced at the reference to Jean's age. Her great-aunt deeply resented being retired.

"I'm…unhurt." Jean's gaze fell to Ro's welts, eyes wide. "Your hands though!" She turned to the sink and flicked on the cold water. "Quickly! Under the water now. Danielle, the aloe vera lotion is in the bathroom cupboard, top shelf. Go!"

Dani sprinted for the bathroom. She flung things aside in the cabinet. God, if this stupid lunch had hurt Ro's career, she'd never forgive herself. Would Ro forgive her? Her gut twisted.

She raced back to find Jean holding Ro's hands under the water and murmuring to her.

Jean snatched the lotion from Dani's outstretched fingers and pulled Ro's blistered hands from the flow.

Ro stared at them and glanced at Dani. "I know it looks a mess, but I heal fast. And I'm sure…" She bit her lip, "…I'll be fine."

"You have superb reflexes," Jean dolloped lotion onto Ro's hands. "I've never seen anyone move that fast."

"Well, it is my job," Ro said with a grimace as Jean worked the ointment in. "They train us to react, not think. Which, as you can see, isn't always a good thing." She gave a wry chuckle. "I was just coming to see if Dani needed a hand and saw a tray coming right at me and reached for it. Pure instinct."

"Your job," Jean repeated. "Yes, I can see you're a professional." She glanced at Dani. "So what's your excuse?"

"Huh?" Dani asked cleverly.

"Your friend is trained to react in an instant. You are not. Your quick thinking was…most unexpected."

"Unexpected?" Dani hid her annoyance. Would it kill Jean to say thanks? Even her compliments sounded like accusations.

"Oh, Dani's always been pretty quick," Ro said. "She trains with me at the local park some weekends. I guess something stuck." She grinned.

"So it seems," Jean said. "Well"—she shook her head—"enough of the dramatics. Everyone will be wondering where dessert is." She waved at the pavlova. "I'll take this out. Danielle, plate up those fruit pies. We can't have Ro's sacrifice being in vain, now can we?"

Dramatics? Oh, and you're welcome.

Jean paused and added, "And plate up that trifle. Fred always enjoys it."

Her face was implacable as she swept from the room, leaving Dani speechless.

"Well, there you go," Ro said. "Your trifle is officially a welcome addition to the feast."

"Until anyone eats it," Dani joked, but her delivery was strained. "Are you really all right? I'm so sorry."

"The aloe's working. It's already hurting less. Can you get me a bandage to cover the blisters, and we can go and try that pav she's so proud of? I won't put myself on Jean's blacklist by knocking it back."

Rhoda was snoring in an armchair. Torn festive paper lay all around from gift wrappings. Dani stared at her present from Jean. A scarf. Tartan. She'd knitted them for everyone. Had it ever snowed in Brisbane once in its entire history?

Peak heat had hit, and the old ceiling fan was now just swirling sweltering air around the room. All the leftover hot food on the table just added to the stifling warmth.

No one could move. The paper party hats affixed earlier on sweaty heads (except Jean's brow, which neither sweated nor permitted party hats) had begun to disintegrate on foreheads.

Mike's red hat stain looked like someone had attempted to lobotomise him.

The conversation had moved on to next to nothing. Occasional spurts and starts of half-remembered things to share. Even Sally had dropped Teddy as a topic and was bitching about her boss.

Jean, however, sat, ramrod straight in her seat at the head of the table, saying little but watching everything through half-lidded eyes.

Dani's nephews and nieces had been roped into dishes duty. They were making a loud, sudsy game of it in the kitchen—usually grounds for an intervention. For once, Jean had not so much as twitched.

Stephen seemed to think he was closing a real estate deal with his brother, John, who actually seemed to be agreeing to everything just to get him to shut up.

The mix tape came to an end. Rhoda woke up, jumped to her feet, and flipped it over on her way out the door while hauling her husband in her slipstream. She gave everyone a breezy wave and promised to furnish them all with updates on her ailments. "Check your emails!"

Dani's mother came around to give Dani a quick hug good-bye. She whispered in her ear, "She's lovely. We'll talk properly later. I'm happy for you."

Dani smiled. Her mother loved all her girlfriends.

Sally's hug was harder, more bruising. "Merry Christmas, sis," was all she said.

Mike's hug followed. "I like your friend." He smiled, then murmured, "And so does my stubborn wife. Not that Sally'd admit how cool Ro is. I hope you're really happy together."

Dani grinned at him. He was one of the good ones. And he obviously had better gaydar than his wife.

Soon only Dani was left, along with Ro, who had disappeared to use the bathroom.

Jean regarded her in a strained silence. It was unsettling. Dani was pinned to her chair by Jean's considering stare.

"Your friend has discipline," Jean suddenly said. "She'd have to, to do what she does."

"I guess."

"A pity it hasn't rubbed off on you."

Dani's eyes narrowed. "You think I'm undisciplined."

"I don't think, I know. Your mother let you get away with far too much. Let you run wild."

"Great…" Dani licked her lips. *Come on, Ro…*

"When I was a young woman, we were taught self-control and restraint. There was little freedom. Ladies were taught to dress and behave correctly. We did not climb trees, ride bicycles, or run riot the way you did."

Awesome. Another etiquette lesson. Just what she needed. She'd value it as much as the scarf. "Well," Dani said, with a tired wave, "I'm sure you aced those lessons as a girl."

"No." Jean studied her. "I did not. It was stifling."

Dani blinked. "I don't understand."

"No, I don't imagine you do." Jean flicked lint off her dress. She appeared to be debating whether to continue. "You've had quite the life, Danielle. Freedom. Possibilities. Opportunities."

"I suppose."

"Even if you've wasted them all. I can't imagine the thrill in shoe sales."

"And I can't imagine the thrill in selling wool and fabric." *Oh crap.* Dani bit her lip. She couldn't believe that had slipped out.

Jean regarded her evenly. "The difference is it was *my* store. I owned it. It was one of few options available to me in the fifties when I arrived in this godforsaken place. I can't say the same for you, who had options galore at your feet."

"Wait, you didn't want to move to Australia?" Since when?

"When I was eighteen, all I ever wanted to do was travel. I wanted to choose my own path in all things, including matters of matrimony."

Dani stared at her in surprise.

"I got a job, over my mother's objections, working in a respectable dressmaking shop and saved up all year. Finally I had the money I needed. I had the tickets booked. My best friend, Maggie, and I were off to see the world. We had organized a chaperone, of course—Maggie's aunt from France. It was terribly exciting. France would be our first stop. Then Italy, Spain, over to Portugal, on to Scandinavia, home to England. The following year, we planned we would save up again and then take on America. North and south."

"Wow." Dani couldn't imagine that. She'd never left Brisbane, let alone Australia. But seeing Europe in mid-last century? She tried to imagine that. It'd still be rebuilding after the war. New stores would be springing up, tourists would be returning to the historic sights. "Was it amazing?"

"Oh yes. Thrilling." Her tone contained a biting edge. "Or so my brother told me."

"Peter?"

"Just before I was due to leave, my mother suddenly took ill. In my day, the daughters were always the ones to tend their parents. It wasn't an option. I was tersely instructed to give Peter my ticket that I'd saved up all year for. He would go in my stead. No arguments."

"That's awful."

"Actually, the particularly awful part was when I discovered, after Maggie and Peter were abroad, that my mother wasn't really ill. She simply didn't wish me to go. She decided she'd be lonely without me tending her. And, again, being the times they were, I was not able to say one thing." Her eyes narrowed.

"Did you get to go to America the next year?"

"No." Jean tilted her head. "I am not a fool. I knew my mother's health would suddenly take a perilous turn then, too. Or perhaps my passport would mysteriously go missing. Or something else. So I made other plans."

"What happened?"

"I chose a husband."

"Chose? You mean you fell in love with Uncle Fred and—"

"No. Listen to what I'm saying: I chose one. Very carefully. I found the first man I determined had the means to move me far from my parents' control. On our first date, Fred expressed an interest in emigrating to Australia, and that's how I knew he was suitable."

"Did your mother approve of you leaving England?"

Jean smiled. It was not pleasant. "Oh no, but she couldn't do a thing to stop me. After all, she had trained me to obey my husband. And if my husband wanted to go to Australia, that's what one did."

Hesitating, Dani was unsure if she was about to cross a line. "Was Uncle Fred good to you?"

"I chose correctly." A hint of steel crept into her voice.

Dani wondered if she dared ask the next question. "Did you…love him?"

"He has been exactly what I thought he'd be."

That didn't answer anything. Dani caught Jean's even gaze. *Actually, it did.* A whole life, sixty years, without any romantic love.

"It is what it is," Jean said, her expression stony. "Every time I look at him, I'm reminded of the scarcity of choices women had in my day. Choices you seem to blithely take for granted."

"You think I take my life for granted?"

"Yes. It's appalling to watch."

Dani frowned. "Why?"

"Your sister is tolerable. Sally never aspires to anything more than the mundane. She doesn't have a spirited bone in her body, an inquisitive thought, a curious nature. You, though…you have all three, and I had to tolerate the unendurable. Watching you grow up without an ounce of discipline or ambition to make the most of your life. You just…" She waved her hand.

"What?"

"Take it all for granted and do nothing with it."

"You're jealous of the opportunities I had that you were denied?" Dani couldn't believe her ears. "Are you saying you are jealous of *me*?"

"I suppose you'd like to believe that. Would it help you make sense of things between us?" Jean's eyebrow cocked in challenge. Taunting her.

"Yes," Dani whispered.

"I'm not jealous of you, Danielle. You are *enraging*. Your life is just so easy."

"So that's why you decided to make it hard?"

"I was teaching you discipline. Your mother never pulled you into line. Your father was never home. What hope was there for you to excel at anything?"

"My parents did the best they could." Dani squared her jaw. "And for the record, you don't have to grind someone under heel to teach them something."

Jean's mouth twisted into cruelty. "Suffered *so* much, have we?"

"Oh, I get it." Dani couldn't believe she'd never seen it before. "You've been punishing me. You had it hard, so I should, too? Otherwise it's not fair." She gave her a bitter look. "Charming philosophy."

"How dare you! You have no idea what my life has been like." Jean rose halfway out of her seat, her twisted arthritic fingers curling into fists.

"I know you were a young woman who felt trapped and so used a husband as a means of escape."

Eyes still mutinous, Jean opened her mouth to speak but instead clamped her mouth shut and resumed her seat.

"But then you got stuck in a loveless marriage," Dani continued. "However, you had discipline. And hard work. Ambition. So you flung yourself into your shop so you didn't have to think about your lonely, sad life."

Jean's nostrils flared. "You are *intolerable*."

"I guess I am. And you're exactly like those glass figurines in your display case that you never let me look at. Perfect, cold, and untouchable."

For a long moment, there was no answer. Jean glared at her, rolling her wedding ring around her finger.

"I'm sorry for what you had to go through," Dani said more kindly, "but how is forcing me to be someone else, someone you approve of, a good thing?"

"Silly girl," Jean said, her voice harsh. "You think I'm taking from your path? I was the only one who truly saw *you*."

"You saw me? Then based on all that disciplining, you clearly hated what you saw." Dani inhaled, dreading the answer but knowing it all the same. "Right?"

"Of course. Mirrors are the ugliest implements to endure."

"What?" Astonishment flooded Dani. She couldn't seriously mean…

"Do you know what my mother called me?" Jean demanded. "Over and over, it's all I heard. An undisciplined *wild child*."

Dani gasped.

"Now do you see?" Jean snapped.

Wait, Jean hated her because Dani reminded her of herself? All these years she'd just seen Dani as a bitter reminder of dreams lost and wasted? But why didn't Jean reclaim her dreams? "Why didn't you ever travel? Later?"

"Fred didn't want to." She gave a faint eye roll. "I follow my husband's wishes."

Screw that. "I don't obey anyone," Dani blurted out.

"I am well aware."

"Do you really resent me, Jean?"

The older woman leaned forward and cupped Dani's cheek, angling her face to the light. Jean's eyes locked on Dani's. Her fingertips bit in. "With every fibre of my being."

Dani flinched, trying to pull away.

Those old, claw-like fingers tightened their grip.

"And I'm self-aware enough to know my resentment of my own circumstances is far greater than my resentment of yours," Jean's eyes bored into Dani's. "This bland existence is my life. You have your own. So my point in telling you all this is whatever you do, don't waste it."

"I don't plan to."

"Then go to England with her," Jean said abruptly.

"What?"

"At lunch, your friend mentioned her team is competing in the netball world cup next year in England. Go with her. See the world. Live. Get out of Brisbane. Do something, *anything* with the opportunities you have. My God, it's physically painful watching someone with the zest for life I once had just scratch away at sneaker sales and little else."

Dani's hand lifted to claw Jean's fingers from her chin, annoyed, yet again, that her choices were being mocked. She met Jean's eyes. Instead of the censure she expected to see, she saw only deep loss.

Against her will, Dani's fingers curled into Jean's, cupping them against her face. "I'm sorry for all you went through," she said honestly.

"One makes do." Jean dropped her hand. "All over the globe are women like me, still dutifully obeying rules the world no longer seems to follow."

"You don't have to keep following them."

"Of course I do. I made vows. Love, honour, obey. Though I know you'll never understand my life."

"No. My world's not the same as yours."

"Finally, something we agree on." Jean's lips curled into the faintest of smiles.

"Yeah." Dani offered a tiny grin back at her concession.

Ro returned. "Sorry I took so long," she said with a hefty sigh. "Figuring out button-flies with bandaged hands is the pits. We ready to go?"

"Yes." Dani looked to Jean. "Um…I guess…until next year."

Ro grinned at Jean and lifted a bandaged hand in farewell. "Yep. Until then."

The suggestion they'd still be together to do it all again in a year's time filled Dani with joy.

"Next year?" Jean queried.

Dani braced herself, wondering if Jean was about to say something hideous. Point out all the ways Ro wasn't family and she was lucky she'd even been invited this year.

Instead her aunt's voice contained the faintest hint of warmth. "But of course. What would Christmas be without *the friend*?"

There was no mistaking that particular emphasis.

Oh shit! She knows. Dani swallowed.

Ro laughed and softly elbowed Jean. *Actually elbowed her.* "Damn straight. This friend will be back, ready to stare at your frizzles and catch whatever desserts Harriet scares my way. Thanks for lunch. It was great meeting everyone."

Jean arched an eyebrow. "Not *frizzles*."

"I know, I know." Ro grinned. "It was crazy of me to call them that. I don't know why you put up with me."

"Your dessert-catching skills, perhaps." Jean's lips were pressed together as if desperately preventing a laugh. Her eyes were bright.

Dani stared in disbelief. Jean did not tell jokes, and certainly not with Dani's girlfriend. A familiar form shuffling down the hall caught her eye. "Bye, Fred!" she called.

He turned, his face wreathed in delight. "Bye-bye, Edith. Lovely seeing you again."

With a faint sigh, Jean shook her head and that ever-pressing sadness seemed to settle back over her. She began closing the door, shooing them out. "Good-bye, Danielle." Then she paused, her eyebrow lifting. Her smile became full and real. "*And friend*."

The click of the door ended the conversation with finality.

"Little Drummer Boy" played on.

Number Five

Monique Carson, Las Vegas's premier CEO sex fantasy expert, straightened the paperwork on her desk in Room 612 of Hotel Duxton. The desk was wooden, solid, and perfectly sized for the taking of women over, or under, it while she dictated her orders for the day, depending on the client's desires.

Her clients were all women. Monique loved seeing women open up and come alive from being intimate with someone who knew how to ignite their bodies. There was something so powerful about looking into a woman's eyes the moment she understood what sex could really be like.

Repressed women, unhappy women, bored women. Showing them how much they could feel was a heady sensation, and, by God, Monique loved her work. All her clients, even the walled-off ones, were fascinating to her.

Which lead her thoughts to her next arrival.

If Monique Carson saw herself as olive oil—languid, evocative, and smooth—June Menzies was brittle as sandpaper. The abrasive, sixty-two-year-old hotel executive existed in a state of constant annoyance and ferocity, approaching her work and life as if storming battlements. Little wonder half the staff at Hotel Duxton Vegas were in fear of their front desk manager.

To Monique, though, June Menzies was utterly delicious. After all, a ball of fury was just something else to play with and pull apart. Something interesting. Exciting. Fun.

And although Mrs. Menzies often suggested she hated everything about Monique's teasing attitude and all the salacious details that her work entailed, it never stopped her from visiting. Often.

A knock sounded.

Right on time.

"Darling, come in," Monique purred, stepping aside to allow entry.

Mrs. Menzies entered and placed a small leather handbag on the chair. It was rigid and black, as formal as its owner in her starched outfit.

Her shoulder-length, slightly damp hair was a rich dark brown courtesy of her doubtlessly expensive hairdresser. She wore her expression and her hotel uniform the same way: stiff and armored. As if just daring someone to take her on.

Mrs. Menzies was rotund, short, with an ample bosom, a thick waist, wide hips and thighs, and a permanently drawn down mouth. Her wrists were knotted into tight fists. She looked even angrier than usual, which probably explained her call an hour ago for Monique to urgently fit her in.

But as much as June Menzies so often resembled an enraged, lethal porcupine, in her dark eyes lay a fire that Monique found deeply attractive.

The woman's rounded cheeks—sporting a rising blush from the awareness of what she was about to do—were as smooth and flawless as the rest of her soft, gorgeously fleshy body.

Every woman was beautiful to Monique—even the ones who never saw it in themselves. Especially those women such as June Menzies.

Mrs. Menzies's husband often dismissed her as nothing, which only made her fight even harder to prove her value in her professional sphere. The more he cheated on her, the more efficient a manager she became. Monique had often thought it would be fascinating to study this link between personal fury and professional prowess…if one didn't mind losing an eye in the process.

Mrs. Menzies's mouth flattened in a sharp line as her intense gaze locked with Monique's. She waved at the damp ends of her hair. "I've already showered."

It was a rule. No one could begin her hour with Monique without showering. All her other clients did so in Monique's suite. June Menzies, multitasking queen, always took care of it before arrival so as not to lose a second of time.

"Number four," Mrs. Menzies announced with an annoyed huff, as if it were difficult admitting aloud what she wanted.

Number four.

Monique had long ago developed a list of five options for clients to select from based on the emotions they wished to evoke. The first three were self-explanatory:

Take Me—a basic lesbian fantasy seduction, usually selected by questioning or straight women wanting to dip their toes in Sapphic seas.

Tease Me—for the delayed gratification lovers, women for whom less was more and a featherlight touch felt like bliss.

Thrill Me—for those who loved hints of danger and daring and being taken to the edge. It had flavors of BDSM, if requested.

Boss Me—number four—was her most popular item by far, given it was Monique's specialty. She would become the CEO of women's fantasies, slide on an executive power suit, and adopt her most imperious attitude, reeling off her orders for the day as she fucked a client any way Monique decided.

The ceding of complete control to Monique was a large part of its appeal to those who chose it. So powerful was this effect, she'd had some women go weak at the knees the moment she'd merely unbuttoned her top button.

Lastly, there was number five. It was an indulgent experience Monique had long thought Mrs. Menzies would benefit from. Once, eighteen months ago, Monique had suggested trying number five only to have Mrs. Menzies erupt in a rage that she was not some "pampered poodle needing to be put on a pedestal and lied to."

What an interesting choice of words. Of course, to choose number five, one had to believe themselves worthy of it in the first place. Sadly, far too many women did not.

"Ms. Carson." Mrs. Menzies's clipped voice cut through her thoughts. "My break times are strict. I don't have all day."

"Four it is," Monique supplied a genial smile. "You *do* love Four."

Mrs. Menzies's head snapped up. "I swear if you suggest Five again…" Her laugh was short and sharp.

"Perish the thought." Monique offered a wry smile. The only person who brought up number five these days was Mrs. Menzies herself.

Monique quickly pushed to one side a pile of notes on her desk, leaving an adequate gap for what she had planned, and licked her lips in anticipation. "Before we begin, remind me of your safe word."

"Chanel."

As in Chanel *Number Five*. Which Mrs. Menzies was also wearing once again. Her subconscious clearly lacked all subtlety.

Monique nodded and removed her navy jacket, slipping it onto the back of a polished wood chair, and then sat on top of the desk, crossing a leg languidly. She leaned back far enough that her breasts strained against her cream shirt.

Mrs. Menzies's nostrils flared. Sometimes she disapproved when Monique made it too obvious and flaunted what they were about to do, even though it was exactly why she was here.

"Feeling annoyed today? Need a bit of venting?" Monique ran a suggestive hand over her own thigh. This particular client needed to get her grievances out before they began, or she couldn't enjoy what followed.

Mrs. Menzies's eyes narrowed. "Yes."

"What's happened?"

"The usual." Her lips thinned.

"You've found out about another of your husband's indiscretions? Or is some pitiful minion giving you grief and not respecting your authority? You want to fuck away your fury?"

"Must you be so blunt?" Mrs. Menzies's lips curled in distaste. "I don't fuck away anything!"

"I beg to differ, darling." Monique plucked at her top button, opening her silk shirt a little. "You want to make the whole world pay when you're angry. But then you come and see me so you won't commit a murder. Your husband should send me a thank-you card. He lives only due to me."

"You give yourself too much credit. I'm still planning on his method of disposal." Mrs. Menzies's lips gave the tiniest concession of mirth.

Monique smiled back. "Well, he's safe for now."

"You think you have me all figured out, don't you?" Mrs. Menzies eyed her, expression darkening.

"I do, darling." Monique plucked another shirt button. Then another.

Mrs. Menzies's eyes fed on Monique's rapidly appearing skin even as her lips tugged down again. "Is that so?"

"I know you'd love me to tear your clothes off you and ravish you the way you deserve, but you will never ask."

"The way I *deserve*." Mrs. Menzies's tone filled with scorn. "Sure. That's it."

"Oh, yes." Monique's gaze slid appreciatively over Mrs. Menzies's body.

"You have to say that. You flatter me so I don't evict my hotel's in-house prostitute."

"You *do* realize most of Vegas's hotels have women like me in them? I'm hardly unique." She smiled. "But…I also keep a low profile, choose only discreet clients, and that enables managers like your good self to look the other way to keep a most excellent guest such as myself. So no, try again."

Mrs. Menzies's jaw tightened, but her eyes signaled agreement. Rules or no rules, no matter the hotel's pedigree, the oldest profession found a way to flourish everywhere. "Fine," she conceded. "So you say nice things about me because I pay you."

"No, you pay me to help you lose control and you pay me to give you permission to let go. And you love it when I do naughty things that would scandalize your employees, because the forbidden excites you. And most of all, you love being at my mercy and not being the one in charge for once. But you do *not* pay me to be nice to you. So when I say a thing is so, it is."

Mrs. Menzies snorted. "I have huge, saggy breasts, a fat backside, not to mention stretch marks and wrinkles and gray hairs. My husband calls me frumpy every day. But you, who've had every type of woman there is, declares that I'm desirable." She leaned in. "*Liar.*"

"I have never lied to you, June," Monique said placidly. "Not once."

"Of course you have. I'm not fool enough to believe any sex worker's flattery. And don't you dare tell me you're some kind of idealist who believes it."

"Not an idealist, darling. I merely look past the ridiculous notion of what society claims is desirable." Monique regarded her. "I'm a seeker of more. I like to understand things. People. And on that note, will you tell me why you're so worked up today?" She held out her hand to tug the other woman close.

Mrs. Menzies accepted the pull with little resistance.

"Tell me?" Monique slid a hand around the back of Mrs. Menzies's waist, hands falling to that fabulously ample rear.

Mrs. Menzies grimaced. "I really hate the upper management at my hotel."

"What have they done now?" Monique rubbed a little harder, enjoying the fleshy swell through the prim skirt.

Mrs. Menzies's outfit comprised a black skirt, tight across her figure, a matching sharp vest, and a long-sleeved crisp white blouse. Pearls at her throat matched her earrings.

The strict headmistress effect always did things to Monique. There was something so deliciously fun about feeling up someone who lived to be *proper*.

"They treat me as a dumping ground for all their stupid ideas."

Monique, still sitting on the desk, tugged Mrs. Menzies between her legs. "How rude of them," she teased as her hands trailed around to the sides of Mrs. Menzies's skirt.

"Exceedingly rude." Mrs. Menzies parted her legs slightly, her only admission of how much she wanted Monique's attentions.

Slipping her fingers under the skirt hem, Monique toyed with the material suggestively for a few moments as she waited for Mrs. Menzies to finish admitting what was aggravating her most.

"They're dumping some hotel trainee on me with no notice. Tomorrow, I have to train her in all aspects of my job and set it up so she can do the same in three other departments. I met her earlier when she came in to sign some paperwork. She's pure ice. Nose in the air, full of herself. Gave me a chill to the bone."

Monique shifted her hand up beneath the skirt, enjoying the warmth and solidness of voluptuous thighs. The flesh under her fingers quivered.

Mrs. Menzies's expression was as hard and cold as it always was, as though Monique's hand wasn't wandering higher and higher. Her jaw, however, clenched.

"I'm intrigued. There's someone capable of rattling even you? And an underling at that? I so want to meet her." Monique allowed the back of her hand to bump into the junction of Mrs. Menzies's thighs. So warm, even through cotton.

"No!" Mrs. Menzies hissed. She paused. "To you meeting her, I mean. Continue…" A red hue crept up her throat. "…the other…matter." Her eyes darted down to convey her meaning, and both their gazes followed Monique's roaming hand swallowed by Mrs. Menzies's skirt.

Monique chuckled. "Hmm. You're certainly enjoying the *other matter*. I can feel that." She fingered a line into Mrs. Menzies's soaking panties.

Mrs. Menzies shot her an aggrieved look. She always reacted as if her body's obvious interest was a betrayal.

"But I definitely should meet her," Monique purred. "I'll call down tomorrow on some silly errand. Send her up to me."

"Oh, I don't think so. She seems to be the sue-everyone sort. I'm not risking you setting her off with your…antics. I think she's come from money."

"I will behave, darling. No touching. Scout's honor. *Toying* on the other hand… Oh, I'm very good at toying, wouldn't you agree?" Monique thumbed her in an exceedingly sensitive spot.

Mrs. Menzies swallowed. "You…have some talent in that regard."

Monique smiled. Mrs. Menzies was almost ready. She just needed to be fired up—in every sense.

Swaying in a little, chasing Monique's hand for friction, Mrs. Menzies surrendered. "Fine. I'll send her up to you, and you can see for yourself how cold she is. Just…*behave*." Her breath hitched as she swayed in again, rutting herself against Monique's knuckles.

Monique nudged aside Mrs. Menzies's panties and assessed her readiness. Wetness coated her fingers. She allowed the faintest tip of one finger to settle at Mrs. Menzies's entrance. It did a suggestive little swirl. "I'm sorry your bosses are throwing trainees at you and don't care how much they add to your workload."

Mrs. Menzies gasped, and her chest rose and fell rapidly. "It's disruptive and unprofessional." Her jaw ground hard. "They don't care. I put up a lot for this company, and they treat me like…like…"

"Frank?" She had the same frustration in her eyes that she usually reserved for her cheating, worthless husband.

"With no respect," Mrs. Menzies finished.

"As if you're disposable and someone barely worth their time," Monique guessed. She withdrew her hand. Mrs. Menzies was quivering with rage and wet as an inland sea. *Perfect.*

"Yes!" Mrs. Menzies spat out. "Yes!" She stepped back, yanked off her vest, chest heaving with rage. She flung the item to the floor. "Enough. I want this now." She wrenched the buttons open on her shirt, exposing a beige bra with erect nipples punching through it.

Turned-on and furious, Mrs. Menzies was always an impressive sight.

Monique's lower stomach clenched in approval. She rose. It was time. Her expression turned cool and imperious as she settled into her CEO persona. She'd dressed especially for Mrs. Menzies, having packed something fun inside her tailored pants today. "Agreed. I think we've had quite enough chitchat."

Mrs. Menzies licked her lips. "Yes." Her voice was now a gravelly croak.

"I have some paperwork for you to review," Monique announced, tone sharp. "My previous assistant was woeful. I trust you'll do better?" Her eyebrow rose in challenge.

"I'm excellent at paperwork, Ms. Carson," Mrs. Menzies murmured. Lust and excitement flooded her face. "Is that *all* you need from me?"

"No. I require some stress relief," Monique replied in her iciest tone. "I want to spread you out and have you on my desk. I trust that's acceptable." It was only barely a question.

"I can assist with that." Mrs. Menzies's chest heaved.

"Take off your bra, then lie on my desk, face first." Monique patted the furniture in question.

Mrs. Menzies's nostrils flared. She did as instructed, freeing her magnificent breasts, and then sank forward over the desk. "Yes, Ms. Carson."

Subservient June Menzies was a beautiful thing to behold. This was the same June Menzies who could reduce her staff to tears with a single stern look.

"While I…avail…myself of you," Monique said, "I suggest you explain to me how you plan to fix my afternoon schedule. And make it good."

Mrs. Menzies gave a faint shudder.

"Well?" Monique snapped at her delay. "Details. Now."

"At two, you have the meeting with the ambassador." Mrs. Menzies's voice was a breathy mess.

Interesting. Mrs. Menzies only selected ambassadors for fictitious meetings when she wanted someone powerful in her fantasy.

Monique's hand slid to the skirt-clad ass in front of her and rubbed it in circles. "Which ambassador?"

"Germany."

"Ah yes, Ambassador Müller. He can be so tedious. Spread your legs for me, June." She waited. "No. Wider."

Mrs. Menzies shifted again after a moment's pause.

Monique stepped in and pushed her groin hard against Mrs. Menzies's ass, confident she'd feel the rigidness of the strap-on.

"Oh-h," she stuttered. "Yes."

"Yes what?" Monique demanded. "Yes, Müller is tedious?"

Mrs. Menzies lifted her ass a little as if to feel the hard shape better. "*Yes*," she said firmly.

Monique slid up Mrs. Menzies's skirt, exposing her backside to cool air. She then wrenched down Mrs. Menzies's stockings, taking in, with satisfaction, the goose bumps that appeared.

Mrs. Menzies wore beige-colored full briefs to match her utilitarian bra. Forceful and solid like their owner. Monique rubbed the garment's heated crotch, cupping all the way under Mrs. Menzies and coming back up again. Her fingers came away wet. "Very good, June."

"Oh," Mrs. Menzies mumbled. "*Fuck.*" The last word was barely a whisper.

Monique loved it when desire removed the other woman's censor button. She could smell Mrs. Menzies's arousal now. *Delicious.* She returned her hand to cup her.

Mrs. Menzies began wriggling beneath Monique's hand, desperately seeking more rigid contact.

Running one firm finger between Mrs. Menzies's legs, Monique pressed hard enough into the cotton near the clit for Mrs. Menzies to tremble.

"All right, June, I'm going to have you now." Monique slowly slid down the final barrier and then dropped the sodden undergarment at Mrs. Menzies's ankles. She ran a hand up the backs of her legs, leaving a trail of quivers in her wake.

The glistening of wet curls greeted Monique as well as a liberal smear of moisture at Mrs. Menzies's upper thighs. Monique leaned in close and inhaled against Mrs. Menzies's folds.

"I'm not impressed you've booked a meeting with Ambassador Müller." Monique exhaled over the exposed heat, appreciating the tremble her breath against vulnerable flesh created. "You know how I feel about him, and yet you did it anyway." She took a slippery lower lip between her teeth and tugged sharply.

Mrs. Menzies gasped in surprise.

Monique released it, tongued it for a second, and rose once more, enjoying the disappointed moan from Mrs. Menzies.

Slowly, Monique slid down the zipper on her pants, making sure it could be plainly heard. "I'm unhappy with you at the moment." She pulled out her strap-on, lathering it with KY Jelly from the tube she kept hidden in her desk.

Monique slid the tip of the hard silicone up and down Mrs. Menzies's folds, making no move to enter her. Over and over she did this, until Mrs. Menzies writhed.

"I'm sorry, Ms. Carson. Perhaps if you…took advantage of the situation before you as my apology?" Mrs. Menzies gasped out the words. "Please?"

Half naked, soaked, needy, in disarray, and now begging for Monique's attention? These were the moments Monique most enjoyed about her job. Making women *crave*.

"Hmm," Monique said, as if considering the offer. "I suppose it will do. You are a most pleasing sight. Your body is so ready." She dipped the strap-on's head the tiniest bit inside Mrs. Menzies's entrance.

Mrs. Menzies shuddered. "Please," she repeated. "*Please.*"

Monique waited just long enough for Mrs. Menzies to squirm in anticipation. Then, she thrust.

The material of Monique's crisp navy pants pressed into the backs of Mrs. Menzies's naked thighs as the silicone was swallowed whole. She went deep and hard. After all, Mrs. Menzies had evoked Germany. If she wanted it light and fun, she'd have mentioned Fiji.

Mrs. Menzies cried out. "Oh. *Oh.*" Her hands turned to fists, grasping at air against the table. "More. Deeper. Oh."

"No, no—this isn't about what my *assistant* wants." Monique sounded bored, but her own desire was now raging. With controlling, uptight women like Mrs. Menzies, Monique was always turned-on when they crumpled. "Now then, tell me what you have planned for the rest of the day. Quickly." She thrust again, harder.

"Oh. I…call down to Accounts for more RS1 forms. I need to…ohhh…" Mrs. Menzies gasped and shuddered as Monique tilted her hips a little, just where Mrs. Menzies liked it. "Collate the new-hire forms and get some…*God.*"

Monique slammed into her. "Such a good employee, aren't you?" Her own clit quivered and her nipples knotted at the sight before her. "You make me so wet, June. Christ, you make me wet."

Mrs. Menzies froze for a moment, her hands uncurling from their fists. "Oh," she cried out.

Monique pulled out of her and ordered her to turn over onto her back.

Redness tinged Mrs. Menzies's cheeks in this new position, and Monique knew it wasn't entirely arousal. Mrs. Menzies's desperate need to come burned in her eyes, warring against her embarrassment. She hated looking this wanton, her swollen folds on display before Monique's hungry gaze. Large, pillowy breasts, legs spread, and wetness smeared all over her inner thighs? *So damned hot.*

"Beautiful." Monique breathed out the word with conviction.

Mrs. Menzies turned away. "You don't have to say that."

She didn't believe it of course. Women like her never did. They believed their intimate partners, the ones who had years to shape their perceptions, not an acquaintance. Just once, Monique wished June Menzies could see herself the way Monique did.

Her fingers found Mrs. Menzies's clit, the tight bud now peeking out between her folds, and she caressed it. *Fast, slow, circle, straight.*

Wet, soft sounds filled the air along with Mrs. Menzies's helpless gasps.

"I need you to pay attention to your CEO, June," Monique husked, leaning in. "I'm going to require a coffee next." She grasped the strap-on with her other hand and slid it back inside as she continued to fondle Mrs. Menzies's clit. "Black, scalding hot, with two sugars." As the silicone pumped in and out, Monique's own cunt clenched in delight.

Mrs. Menzies watched her through half-lidded eyes. Her lips were slightly open, sipping in air, her nose flaring, but she was studying every twitch on Monique's face. As if she was searching for the truth as to whether Monique was aroused by this too.

Aroused wasn't even the start of it. Monique was so damned close.

Mrs. Menzies's intense scrutiny only heightened the experience. Monique's jaw tightened in a bid to hold back an audible grunt of pleasure. She should not be this near the edge, not when her client's needs were paramount. "And then shift my appointment with that idiot ambassador—I will not do *anything* I don't find enjoyable. I never do. Do you understand?"

That was an important message.

Mrs. Menzies didn't answer, but her hands fell to her wide, dusky-colored areolas, plucking at her fat nipples as Monique thrust into her, reveling in her illicit sounds of excitement.

"I'm selective about who I spend time with," Monique added, her breath coming in sharp pants. "I'm choosy about my assistants, for instance. I expect them to be available to cater to my *every* whim." She punctuated the words with a hard press of Mrs. Menzies's clit. She was rewarded with a deep, low groan that made her twitch.

"Yes, very good," Monique gritted out. "I appreciate how you give your CEO your all."

Mrs. Menzies's thighs were beginning to tremble.

"I'm going to need that report on my desk within an hour. And I warn you: next time, I won't go so easy. I'll use my mouth on you. I'll slide my tongue all over your pretty little cunt. I'll make you lose control and moan, no matter how hard you try to be *oh so professional*, and everyone will hear you. You'll be helpless and laid bare, with me watching. With your *staff* listening." She dropped her voice to a lower, seductive register. "And then I'm going to *fuck* you again. And that time, maybe I'll let them watch."

Mrs. Menzies's wail filled the air. Her eternally furious mask fell away, and a shining, naked expression of ecstasy flooded her features.

Stunning. How could anyone doubt the beauty of women?

Achingly slowly, Monique pulled out from Mrs. Menzies, bent over, and kissed her clit, slipping her tongue all over the slippery flesh in a sensuous, drawn out farewell. Then, she straightened. "You are an *excellent* CEO's assistant, June. I'm very pleased."

Mrs. Menzies's breath was coming in heaving gasps, her eyes still screwed shut.

Monique reached to the desk for a tissue and wiped down the dripping strap-on. After removing it, she pulled up her pants. Finally, she stood back and reviewed the magnificent disarray before her.

Mrs. Menzies lay sprawled on her back, panting, those generous breasts rising and falling, her whole body on display—swollen, aroused, and very much taken. The view was exquisite.

Monique's cunt twitched harder. Honestly, if Monique didn't have another client soon, she'd be sorely tempted to play with Mrs. Menzies some more and give herself her release. God, how she loved women like this. Rarely did she encounter anyone with walls so high who would become so vulnerable in front of her.

"Are you really wet for me?" came a murmur.

Monique's gaze drifted back to Mrs. Menzies's face. "Hmm?"

"You said you were wet." Mrs. Menzies sat up. Her direct gaze was back to sharp and suspicious. "That was just a line to get me off, wasn't it?" Her mouth pulled down.

Monique regarded her. "So wet I almost came. That's the truth, June. I'm still so close, thanks to you."

Unlike other women in her business, Monique never lied to a client about whether she'd orgasmed. Women often knew anyway. And besides, Monique's honesty was one of her selling points. In fact, some clients liked to make it their mission to get her off. She never let them succeed, because for them, the thrill lay in the chase.

For Mrs. Menzies, though, this was no game. Her entire self-esteem was bound in her idea that she was in no way beautiful or worth Monique's sexual interest.

It was why she hated the mere idea of number five: *Worship Me.* Because, in Mrs. Menzies's mind, for Monique to ever worship or desire her would require Monique faking the entire encounter.

How little she understood. Monique truly did find every woman had an attractive quality about her. It wasn't some glib line. They all had something about them she was drawn to, inside or out. Most beauty wasn't on the surface anyway.

"It *is* the truth," she repeated.

Mrs. Menzies found her feet. She looked a little shaky. "Well. Thanks for telling me what I wanted to hear." A faint, embarrassed blush tinged her cheeks as pulled up her underwear and stockings. "You're good for my ego at least after half the shit Frank says to me."

Monique watched her jerky movements. "June," she said quietly, "if anyone could get me to come, it'd be you. I love bossy, confident, controlled women more than I can say."

"Well, I'm certainly that." Mrs. Menzies snorted.

She doesn't believe.

How…disappointing. Monique cocked her head and offered something she never did. "June? Would you like to feel the effect you have on me?"

Mrs. Menzies froze and glanced up in surprise. She swallowed, her desire and interest clear in her eyes. "Yes."

With a head tilt, indicating she should come closer, Monique lowered her tailored pants to mid-thigh, then drew down her panties a little. She clasped Mrs. Menzies's hand, drawing it to cup her soaked center. "Feel for yourself."

Mrs. Menzies's fingers slipped through Monique's wetness, her face filling with a look of wonder. Boldness overtaking her, she slid a thumb higher, nudging Monique's clit, then circling it.

That was all it took. Monique moaned, snapped straight as her thighs quivered, and with a delighted exhalation, she came in a rush of wetness all over Mrs. Menzies's trembling hand.

Well. That was unexpected. Monique blinked as she caught her shaky breath. "June," she murmured in awe. "How delightful you are."

Mrs. Menzies looked absurdly pleased as she removed her hand. She stared at the wetness soaking her fingers as Monique adjusted her clothing again.

They didn't speak for a moment.

"My husband thinks I'm ugly."

"I know," Monique murmured. She met Mrs. Menzies's gaze. "And he's wrong."

"He tells me I'm lucky to even have him. That no one else would put up with me or find me attractive."

Monique lifted Mrs. Menzies's wet fingers to the light. "And yet…all evidence to the contrary."

"That didn't escape me." Mrs. Menzies's voice was tight. "I honestly thought you were lying."

"You have the proof of my desire. Trust your eyes."

Mrs. Menzies hesitated, as if thinking about it. "All right."

Finally. "Good."

"I think maybe next time…" Mrs. Menzies inhaled. "I might like to try number five." Her eyes narrowed in warning. "As long as you're not too smug about it."

"Never." Monique smiled. "And an excellent choice. You deserve it."

Heat rose up in Mrs. Menzies's cheeks, giving them an attractive glow. "Maybe."

"It would be my pleasure to worship you for an hour. And you now know that's the honest truth."

Mrs. Menzies's eyes crinkled. "Thank you." Her almost-smile fell away as her thoughts clearly drifted back to work, life, reality. She finished dressing quickly, her shoulders already sinking as though she were preparing for battle.

"Next time," she said when finished. She swallowed, then turned to the door. "You know what I need."

"Yes. I can't wait." Pleasure infused Monique's voice. "Number five it is."

Discover how Monique Carson is first introduced in Lee Winter's *Hotel Queens*, about two rival hotel executives vying for the same dream deal.

Flashbang

Daily Sentinel reporter Lauren King might have spent over a year covering the outlandish parties of LA's rich and famous, but she had never experienced anything like this. Hell no.

In the center of the Pacific Grand Hollywood's Arctic-hued ballroom sat an enormous bed, upon which was arranged a half dozen A-list actresses, barely dressed in scraps of white, tapping away on their cell phones and sipping colorful cocktails.

An Icelandic girl band was on a corner stage, swaying and singing a quirky folk-pop repertoire, their faces barely visible above shaggy white coats. They looked like blue-haired polar bears.

"Radiator Fluid, ma'am?" asked a passing muscle bound waiter wearing nothing but white boxers and suspenders. He offered her a noxious-looking yellowy-green drink with a white umbrella in it. He was on roller skates. White.

"Ah, I'll pass." Lauren winced. "I'd prefer not to drink my car."

He rolled off, and she turned to study the glitterati, their shiny cocktail outfits flashing under a dozen mirror balls.

She shook her head. Only a bunch of overindulged celebrities would think that a 600-person white party with 100-proof cocktails would be a great way to launch their fashion blog, Flashbang.

A *blog*, for God's sake.

"Appalling, isn't it?" a sotto voice murmured near her ear. Lauren turned to find her good friend by her side. Los Angeles's top publicist was a vision tonight, draped in white satin, like some Rubenesque goddess commanding a toga party. Her scarlet slash of lipstick matched her vivid red hair.

But Mariella Slater wasn't just any publicist. She had a reputation for genius and could turn any celebrity's worst indiscretion into a publicity triumph. Such as last week when bad-boy action star Jordan Klauss tossed his personalized, handmade rubber sex doll from an eighth-story apartment window. It landed, with shattering effect, on an elderly resident's BMW parked below.

Mariella had spun it to the breathless media as a "highly technical stunt rehearsal with a minor gravity malfunction." She praised the star's "unquenchable work ethic" and noted that the car owner had scored not only a new BMW but, most importantly, free tickets to Klauss's next movie. Which was called *Slammmer*—with three Ms. Coming to a theater near you this fall.

She was that good. Who else could induce every entertainment reporter from 278 publications worldwide to dutifully name the movie amid their sex-doll-scandal copy? And they all spelled it right.

Lauren glanced around the room. She knew from her VIP invitation that her larger-than-life friend was the mastermind behind tonight's eyeball-bleeding monstrosity. It's just that she couldn't believe it.

"Mariella?" Lauren asked, dazed. "What on earth? It's like end times—in Siberia. Without clothes."

"I know, I know. Problem was it was planning by committee," Mariella admitted. "Froesha wanted everything white. Francine insisted on the roller skates to add a 'kinetic frisson.' Heddy wanted topless hunky men, because, well, it's Heddy. Veronica's mechanic-turned-spiritual advisor wanted the car-themed cocktails. Et voilà." She snapped her fingers.

"And the bed?"

"Trisha's new water and air diet has made her too weak to mingle, and Heddy's got a permanent hangover. The others like the way they can keep their dresses from wrinkling by not actually moving. And Francine can't even do up her dress at the back, so that's why she's lying the way she is. Besides, they do look gorgeous in the photos. Anyway, sweetie, enough of my brilliance. Let's talk about you. I'm so glad you came."

She gave Lauren a breezy pair of air kisses.

"Well it's kinda my job, so…" Lauren shrugged. Her off-the-shoulder, midnight-blue cocktail dress—a second-hand-boutique find which suited both her athletic figure and threadbare budget—shimmered.

"Not for much longer," Mariella said. "Am I right in thinking this is the last party you'll ever have to cover before you head to DC? Then it's just dull reporting on dreary people with no fashion or financial sense?"

"Yep." Lauren was unable to hold back her delighted grin. It was only her dream since she was a girl. From Iowa to DC. *Hot damn.* And all it'd taken was the exclusive of the decade.

Mariella gave her an affectionate smile. "Anyone would think you're happy to leave behind our decadent land of shallow dreams."

Lauren's head bobbed adamantly.

"Hell yes. Sorry, Mari, I know you love this crazy place, but I can't wait. I'm blowing this popsicle stand in two weeks, eleven hours." She glanced at her watch. "And fourteen minutes—give or take."

Mariella laughed so hard that her arms, ringed with a riot of shiny bangles, jangled. "Speaking of popsicles, where is your frosty, world-scoop collaborator? Isn't Ayers here tonight?"

Lauren's heart sank at the reminder.

"Catherine finished up her *Sentinel* contract a month ago, so she's off the hook on the party beat. And no, I have no clue what's she's been up to. I'm not her minder, so how would I know?"

Okay, so that was more defensive than she'd meant it to be. But it was a sore point. They'd both been flat out packing for their new jobs that had come about from their joint exclusive. And then, two weeks ago, Catherine had disappeared to work out some logistical issues at her next post. The occasional text message had been all Lauren had heard from her. And while her head knew how hectic things were for Catherine, her heart preferred whimpering pathetically in the corner.

Not that she'd shared that with anyone. Besides, she couldn't, given that they hadn't told a soul they were dating. They hadn't even talked about telling anyone. It was on Lauren's to-do list. But right now she was becoming adept at slapping on a happy face and pretending not to care what her prickly, former arch-nemesis got up to.

It wasn't even that hard. Everyone just assumed they still couldn't stand each other. Well, *almost* everyone.

Mariella leaned closer and whispered conspiratorially, "Lauren, sweetie, I know something's changed between you two. I can practically taste it. You vibrate on a different frequency when she's around. You light up like a C-list actress near the paparazzi. Don't bother denying it. What do you take me for? A *studio* publicist?"

A stain rose up Lauren's cheeks. Damn, Mariella was good. She looked into her friend's perceptive blue eyes and huffed out a breath. Then she finally gave in.

"It's still…new," she confessed with a sigh. She folded her arms. "And I haven't seen Catherine in two weeks while she's getting her new office ready. It's driving me crazy."

She felt a blissful amount of relief in admitting that.

"Ah," Mariella said with a sympathetic nod, and then glanced over Lauren's shoulder. "Well, this should help." She waved a red talon toward the door.

Lauren's gaze followed the finger. There stood Catherine Ayers. Elegant, aloof, glorious. Lauren tried not to swallow her tongue, but hell, she was only human. Her lover was dressed in a pale-lemon cocktail dress with pearl drop earrings, her auburn hair coiled up. Tendrils curled around her ears, showing a tantalizing amount of neck.

Lauren watched, transfixed, as Catherine's sharp gaze swept the room. When their eyes met, Lauren exhaled shakily. Then grinned like a complete fool.

Mariella laughed. "I see I was right. So here's the CliffsNotes—Your sneaky, secret paramour asked me for a ticket tonight because she wanted to surprise you at your last LA reporting gig. Who am I to stand in the way of the infamous Caustic Queen?" She dropped her voice to a whisper. "Or deny the woman she so clearly loves?"

Lauren's head snapped around to stare at Mariella. That was another thing on her to-do list. Declarations of feelings beginning with the letter L. Well, she knew how she felt…but, oh God, was it *that* obvious?

Mariella patted her arm and winked.

"Now, hon, I know that face. Don't overthink it. Okay, go on, have fun. Mock us and our silly, plastic world, and get drunk on Radiator Fuel and Dipstick Daiquiris."

She gave her an engulfing hug. Lauren felt the bruising press of her studded bangles and the powerful jolt of her perfume.

"I *will* miss you," Mariella said with a dissatisfied huff. "Very much. You always spoke the truth in a town where everyone lies to your face. And you always let me rant about those horrid little sacks of hormones turning my hair gray. Now *there's* some sage advice—never, ever agree to promote a boy band. And don't forget me when you win that first Pulitzer."

Lauren gave her a fond squeeze. "Never. You're unforgettable. All the best on keeping your hell clients out of the tabloids."

"Don't I always? Now, I'm going before I get all sentimental and rue my unwaterproof mascara."

Mariella gave her a kiss on the cheek—a real one for the first time—then wiped her lipstick away affectionately. Lauren's heart caught as her friend slipped into the crowd with a loud, bangle-clanging wave.

Her attention was soon distracted as Catherine arrived at her side. The formidable ex-Washington bureau chief might once have been banished to LA's gossip-writing beat to serve time alongside Lauren, but it had never dulled her fierce intellect nor silenced her biting tongue.

And God she was stunning.

"Well, well, Lauren King, goat botherer and entertainment hack," Catherine greeted her with her usual cool expression. Her eyes, though, twinkled. "What a surprise seeing you here," she drawled.

Lauren groaned. "Are you ever going to let the goat thing go? It was one story, like, a hundred years ago."

"Unlikely. The ground's much too fertile." Catherine leaned forward to air-kiss her but hovered for longer, lips drifting over Lauren's cheek until the fine hairs leapt to attention. Lauren suppressed a shudder.

Catherine gave her a small, knowing smile and then stepped back.

They regarded each other.

"You look phenomenal tonight," Lauren said after a few beats, eyes tracing the fall of luxurious fabric. And damn, she really did. A girl's hands could get lost mapping out the stunning lines of her dress.

"Lauren," Catherine whispered against her ear lobe, "if you wish everyone in the room to know what we mean to each other, keep looking at me like a steak you could devour raw."

"Can't help it. You're a sight for sore eyes. It's been *way* too long."

"Only two weeks," Catherine said. But her intense gaze belied her words, roaming across Lauren's form. Her expression grew appreciative as she took in the dress which so effectively accentuated her curves.

"Have you been clothes shopping with your neighbor again?"

"Yep. Joshua said I was looking like 'a sad, bedraggled hobo.' Direct quote. *So*… you like?"

Lauren smoothed her hands down her flat stomach, enjoying the way her lover's eyes followed them closely. Catherine's gaze slid up to her toned arms and came to rest near the swell of her bust.

Catherine's gaze was burning as she tilted her head and said with deceptive softness, "I believe Marc Jacobs should pay you to wear his label."

"*That's* who I'm wearing?" Lauren asked feebly. Her mouth was suddenly dry. "Okay," she said with a squeak.

There was a soft snort. "How is it you could write about this surreal nonsense for an entire year and not retain a single designer name?"

"Just lucky, I guess." Lauren gave a chuckle. "Besides, I had other things to think about. Vital things."

Catherine's eyebrows lifted. "All I recall was you trying to needle me to the point of rage for twelve exasperating months."

"Yeah. Like I said—vital things." She grinned unrepentantly, and Catherine's lips twitched in amusement.

A roller-waiter slid up and offered them a platter of appetizers with an over-the-top flourish. Lauren sighed. *Was* everything *overproduced in this town?*

"Charcoaled carburetor ball?" he asked with a straight face.

Lauren studied the blackened crispy spheres. "Does it contain *pure* carburetor?"

He peered at her in confusion, then gave up and turned to Catherine. "Ma'am?"

"No car parts before nine," she said drolly.

He gave them both an unimpressed glare and rolled away.

"The madness of LA," Catherine said. "Can't say that I'll miss it."

"What? You won't miss anything at all? What about the waitstaff at restaurants who give you their resumes just on the off chance you're a big-shot producer? Or Velveteria—the Museum of Velvet Art? Sad furry clowns for the win! Tanning studios on every other corner? Come on!"

"Shocking, but no," Catherine said before pausing. "Perhaps…well, I think I'll feel sorry about leaving my home. It was a sanctuary in this frivolous hellhole. Tad's expressed an interest in renting it from me at 'struggling artist rates.' Which I take to mean that he'll pay me random sums of rent if and when he ever finds an acting job." She rolled her eyes. "But I will miss my place."

Lauren smirked. "Well a lot happened there, no wonder you're fond of it." She gave her eyebrows a suggestive waggle. "I particularly think the guest bathroom should have its own shrine."

Catherine exhaled, her cheeks reddening. "God, you're impossible."

"Yup." Lauren grinned, but then her mood dropped. "These last two weeks have been terrible. Did you know that?"

When Catherine's eyes gleamed a little too smugly, Lauren added, "I've had no one to tease or work my evil schemes on at VIP events. Everyone's narcissistic and as shallow as a butter dish. It's been boring as hell."

"Did you really only just notice how shallow this place is when I wasn't here?" Catherine's eyebrow slid up to a preposterous angle.

Lauren considered that. "Yeah," she said. "I really only did." She brightened. "So…you came back early? For me?"

Catherine flicked invisible lint off her dress. "Hmm. Well, it was either that or take up an offer from Joe Biden to discuss his vision for growing Delaware's agricultural sector. Even my tolerance levels aren't that high."

"Gee, thanks." Lauren scowled. "It was me or tractors?"

Catherine gave her a smirk. "It was a close call. By the way, I'm reliably informed that your replacement on *The Sentinel*, that blonde creature with the unironic side ponytail, is here tonight."

Lauren frowned, trying to follow the conversation. "Uh, so?"

"So, I may have informed her that she has to update the paper's website on your behalf tonight. Therefore," Catherine said as she studied her, "your services here are no longer required. At least, not in a professional capacity."

Lauren blinked. "What? Candy agreed? Just like that?"

Catherine's smile became positively feline.

"It won't take her more than fifteen minutes. And I may have couched it in terms of being a smart career move never to argue with me. Ms. Summers proved her IQ might actually be out of double digits by agreeing immediately. Now then, I came tonight because there is something I wish to urgently discuss with you."

"Oh?"

Catherine placed her hand on the small of Lauren's back and propelled her through the blinding whitescape, past the industry insiders, VIPs, and socialites downing their colorful concoctions, and beyond the bed of pretentious, *Flashbang*-blogging celebrities.

They came to a set of double doors with shutters covering the glass. Catherine opened it and pulled Lauren through, closing it behind them with a snick.

"What are you…?" Lauren stopped. They were on a balcony packed with pots of ornamental trees of various sizes and shapes. Lauren realized these were probably from the hotel's ballroom, but had been hidden here to make room for tonight's all-white event.

Catherine led the way, and they picked a path past the potted forest until they emerged at the front of the balcony, next to one of two facing concrete pillars that edged the area. Far below was the darkened, outdoor swimming pool. Beyond that lay the bright lights of LA.

Lauren glanced back toward the door but saw only trees. It was like being dropped into an instant jungle. Even the air smelled different, no longer having the constant, smoggy bite she'd become used to permeating the pores of LA.

She stared around her in wonder. Catherine smiled at her awed expression.

They could still hear the distant tinkling laughter and music from inside the ballroom and low murmurs of people on other balconies, out of sight, on the other sides of the pillars.

"Uh, what…?" Lauren began. "I mean, why—"

Catherine stepped inside her space and backed her against a pillar, a predatory glint in her eyes. "Why?" she asked. "Well, I would hate for your last LA event to be unmemorable."

"Oh, um, yeah," Lauren said, eyes wide. "That would be terrible."

"Mmm." Catherine traced her fingertips down her face, the barest grazing of tips across her skin.

Lauren swallowed.

Catherine's fingers floated back up to her hairline, then disappeared into her shoulder-length brown hair. She combed them down to Lauren's ears, tucking any loose strands behind them. Catherine breathed against the shell of Lauren's ear, the tip of her tongue sliding along its edge.

"Oh," Lauren said with a whimper, finally grasping what their "urgent discussion" was about.

"We have to be *very* quiet," Catherine warned, eyes half-lidded. Then she pushed her body firmly against Lauren's. Her lips were tantalizingly close but did not touch, staying just out of reach.

Lauren felt the softness of Catherine's delectable breasts and the press of her hips and muscled thighs. She could feel the heat radiating off her—so ironic for a woman famous for her icy edge. Right now she was searing hot.

Lauren shivered at the thought of Catherine being aroused, and her nipples hardened.

"Are you cold?" The honeyed timber of her lover's voice made Lauren's stomach flutter.

Catherine's knowing gaze slid down to study the two hard knots now jutting out against the midnight-blue confinement of her dress.

Lauren flushed. Her brain was flailing too hard to articulate complete thoughts. Or any thoughts, for that matter. She shook her head mutely.

"You certainly *seem* cold," Catherine continued teasing softly. "If only we could warm you up somehow."

Lauren's chest rose and fell rapidly. "Warm? Uh…I…" Her cheeks grew even redder as her voice faded out.

Catherine smiled wickedly and skated her fingers across the top of Lauren's dress, which was a straight line of glossy, strapless satin. Lauren felt the faintest whisper of warmth as the fingertips strayed off the dress and to her chest. Catherine leaned closer, and her breath dusted across the bare expanse of skin. Then, achingly slowly, she lowered her mouth to Lauren's chest. Small, teasing puffs of warm air sent goose bumps rippling across her skin.

"Poor Lauren," Catherine said into her chest, her words dripping with promise, "suffering so much."

Catherine's head dipped lower. She blew across Lauren's aching, erect nipples and then pressed her mouth against one through the dark blue fabric.

The instant moist heat was explosive.

"Oh *fuck*!" Lauren's eyes widened.

"*Quiet*," Catherine murmured into her nipple. "*Not a sound*."

Bolts of arousal shot through Lauren as she watched Catherine mouth her breasts, swapping between nipples, thoroughly wetting the satin with her tongue.

She bit her lip, desperate to stay quiet.

Catherine's head lifted. "Hmm. I'm not entirely sure that's getting the job done," she said, examining the darkening wet spots. "Perhaps more direct methods are required to warm you up?"

"D-direct?" Lauren said. "Um…you mean…you want to… *Here*?"

"That's exactly what I mean," Catherine said and tossed her a haughty look. Her dark eyes were filled with the promise of every gloriously, naughty deed Lauren could ever imagine. And probably a few she couldn't.

She gulped, making an odd, strangled noise that had never before come out of her mouth.

"*Quiet*," Catherine said again. It became like a murmured mantra as her hands slid down Lauren's dress. They skated to her waist and then drifted back up to her chest. "*Quiet.*" She whispered kisses along her collarbone and ran her tongue down Lauren's cleavage. "*So very quiet.*"

Then, without warning, she pulled away and wrenched down the bodice of Lauren's dress with both hands. Lauren's full, naked breasts bounced into sight.

Catherine gave a pleased hum at the lack of bra, as her scorching gaze studied her find. Her fingers lifted once more to run lazy circles around a coral-pink nipple. She flicked it, and they both watched as the swollen flesh puckered.

"Delightful." Catherine's voice was low to the point of gravelly. It was doing funny things to Lauren's insides.

Catherine's lips landed on the nearest bare nipple, and she scraped her tongue across it.

"Oh *God*," Lauren said.

Her lover's white teeth nipped and nibbled at the sensitive flesh, and Lauren's hips began to buck forward. She wondered if she looked as desperate as she felt.

"Feeling a little needy?"

Well, that answered that question.

The tongue laving her breast paused, and Catherine's head angled up. The gleam in her eyes was positively dangerous.

"*Please*." Lauren gasped. Her hips bucked again. *God, did she have* any *self-control?*

"Please, what?" Catherine's nimble fingers reached for the mid-thigh hem of Lauren's dress and waited. "Was there something you wanted? Something you needed?"

"*Catherine*," Lauren said in a whisper. She swallowed.

The air around them felt charged. She could smell arousal and a hint of Catherine's perfume and a sweet peatiness from the press of ornamental trees. Her nerve endings felt as though they were misfiring. Every part of her skin was hypersensitive. A hint of breeze felt almost painful. And whenever Catherine's tongue slid teasingly across her flesh, Lauren's center clenched, craving so much more.

The hands on Lauren's thighs were stroking now—firm, even motions that were sending electric jolts straight to her core. The vision of what lay ahead was Lauren's final undoing.

Catherine—*the* Catherine Ayers, all uptight, Boston elite, fancy pearls, and superior attitude—was about to fuck her up against a wall at Lauren's last LA party. It was so damned illicit. So…*oh hell*…so *wrong.*

"God yes," she moaned.

So right.

"*Quiet.*" The lips against her breast said as they curled into a smile.

Feathering fingertips reached high up the inside of Lauren's thighs, and her muscles trembled in anticipation. She wasn't sure she would be able to hold her own weight if Catherine kept up such torturous games.

"Please," she whispered again, not even bothering to hide her wantonness. "Please touch me. God, I've missed you."

Catherine responded instantly, and by the time her fingers reached their goal, having first detoured past every inch of soft skin along the way, Lauren's panties were a soaked mess.

Catherine rubbed Lauren's cleft, outlined against her sodden lingerie, and groaned approval against her neck. "Good," she said softly. "I'd hate to be the only one."

Lauren gasped at the implication and, stung into action, reached for her desperately, drawing up the lemon-colored designer dress pressed against her.

There was a small gasp, so soft that Lauren almost missed it. She loved the way Catherine's breathing changed the moment she touched her. She hooked the dress in her fingers, drawing it higher and higher, the tips of her fingers playing over the slipperiness of silk stocking under it.

She paused when she felt something unexpected. A pair of lacy bands? Catherine was wearing thigh-high stockings?

She glanced at the woman who was settled against her neck, dragging her teeth across the skin, nibbling possessively. Their eyes met, and there was no mistaking Catherine's desire. Her lips curled up into a cat-like, possessive smile that was part smirk, part power play.

Those teasing fingers between Lauren's legs did a mischievous twiddle, causing her thumb to bump against Lauren's clit, reminding her that they were still there.

Lauren groaned at the gush of moisture under those maddening fingers and tried to distract herself. But those twirling fingers were playing serious havoc with her concentration.

Two could play at this seduction. She shifted her hands higher up Catherine's thigh, farther up under Catherine's dress, and then paused in amazement. All she felt was Catherine's warm thighs and then… Even *more* warm skin. *Wet*, warm skin.

"Catherine? Did you forget to put something on this evening?"

"On the contrary," came the arch reply. "Forward planning is an essential skill. I thoroughly recommend it."

Lauren swallowed. Her fingers rubbed against the slippery skin, mapping out Catherine's petite tucks and folds, relishing how much heat and liquid she could feel.

"Oh," Catherine huffed near her ear in a voice that sounded uncharacteristically ragged. *"Inside.* Now. *Oh Christ."*

The plea was the most erotic sound Lauren had ever heard. She entered Catherine with two fingers, pushing inside the pulsing, obscenely wet heat, and set up a consistent rhythm. *In and out.*

A gasp.

A tremble.

In and out.

A soft hitch.

Lauren pressed her legs together, desperate not to come herself.

A small cry.

In and out.

It was the most alive Lauren had ever felt, these moments where she claimed as hers this beautiful woman. A woman that everyone dismissed as distant. Cold. Unfeeling.

If only they knew.

Catherine rocked herself against Lauren's hand, making pleas for *faster*, *more*, and *yes*, *there*, *oh*, *oh yes*.

Lauren loved the clenching sensation as Catherine's body pulled her fingers deeper, demanding more of her. Her heart pounded at having such an intimate experience, knowing that Catherine was as aroused as she was, as hot and frantic and needy, and even if she wanted to, she couldn't hide it anymore. There were no more games. Not when she was like this.

She pressed the base of her hand against Catherine's clit and almost unravelled on the spot as a low, primal moan filled the air—erotic and raw.

Lauren's fingers were soaked in Catherine's essence, and she revelled in the proof of the effect she had on this enigmatic woman.

Catherine's hand between Lauren's legs suddenly twitched back into life. Without a word, two fingers were inside her. Lauren squeezed her eyes closed at the overwhelming sensation, combined with the intoxicating sounds of slippery flesh being stroked.

A teasing thumb snicked across her clit, circling it, flicking it, torturing it. Lauren quivered and felt herself clench, and then Catherine's wicked lips were on her mouth.

Catherine usually kissed her as though she had all the time in the world. As though playing and kissing were the same thing, a way of showing her skills at arousing another. But this was new. She plundered her mouth. There was no trademark finesse. It was like she was drawing her life force from Lauren. It was desperate, frenzied and so, *so* damned hot. They tangled tongues, aroused by each other's soft moans as their fingers drove each other's desire higher and higher.

Lauren was nearing her tipping point as the pressure built. Curling, coiling blasts of ecstasy were starting to radiate out from her clit, and her brain had turned into a sloppy, euphoric mush.

The smell, the sounds, the taste of those lips. She pressed closer into Catherine, holding on, clinging to her.

To Lauren's surprise, Catherine succumbed first. She crashed against her, pinning her against the pillar, and surrendered with a low, long moan.

Lauren lived for this. Seeing the walls crash down that kept Catherine apart from the rest of the world. Seeing the distance vanish, the guarded look fall away and just honest vulnerability reflecting back from her icy blue eyes.

Sometimes Lauren wished she could freeze time to that heartbeat when Catherine came undone, the first twitch where all her fears and hopes were exposed. Almost close enough for Lauren to touch and smooth away like a tear.

Catherine's eyes fluttered closed as she bucked again. The lost, helpless cry was enough to unravel Lauren. When Catherine's fingers sought out her clit once more, she shuddered and came with punishing force, practically crushing the hand stroking her.

There was a moment's silence. Fingers still held by the other's warmth, pounding with staccato pulses.

Lauren didn't want it to end. She never did. And after two weeks apart, it felt even harder to let go.

She felt the loss of Catherine's fingers and, with great reluctance, slid her own out from beneath Catherine's dress. They straightened their own outfits a little sheepishly. Then Catherine pressed herself gently back into Lauren, arms wrapping around her, holding her. Tight.

It conveyed more emotion than she'd ever openly said out loud. Maybe Mariella was onto something? It was a thought to dissect at another time. She felt those teasing, naughty teeth scraping against her neck once more. A reminder of who Lauren had just been claimed by.

"Wow," Lauren exhaled. "*Never* leaving. This is perfect right here."

A smile twitched against her neck. "Then you would have to explain to your new editor that you're passing up a career-making opportunity in order to satisfy your lover over and over against the wall of the Pacific Grand."

"Sounds feasible."

They both laughed.

"Lauren?"

"Mmm."

"Why are the waiters on roller skates at this thing?"

"Not sure. I think it's Heddy's fault. Or Francine's? I lost track."

"Ah."

There was a lengthy silence, and then the arms around her gentled and stroked her back. "Lauren?"

"Mmm?"

"I missed you, too."

Lauren smiled and exhaled shakily against the head burrowed into her neck, knowing Catherine would never see her relief.

"I could tell," Lauren said lightly. "And I missed you more."

"Must you always argue with me?" Catherine asked curiously.

"Ha. You like me like this," Lauren told her, dropping a kiss on her temple.

"Sadly. It's clearly a madness." Catherine caught her eye and then kissed her thoroughly. She pulled back, studying her. "Although I could get very used to this kind of madness."

Lauren felt soothed and a little giddy. "Yeah." She grinned. "I know the feeling."

Lauren King might have spent over a year covering the outlandish parties of LA's rich and famous, but she had *never* experienced anything like this.

*

If you enjoyed *Flashbang*, check out *The Red Files* and experience Lauren and Catherine's journey from arch rivals to lovers.

When DC Met Iowa

Cynthia Redwell awoke with a grimace and a mouth as dry as her last Economics in Journalism conference.

Christ, that must have been some wedding reception.

It was a bit hazy now. There had been imbibing. Party games. More imbibing. Cynthia offering her fabulously biting snark about the perils of the Midwest to… to? A blurry face swam in and out of view. Whoever. Someone.

Oh well. What's the worst she could have gotten up to? Besides, what happens in Iowa stays in Iowa, right? Wasn't that a thing? It should be.

Yawning, she glanced around as her brain slowly dithered into focus. She frowned. Unless the Grand Millennium was now stocking up on Smurf-blue Target sheet sets and decorating walls with butch female sport stars, she'd gone home with a…new friend…last night.

Glancing uneasily to her side, Cynthia discovered a human-shaped lump in the bed. Oh. Well, it wouldn't be the first time, but she usually carefully vetted her one-night stands for discretion first. God only knew what this one's predilection for spreading gossip was. She bit her lip.

Of course, she could be overreacting. There might be an innocent explanation. A lateness issue? Some friendly local had explained they only lived around the corner and would she like to…bunk in?

For God's sake. Even hungover and with a brain firing on half a cell, that sounded about as believable as her best friend's insistence she wasn't into some brash Iowan. And look where they were now. Enduring the headache-thumping washup from Catherine's wedding to said Iowan girl, Lauren.

Still, a good reporter checks her sources and examines the evidence.

Lifting the sheets cautiously, Cynthia ascertained her own body was indeed entirely naked. And, given some twinging muscles as her thighs shifted, it appeared she'd done more than cuddle up for warmth last night.

Cynthia huffed out a breath. Well. It'd be nice to remember her apparent night of chandelier swinging. Unless her bed partner had been unspectacular? Maybe that was it?

She prodded the buried lump through the thick comforter. "Hey."

"Mmph. G'backtasleep."

"Where am I?"

"With me. Sleep now."

"And you are?"

The lump flung back the sheets a foot and revealed itself to be a thirty-something brunette with a freckled face, wide, full-lipped mouth, and broad shoulders. Short, squat, and solid. Like a weight lifter, only rounder.

Cynthia blinked. This nuggety woman with a proud, strong jaw and flashing brown eyes was the antithesis of every perfectly manicured stick insect she'd ever bedded. Since she usually only bedded colleagues, she supposed that figured. There was a bland conformity to TV women, right down to the blonde hair, lean limbs, and dazzling white teeth. Cynthia was right out of the same mold herself.

She wasn't sure whether to be surprised at her unexpected choice under the influence of local swill, or ponder her drunken ass's sense of humor.

"Well… you're different," she muttered.

"And by that you mean to say 'good morning' and 'you're cute'." The woman elbowed Cynthia. "Right?"

She actually *was* cute, in a tomboyish sort of way. Compared to Cynthia's lean exclamation mark of a body honed with Pilates, spin class, and green shakes, this woman screamed strength and solidness in a way Cynthia found appealing. Her edgy spunk was excellent too. She'd be no pushover. Christ, how Cynthia disdained weak women. So maybe Cynthia's drunken ass knew more about her tastes than her sober ass realized.

But there was no point encouraging the girl by offering random compliments. That might spark an expectation of round two of more forgettable bedroom calisthenics from this robust Iowan.

Cynthia had no time for that. All she wanted was to get caffeinated, dressed, get on a plane, and get the hell out of Iowa for good… Even if the woman's wide, curling mouth was all sorts of alluring.

Enough of that. Time to commit to the exit strategy. "Right, well, um…" Cynthia peered at her bedmate, hoping a name would leap into her synapses. The silence dragged on for an uncomfortable beat.

"Suze," she supplied with a knowing look. "Seriously, Cynthia? After last night, I'd have thought you'd at least remember my name."

"I can't even remember last night, let alone the finer points on names, occupations, or various pets." Cynthia's gaze roamed the room. *Where in hell are my clothes?*

Suze sat up, the sheet falling away, revealing an ample pair of bare breasts. It curtailed whatever grumpy inner monologue Cynthia was working up to as she stared at the impressive sight.

Oh my. Why couldn't she recall playing with those? Cynthia's brain gave a pained whimper at the loss.

"You don't remember your awesome beer pong buddy?" Suze snorted. "Or the rest?"

Good God, Cynthia would dearly love to remember the rest right now.

"Name's Suzette Beringer. Occupation: former softball legend. Currently: mechanic and bed buddy. Also: Lauren's best friend from college and highly sleep-deprived. Pets: one pug named Buttcheeks. Do *not* start on his name. My ex named him, and I can't change it, because it's all he damn well answers to."

I hooked up with a beer pong player who owns Buttcheeks the dog.

"You think less of me now, don't you?" Suze asked, giving Cynthia a quizzical look.

"Yes, definitely," Cynthia confirmed. "But don't worry; the bar was set low. You being an Iowan and all." Her smirk was as wicked as her words.

"You know, the cracks about my home state were funnier when I was trying to get in your pants."

Cynthia blinked. Rather than sounding offended, as most people were by her deliberately acidic tongue, Suze looked faintly…amused. Suze shrugged and ran her fingers through cropped brown hair, doing little to erase the bed hair at the back.

Okay, what is happening here? Cynthia tried again. "So, *Iowa*, you're a mechanic? You're a walking oil slick like Lauren's knuckle-dragging brothers?" Cynthia was almost impressed at the dollops of disdain she'd managed to inject into just two sentences. Not that she had anything against mechanics; after all, she loved George back in DC for keeping her beloved Audi purring. But how on earth was some cute lay from Outer Hicksville immune to her finely honed slings and arrows?

"I'm a *flight* mechanic. I work at the airport. Why? Need some duty-free?" Suze drawled, dragging her sheet back up to cover her chest.

Cynthia's brain all but pouted as the glorious sight disappeared from view. *Focus.* Her evil superpower was failing. That had to be it. Maybe she needed refueling. "I need coffee." Where was the kitchen anyway? She looked around again. "Is this your place?"

"For an economics expert, you're pretty slow, aren't you?" Suze tutted, eyes gleaming with amusement. "Who else's?" She waved at the walls.

Cynthia's gaze took in the various knickknacks. A University of Iowa college degree, the writing too small to ascertain the subject. Smart-ass Comebacks 101 probably. Numerous softball trophies. A framed poster of the singer Pink. Signed team poster of the US national softball squad. *Wait… Did that upstart just call me slow? Me?*

Her eyes narrowed. "I've written three books on the economy," Cynthia blurted before she could stop herself. Oh God. That sounded almost…desperate for approval.

"I wrote a pamphlet once for work," Suze retorted. "*Safety Tips for Employees Working in the MRO Hangar.* It was well-received by critics. Five stars all round."

Oh my God. Not only have I lost my killer touch, I'm being mocked.

Not that she didn't deserve it. After all, Cynthia had been the one to start this bitchy dawn duel. She needed her A game. "Coffee," Cynthia ground out. "Oh, and that's a requirement, not a request."

"Make it yourself." Suze's lips twitched. "Kitchen's downstairs. It's too early for me to move. Besides, I'm not the best at hopping to orders from stuck-up DC chicks trying to rile me up for shits and giggles."

Total. Superpower. Fail. She'd been outsnarked by a damned Midwest grease monkey. It was end times. "Fine." Cynthia threw back the bedcovers to get her coffee, too irked to consider that she was stark naked.

She only paused, midway to the door, when she realized Suze's appreciative gaze was roaming over her. She puffed out her chest a little, relieved she had at least some power left. "Like what you see?"

"You bet. But I've got simple tastes. Being an Iowan and all."

Okay, that was a surprisingly excellent riposte. Cynthia tried hard not to laugh—one's debating rivals should never know when they've won a point—and instead rolled her eyes.

After snatching a red silk robe off a hook on the back of the door, she put it on. It was far too short, only an inch away from breaching public decency laws.

That's what you get for dallying with a garden gnome, she snorted to herself, heading downstairs.

She padded to the kitchen. Before long, she found the necessities and studied the coffee maker. The machine was surprisingly high-tech, but then again, wasn't Suze some sort of engineer? Mechanic? Whatever. She'd know her gadgets.

Cynthia set to work figuring it out and made a coffee. Then, feeling somewhat benevolent on account of having a good sparring partner, reached for a second cup.

She carried the coffees back upstairs and placed Suze's on the bedside table next to her.

Suze lifted an eyebrow. "I've been lying here debating whether you'd bring one cup or two. I was planning on basing my entire opinion of you on it."

Cynthia snorted. "So pleased I passed your little test."

"Nah, that remains to be seen." Suze took a sip from the cup, and her eyes widened. "I'm probably going to regret asking this, DC, but how'd you know how I like my coffee?"

"Simple. Black because it matches your soul, and three sugars because I can tell you have a sweet tooth."

"A fat crack? How original. I'll have you know there's muscle under this mass."

Cynthia frowned at Suze's interpretation of her words. No, it hadn't been a damned fat crack. At least Suze didn't look put out as she patted her rounded stomach over the sheet. But then people usually hid their insecurities well. Lord knew Cynthia hid them by the U-Haul load. Trust issues, ten-foot-high walls, and self-loathing lesbian pretty much covered them.

While she ordinarily wouldn't give the slightest flicker of concern about what people thought of her commentary on their lives, for some reason, it bothered Cynthia that Suze might feel judged for her body. Which, as her brain had already made clear, Cynthia found decidedly appealing.

"It wasn't a comment about your weight," she murmured, sipping her own coffee. "I appreciate your body. It's you."

Suze's eyes narrowed with suspicion as she turned that over. "Are you making fun of me?"

"No. I've decided I rather like you, in spite of your atrocious taste in birthplaces. You're different. And trust me, in my world, that's as scarce as an honest politician."

"So we're doing honesty now?" Suze chuckled. "Okay. I can do that too. I'm flexible."

"Are you?" Cynthia purred, wishing very hard she could remember what they'd gotten up to last night.

"You really don't remember, do you? Any of it?"

A faint blush warmed Cynthia's cheeks, much to her annoyance. "Not so much." She sighed. "Which is to say, not at all."

"Ah."

"But if I was to take an educated guess," Cynthia began, smiling, "I'd suggest we drank a lot, played beer pong, I thrashed you at that, and we made out in some discreet location. Then, overwhelmed by my sensational kisses, you invited me home. After…hmm…*three* glorious orgasms, you fell asleep in a tangle of sheets, knowing you'd never been had so well. Am I close?"

Suze laughed hard at that one. Actually…a little too hard.

"Well, you were right about the beer pong. But I *let* you thrash me."

"Unlikely. I'm very competitive."

"And I'm a former softballer, remember? I can whip anyone at a throwing game. Well, anyone except Lauren. So, yes, there was beer pong. And you won. And you were so happy that you kissed me. And it was sort of a sloppy, messy kiss, if I'm being honest…"

Cynthia shot Suze a withering look.

"Hey, I doubt my kissing was much better." Suze laughed at Cynthia's outrage. "We were both barely standing by that point. Then we might have dirty danced around the fire pit at one a.m., giving all Lauren's ancient older relatives a bit of a show, but her brothers certainly appreciated it. I'm deaf in one ear from all their hollering."

"God." Cynthia's mouth fell open.

"Then Lauren's dad suggested maybe it was time to call it a night because some of the oldies had weak hearts. Which made you laugh and laugh and announce that I'd take you home to my place."

"How magnanimous of me," Cynthia observed. "I gather you were okay with me cavalierly inviting myself over?"

"Oh, yep. I may have said 'hot damn' a little too loudly. So Lauren's dad drove us back to my place on account of us being fifty sheets to the wind. The whole way home, you were singing songs with dirty lyrics about big-boobed women. Owen was blushing redder than a tomato."

Poor man. Did they make cards that read, *Sorry I Was a Horndog In Your Earshot*?

So much for discretion.

"Right, so we got inside, and you kissed me against the door, then started flinging your clothes off downstairs. By the way, your bra's on the TV…"

So *that's* where her clothes were.

"We got upstairs to the bedroom. I applied my signature moves…" Suze waggled her eyebrows. "You swooned and had a mind-blowing orgasm, courtesy of yours truly, but then passed out halfway through reciprocating. No follow-through." She scowled. "Like, shit. It was seriously disappointing."

"Reciprocat…" Cynthia frowned. She'd been a lousy lay?

"*Reciprocating*. That means I missed my turn. Aren't you DC economics types supposed to know the big words?" Suze nudged her.

"I know what it means. I'm just a little unsure what to make of it. I've never, ever…"

"Well, now you have," Suze said. "Don't worry. I'm sure it could happen to anyone. Not performing."

Not performing? Cynthia prized herself on being as competitive as the next blackened soul that inhabited DC. There was no challenge she'd not crushed. This was completely unacceptable.

"Holy shit, you look so appalled!" Suze sat up straighter, her eyes blinking in surprise. "Like this is some failing of personal honor."

"It is." Cynthia said darkly. She gave Suze an arch look. "Satisfaction guaranteed is my motto. Even if I don't like the woman that much, she always leaves with a smile on her face."

That brought Suze up short. "Wait, what?" She peered at her. "Why would you take home someone you don't even like?"

Cynthia's head snapped up. "What do you mean? Do you like everyone you sleep with?"

"Of course!" Suze gaped at her. "Why else would I want them in my home? In my bed?"

"For release?" Cynthia suggested with a shrug. "A way to pass the time?"

"Then use a vibrator!" Suze side-eyed her. "Is that what I am too? Someone you didn't like very much but wanted to pass a few hours with before your flight left?"

Cynthia would have loved to dismantle Suze's self-righteousness with a snarky "yes." But that would have been a complete lie, and Cynthia was allergic to lies most of the time. "No." She sighed. "I already told you. I like you. God knows why right at this minute. You're more annoying than bikini-line regrowth. And I swear if you tell anyone about us…"

"You mean anyone *else*? Beyond Lauren's huge extended family who all saw you plant one on me and dirty-dance me around the fire pit? Not to mention Lauren's friend, that LA publicist? And her other friends from LA, Josh and Tad? And…"

"All right, Jesus, I get the picture. The horse has bolted." She waved her hand and added, in deference to their location, "Or cow. Whatever." She was screwed. A churning cocktail of emotions began stewing, containing everything from horror and fear to resignation. *Truly screwed.* Cynthia rubbed her face. *Fuck.*

"Why do you care so much?" Suze gave her a curious look. "You're not 'out' at work, I take it? Because you work in TV?"

"I'm not out at all. Anywhere. Or, rather, I wasn't. Apparently Iowan weddings change a person's settings from discreet to raging queer."

"I'm fairly sure it's in the brochure in your hotel room. Should have read the fine print."

There was a pause as Cynthia digested that, and finally she laughed. It sounded hysterical to her ears. "God! Oh God." She sank her head into her hands.

"Look, seriously, stop freaking out. Lauren's and Catherine's LA friends won't tell. They're really nice. And who is Lauren's family going to talk to? No one even knows who you are around here anyway. You're fine, okay?"

Tension eased from Cynthia's shoulders a little. That was true. "You know, the irony of this is rich. For two years, I've been getting some hilarious mileage out of Catherine getting together with an Iowan ex-softballer. *Now* look at me."

"Slumming it, are we?"

"Hardly. I've just lost my mockery advantage. It's…inconvenient. And I'm usually so much better at impulse control. Beer pong? Bedding the cute butch at my best friend's wedding? Not so much."

"You think I'm cute then?" Suze grinned.

"Regrettably for my once-stellar straight reputation, you are appallingly cute."

"You're not bad yourself. For a snooty DC bitch."

"You think I'm a bitch?"

"Oh you are. And you love it. Tell me I'm wrong."

"You're not."

"Why do you do it?" Suze cocked her head, looking intrigued. "The mega-bitch routine?"

"It's just easier."

"Than?"

Cynthia sighed. "Dealing with people. Entanglements. Interpersonal nonsense. Enduring assholes at work. They all steer clear of me, which is how I prefer it. Oh, there are *plenty* of assholes in my industry."

"Yeah?"

"Definitely." Cynthia set her coffee cup down to curtail the urge to hurl it. "Christ. Do you know I used to be a 'valuable resource' and 'top on-air talent'? That's what my boss called me. Then I hit forty. I was moved into minor management with only occasional on-air slots. I suppose it was to avoid viewers having their retinas burned by the shocking sight of an older woman analyzing economic data."

"That'd suck." Sympathy edged Suze's eyes. "Fortunately, Boeing aircraft don't give a fuck how old or pretty the hands fixing them are."

How weird would that be? To have a job based solely on ability? Cynthia couldn't even imagine it. "Did you find it hard, working in such a male-dominated industry? Especially around here?"

Suze shrugged. "Any of the boys who gave me shit in the early days got a wrench waved around for their trouble."

"They were scared of a wrench?" Cynthia couldn't picture it.

"I never said *where* I threatened to use it." Suze cackled. "Now I'm just one of the boys. It's fine." She drained the last of her coffee and set the cup aside. "Tell me, how'd you meet Catherine? She's not on TV. Or into economics."

"We go way back. Back to when we were both young and working at the same newspaper together. As the only two women on staff, we gravitated toward each other. And we each had something the other wanted."

"Oh?" Suze leaned forward. "Wait, you two didn't ever hook up?"

"Never." *Not for lack of trying on my part.* "I taught her how to handle the macho culture in newsrooms. How to stand up for herself better. She was so withdrawn and dedicated, used to saying nothing, just giving off these lethal glares if anyone gave her a hard time. But a vicious look doesn't cut it. I was the one who told her it was okay to say what she was really thinking. She became the Caustic Queen because of me."

"You gave her courage?" Suze asked.

"Oh no. Cat's one of the bravest and strongest people I know. She's been to hell and back and survived. No, I simply gave her permission to let herself off the leash."

"And what did she do for you? You said you each had something the other wanted."

Cynthia debated whether to answer. Well, it's not as if she'd ever see Suze again. With a wry smile, she admitted, "She taught me how to talk the way she does. I had TV ambitions but didn't sound the part. My first lesson in speaking properly came straight from Catherine's correctly enunciated Bostonian vowels."

"No shit."

"Mmm."

"How did you speak before that?"

"Let me put it this way: I learned that if you ever want to be taken seriously, don't sound like something the redneck dragged in." She wagged a finger at Suze. "It's a lesson for us all. Especially those in Middle America."

"This again?" Suze snorted.

Cynthia shrugged. "It's a reflex. I'd apologize, but I don't say things I don't mean."

"Pissing all over the Midwest is like a party trick for you, though; you do it so often."

"It's just too easy." Cynthia grinned. "Like shooting fish in a barrel. Or eating buffalo chicken pizzas at Casey's, if you want the local equivalent."

Suze's eyes went wide. "Holy shit."

"What?"

"Now it all becomes clear."

"What does?" Cynthia was mystified.

"Only a local would cite Casey's. Is that why you harp on Iowa so much? How long did you live here for anyway?

Cynthia would so love to deny it. To wipe away the memories that shaped her…and stained her.

Suze's hand reached over and clasped Cynthia's. "Come on. Share?" Her tone was shaded into concern enough to make Cynthia hesitate in shutting the conversation down instantly.

Would it be safe enough to say the words out loud?

The difficult words had such painful, sharp edges that they always stuck in Cynthia's throat. Only Catherine knew her past.

"I moved around a lot as a child. Not just place to place but family to family."

"Family to…" Understanding lit in Suze's eyes. "Foster kid?"

Cynthia nodded grimly.

"So you wound up here at some point?" Suze guessed.

"Unfortunately."

"For how long?"

"I was actually born here," Cynthia admitted through gritted teeth, "and I stayed only until I was old enough to bolt." Fear and wariness filled her at the thought that Suze might ask for more details. Her hand tensed under Suze's.

"So, your voice," Suze asked instead. "You used to sound like an Iowan? And Catherine taught you to sound like her?"

"Something like that." Cynthia exhaled, relieved to be on safer ground.

"And now you just endlessly poke sticks at the Midwest? Like your subconscious is striking back?"

"It's common to criticize what we hate about ourselves. To be honest, it's not the place I hate as much as the asshole family I lived with. It's hardly Iowa's fault. But I think part of me blames it for even existing. When I left here, I rid myself of all of it. From the dust on my shoes to the pedestrian brown of my hair." Cynthia waved at her blonde bob.

"I get it." Suze's voice was sincere.

"You do?"

"Yeah. You didn't just want an oil change when you got out of here. You wanted the whole engine overhaul. New place, voice, look, everything, right? So you became someone else. Someone opposite. Although, y'know, you can completely rebuild a Dodge, but there'll still be a bit of it left under the hood."

"Perhaps. But every day I get closer to finally getting out of Dodge."

"Ha!" Suze laughed. "Damn, that's clever."

"Thank you." Cynthia smiled and flicked at the tie on her borrowed red robe. "And you have an eye for quality."

"Modest too." Suze shook her head. "Anyway, here's what I think. Part of you has unresolved shit about where you grew up. You even took an Iowan to bed, someone you'd never, ever consider back in DC, right?" She lifted her eyebrow. "I'm a little roll around in your past, aren't I?"

Cynthia stared at her. She had no idea *what* any of this was about. Even this conversation was surreal. Was Suze right? Possibly. "Who can say? All I truly remember of last night is meeting you."

"I should be offended. But knowing you, you'd like that." Suze snorted.

"Ordinarily true. But for some reason, I actually think I want you to like me."

"It's not an urge you get often, I guess."

"Not at all." Cynthia sniffed. "Can you imagine where that would end? Small talk. Book clubs. Socializing with people who want to *catch up soon*."

"How awful." Suze laughed. "So now what? You've had your Iowan hookup and you'll be on the plane to DC within the hour?"

Cynthia considered Suze's words, curious as to the faint stab of regret at the thought. "No. Well, not quite." She pursed her lips. "I'm going to give you my e-mail address. And we will stay in touch."

"We will?"

"Yes. For some reason, I wouldn't object if I heard from you again."

"Do I curtsy to your Majesty at this news?"

"You should."

"Ha!" Suze did a sort of twisted half curtsy in bed that only succeeded in making the sheet fall down again.

Cynthia appreciated the view all over again. *Well.* She licked her lips. She could always catch a later flight. Not as if planes didn't fly out of this regional armpit on a regular basis. She cleared her throat. "Just to tie up any loose ends, I apparently owe you some reciprocation. For certain pressing things left unfinished last night."

"Oh, you don't have to." Suze gave a dismissive wave that looked far too indifferent to be believable. Her hungry gaze diving into Cynthia's cleavage was telling.

"Oh, but I insist." Cynthia said with a purr. "I'm a type A gal. I never like to leave things undone. Unless you'd like to…come undone?" She raised her eyebrow suggestively.

"I…" Suze's cheeks reddened. "I think I would like that a lot." She held out a hand, and her wide mouth curled into a teasing grin. "Slide right on over here, DC. I think it's time you put your mouth to better use than troublemaking."

Cynthia snorted. "Well, I suppose." As she gathered the impertinent woman in her arms, she decided she could think of far worse ways and places to wake up.

Have you read Lauren and Catherine's adventures yet? Two warring reporters find more than a story when they work together. Check out *The Red Files* and the sequel *Under Your Skin*

First-Class Villains

Hour one

Natalya Tsvetnenko strode into the British Airways first-class lounge at Heathrow Airport, her rare Charles Adolphe Maucotel cello in tow. A grey wintry day in London pressed against the tall windows, the fog settling across the runways with a bleakness that matched Natalya's mood.

She was over this European tour. Tired of her fellow Vienna Philharmonic Orchestra members, whom she'd left back in the economy area while she'd paid for an upgrade. And ever since she'd recently started her new life in Vienna, she was especially tired of missing Alison.

It was now a constant craving, this need to be near her, to share thoughts and observations, even if Natalya loathed admitting it. How curious that Alison, whom she'd once dismissed as a mouse, had so much power over her.

Natalya had believed leaving the woman behind in Melbourne would be the end of her passing distraction. Except her sense of loss was getting worse, not better, the longer Natalya was gone.

A staff member with a bright smile and too many teeth greeted her outside the exclusive Concorde Room and offered to stow her cello somewhere while she awaited her flight. Natalya's small sneer of incredulity sent the woman scuttling away. If someone was prepared to pay thousands for her instrument to have its own first-class seat on a flight, she would not be parted with it at an airport lounge either. *Obviously.*

Speaking of lounges, this one was certainly different. The general area with dozens of individual seats was full, but along the walls sat a series of cabana-like zones with flowing cream silk curtains attached on three sides to a timber frame. In the middle of each squatted a beautiful three-seater couch bookended by two ornate armchairs angled towards each other.

One armchair remained empty. Three women had taken the nearby seats, all studiously ignoring each other. It would do.

As Natalya placed her cello and bag within arm's reach and settled into the vacant chair, a British Airways employee appeared, bearing a tablet.

"Good afternoon, ladies. Sorry to interrupt. I'm Jo. I'm just letting passengers know the fog is worsening, and delays are likely. I'll return with updates when I have them."

That earned quiet groans.

Natalya inhaled. *Great.*

Jo reminded them to avail themselves of free drinks and beckoned a hovering waitress over.

Ten minutes later, Natalya was appreciating a vodka as she studied her fellow cabana hostages. Opposite her in an armchair sat one Grace Christie-Oberon, an actress who'd not only informed Jo that she was off to LA but also added it was for the Oscars. Because the English film she'd recently starred in, *The Missing Sky*, had been nominated. So far, she'd turned every conversation into a monologue about herself. When Grace's drink arrived, she'd claimed the waitress had misheard her order for tea.

Natalya, who perfectly remembered Grace's brisk cut-glass instructions for a short black, no-sugar coffee, had been tempted to call her a damned liar before she remembered she didn't care.

Grace was beautiful, with an otherworldliness that was both unsettling and familiar. Natalya had known a manipulative woman just like this: a cocktail for broken hearts and blind obedience. For a moment, Natalya pitied anyone who had the misfortune of loving this actress because, of course, the entire universe would revolve around her.

Grace seemed to sense Natalya's gaze, and the coolest of blue eyes fixed on Natalya. Grace's appraisal contained a sly awareness. She smiled then, a dazzling, magazine-worthy smile that Natalya met with indifference before looking away. Pretty little vipers were only dangerous when you let them be.

Natalya regarded the woman nearest Grace. Emmanuelle Lecoq had initiated a round of introductions with the other women, which Natalya had studiously ignored. The regal creature was perched on the edge of the couch, posture impeccable. Her destination was New York. She spoke with her hands in large, showy gestures designed to capture the attention of those around her. Her close-fitting skirt suit and handbag seemed designer. Lecoq's shrewd gaze darted about, as if she were seeking a conversational companion.

Natalya turned away from her too.

The final woman was Michelle Hastings—flying to Washington, DC. Her voice was the only soft thing about her. Hastings's features were sharp, and her icy eyes revealed little. It was hard not to be drawn to her despite a pantsuit almost designed to blend into backgrounds. She was arresting—compact, attractive, and obviously used to having power.

Grace's replacement drink arrived, and she used the opportunity to explain to the waitress that she was sticking to tea because she wanted a clear head while she worked on her Oscars speech.

Again with the Oscars? Natalya shot her a look so mocking that Grace stuttered to a stop midsentence.

Hastings smirked.

Natalya took another sip of vodka and pulled out her latest issue of *The Strad* to catch up on the classical string world's latest developments. She choked when she saw violinist Amanda Marks had a major feature article: *Meet Australia's String Sensation*. She growled and reminded herself that killing colleagues, past or present, was still a no-go zone.

Regrettably.

Hour two

Natalya's back was aching from the unnaturally upright armchair. Design over comfort, clearly. Her phone pinged. She pulled it out to find a text from Hailey, Alison's scamp of a teenage niece. The girl had admitted getting Natalya's number out of Alison's phone many months ago, and as a result, Natalya often received random ramblings. If pushed, she might admit they were amusing.

Hailey had never stopped worshipping Natalya since she'd saved Hailey from kidnappers a few years ago. It didn't seem to occur to Hailey how absurd it was for a professional cellist to burst in on a hostage scene and take out the kidnappers with a series of brutal moves. The girl had simply decided that Natalya was a "badass" and that explained everything.

Natalya approved of Hailey a great deal.

Natalya! I saw ur concert @ Madison Sq Gardens on YouTube! You were the best one there! When are you leaving UK? luv Hailey xxxxxx

After this followed a stream of little symbols including a fist and a fire. Perplexing.

Natalya typed back. *And how would you know I was the best? Am at Heathrow waiting to leave for Spain; however, fog has set in. There will be delays.*

A few minutes passed and then: *I just KNOW. Sux abt the delay.*

Typical Hailey logic. Natalya was the best because Hailey declared it so; The End—although Hailey wasn't wrong on this occasion.

Natalya's phone beeped again.

Btw this boy at school keeps punching me + saying OH SORRY + laughing wen I get mad. Mum says its cos he likes me + 2 ignore him. I hate his guts. btw he is HUGE. What do I do?

Natalya's eyes narrowed to slits. Some violent, hormonal reprobate was laying his hands on Hailey? *How dare he?* And Hailey's weak-willed mother was endorsing capitulation?

She slammed out a reply.

1. Ensure your environs contain no witnesses.

2. Kick him in the groin and say OH SORRY loudly.

3. Look him directly in the eye as you do, imagining the angriest thoughts you can. Psychological warfare is important.

If there are any further incidents, explain to him that the woman who took down your underworld kidnappers cares a great deal for your wellbeing and WILL find out where he lives. As you say that, be sure to smile. This should solve the matter. If not, contact me ASAP. N

There. She sat back, satisfied. Honestly, why did some people make such a big deal about parenting? It wasn't that hard.

A beat passed, and then her phone pinged once more: *Thanx. I knew you'd know what to do. Ur the best. luv Hailey xxxxxx*

Further perplexing symbols appeared, including a heart shape.

Well. Natalya was gratified Hailey had the sense to go straight to the top for advice. Clearly she took after her Aunt Alison more than her mother.

Thinking of Alison made Natalya's lips curl slightly. What was she doing right now? Was she tucked up in bed, reading, adorned in some doubtlessly respectable nightie that came down to her shins and only rode up her soft, pale thighs when she tossed and turned in her sleep?

Natalya swallowed.

With an impatient snap, she reopened her magazine and tried to focus on an article about the craft of German bow making.

Hour three

Natalya was nursing her second vodka, had grown bored with *The Strad*, and was now observing Lecoq over the pages of her magazine. The Frenchwoman had gone through a considerable number of Chambord Royales—a vile, sickly cocktail if ever there was one—certainly too many to be safe.

The actress…Grace…had run out of strangers to mention her Oscar nomination to and had made a round of phone calls that each included one breezy, flippant, "Oh thank you, darling! Well, it's just an honour to be nominated."

Natalya scowled at her. She'd looked up the woman's movie out of boredom. Grace wasn't nominated for a damned thing. Her film was up for a minor technical Oscar and nothing else.

Michelle Hastings ignored everyone, tapping on her laptop, jerking it away when Natalya slid her gaze to the screen.

Suddenly, Lecoq stood and threw up her hands. “Three hours! This delay is intolerable. *Merde!* I have important places to be, and this does not help.”

“Doubtful.” The soft murmur came from Hastings, her attention still on her screen.

“Pardon?” Lecoq’s hands flew to her hips. “What do you mean by that?”

Without looking up, Hastings retorted, “You’re a former fashion magazine editor who was fired after publicly outing a media mogul and defaming her girlfriend, which resulted in an outcry. Now you swan around fashion events, attempting to network or find a job or relevance. But you don’t have anywhere *important* to be. So sit down and be quiet. You’re disturbing my concentration.”

Lecoq’s expression turned venomous as she sank back to the couch.

Grace laughed and patted Lecoq’s knee. “My, my, you have been busy. I have to say, dear, outing anyone is a spectacularly foolish career move in this day and age. To do it to someone with so much power while working in the fashion industry, which is not exactly known for being straight?” She smirked. “Idiotic.”

Lecoq swore in French. Something about indecent relations with a donkey.

Natalya had to appreciate the originality of the insult.

Hastings closed her laptop with a soft, deadly click, and then she raised her head. “Apparently peace is too much to ask for.” She sighed and pinned a steely gaze on Lecoq. “All right, since we’re on the topic, I’ve always wondered why you did it. Despite what the actress thinks”—she waved at Grace—“you cannot be stupid. You once ran the world’s top fashion magazine. Now? Last I heard, you write online worst-dressed lists about B-grade stars.”

“You know nothing.” Lecoq glared. “I named no names! Everyone assumed it was Elena Bartell I intended to out, but my quotes could have been referencing anyone.”

Hastings snorted. “Anyone with a round building, a helicopter, and a hot younger girlfriend who was formerly her assistant? Your own staff turned on you over this. *They* knew. Why lie to us now?”

“So high and mighty.” Lecoq waggled a finger. “My God, this is what I cannot stand. The absolutism of people—it’s all good guys and bad guys, nothing else. And this cancel culture is toxic. For years, I was always front row at London Fashion

Week. This week, they put me in the fourth row at Stella's show! *Fourth!* None of the designers would even talk with me. My so-called disgrace was months ago. So I misspoke! So what? But no one forgets. I'm now the fashion world's villain number one!"

Ah. Natalya had vaguely heard about the outing of this American media mogul. So Lecoq was the grubby little cockroach who'd done it?

"Misspoke?" Hastings asked with a purr, but her eyes were flinty. "You told the entire world Bartell was having a midlife crisis, screwing her gold-digger 'assistant'—when Bartell's partner is actually an internationally acclaimed journalist. So cancel culture got it right. Suck it up: you *are* the villain of this piece."

"Have none of you ever made a mistake!" Lecoq's head swivelled from woman to woman. "You've never been a villain even once?"

"Not me," Grace said with airy confidence. "Oh, I've played a few on stage and screen—"

"I swear if you mention that Oscar one more time," Lecoq said with a snarl, "I *will* slap you."

Grace blinked. "Excuse me?"

"Four times you've mentioned it!" Lecoq flung her hands up again.

"Five," Natalya inserted dryly in the interests of accuracy.

Hastings chuckled.

"Five!" Lecoq eyeballed Grace. "Why are you judging me? You're an actress. You should know what it feels like to have the media twist your words."

"Except it seems that your words weren't twisted." Grace's gaze sharpened. "Play stupid games, win stupid prizes."

"I'm not stupid. Nor am I homophobic, despite what they said."

"Jealous, then?" Hastings suggested.

"Of Bartell? Don't make me laugh." Lecoq glowered at them through glassy, booze-affected eyes. "My God, when that woman started at *CQ* magazine, she was Elena *Bartlewski*. She was some dirt-poor, Polish-American brat who hemmed clothes for petty cash. She assumed her mentor's editor job would be hers when the woman retired."

Lecoq gave a disdainful cluck. "*Imbecile*. I outmanoeuvred her and became editor instead. And yet somehow, that backward creature ended up running half the publishing world! How does that even happen?"

Natalya lifted an eyebrow behind her magazine. Someone destroying themselves while believing they were eviscerating someone else was always entertaining.

"I was on my way to do a newspaper interview when an e-mail arrived on my phone with the numbers," Lecoq continued. "Bartell's rival fashion magazine had just beaten mine in circulation. Her better than *me*? I trained at the best design schools in Paris, and she just crawled in off the curb! I thought I'd remind her of who she really is. So sue me if I was so furious that I didn't realise my hints would be obvious to everyone else. Then the world rained acid on me. *Merde*. I should have fucked her over properly and told the world her real origins."

"Yes, dear, that would have played *so* much better," Grace said with an eye roll. "Elitist, anti-Semitic xenophobe is much preferable to homophobic. How charming you are."

"I'm none of those things!" Lecoq snapped. "And a narcissist judging me? That's rich."

"I'm no narcissist." Grace's expression lost its mirth.

"Oh please." Lecoq's lip curled in contempt. "Everything's me, me, me. You're never wrong either. You'd be insufferable to work with."

Grace's head took an imperious tilt. "Do you have any idea to whom you are speaking? I have won BAFTA awards, I'm England's national treasure, I'm in line for a damehood. I'm—"

"Go kiss a photo of yourself then! You're not special. If you were, you wouldn't try so hard to impress everyone. Face it; you're a has-been."

"Oh my, insults from the woman who outed someone to millions?" Grace scoffed. "You are the villain here, not me."

"So self-righteous. If I'm a villain for one mistake, then everyone is. Everyone's done something awful they shouldn't have. My misfortune was that mine happened publicly. All of you"—she waved a finger at her audience—"have had the luxury of doing your worst in private. That doesn't make you better than me; it just makes you lucky."

Grace shook her head. "Nonsense."

"It's not." Lecoq reached into her bag and drew out a bottle of champagne. She slid it onto the table. "And I have a 1995 Krug Clos d'Ambonnay that says I'm right."

Hastings inhaled sharply, eyes bright, and examined the label, then glanced up. "I know my champagne. This is worth over $5000. How on earth did you get this?"

"I won it in the Vivienne Westwood afterparty charity raffle. Only thing that went right for me this week. Apparently it's the rarest champagne in the world, and I'm prepared to sacrifice it to prove you all wrong."

Natalya slowly put down her magazine. Alison had once confessed she loved champagne but couldn't afford it often. A rare bottle like this… She pictured turning up at Alison's apartment—claiming she was there for another proof-of-life check on the African violet Alison was plantsitting for her—and just sliding the bottle across the coffee table. Casually, as if it were nothing. Natalya imagined Alison's eyes lighting up in wonder.

Of course, the fantasy was ridiculous. Natalya had no plans to ever see Alison again. And yet Natalya found herself leaning in, waiting for the terms.

Lecoq regarded them. "I challenge you all: tell us your most awful deed, and the worst one earns the woman who did it the bottle."

Natalya let out a sigh. The irony. A contest she was perfectly placed to win, yet she couldn't just admit to assassinating three dozen of Australia's worst criminals.

She sat back again.

"Are you serious?" Hastings asked incredulously. "Your pride matters to you more than the world's rarest champagne?"

"Yes."

"How is it even possible you have this in carry-on luggage if you didn't purchase it at the airport? It's not allowed unless you check it in."

Lecoq snorted. "It's not hard. All you need to do is threaten to sue the airline for thousands if the world's rarest champagne is damaged in transit. My lawyer got me a waiver allowing it under the 'unusual or fragile items' carry-on luggage clause. A bit cheeky since that section's usually for musical instruments." She slid a glance at Natalya's cello. "But it's simply amazing how effective the threat of a public lawsuit is when a famous magazine editor makes it." Lecoq offered a triumphant smile.

"Former magazine editor," Hastings corrected. "And more infamous than famous."

"Do you want to win this or not?" Lecoq's tone turned icy. "If so, fewer insults, more confessions."

"How do you know we won't just make up evil deeds?" Hastings asked.

"Well, I'd certainly have to." Grace smiled.

She was ignored.

"We'll know." Lecoq eyed them all. "I suspect this particular group has an excellent nose for who is lying. Yes? And remember we'll have mutually assured destruction. That means if you tell someone's secrets, we can tell yours in return. So no one shares anything said here. Agreed?"

Grace's smile was angelic. "I really don't have anything to contribute here. Although it is certainly tempting to prove I'm due that Oscar by inventing some dramatic story."

"Bah!" Lecoq faced her. "Again with the Oscar? Do you truly wish to be slapped! I *will* do it."

"So violent." Grace sniffed but leaned away, eyes uncertain. "I can't help it if I'm not a bad person, even if you need to believe everyone is to feel better about yourself."

Natalya let them bicker and mentally cycled through her life. Not everything destructive she'd done came down to killing. She cleared her throat, gaze sharp on the bottle. "I'll play."

"You?" Grace laughed. "Goodness, the cellist thinks she's done something terrible."

"She has," Hastings murmured. "One look will tell you she's more than she pretends."

Natalya frowned. A little too perceptive.

Lecoq's expression turned speculative. "All right." Her green eyes fixed on Natalya. "Tell us, what dark deed have you done?"

Natalya inhaled. Guilt nudged her. The one regret she had. She assessed the room for eavesdroppers, found none, but lowered her voice anyway. "A young woman who looked up to me and had a crush on me tried to hurt me. In retaliation, I decided to teach her a lesson. I fucked her in some dark alley, reminding her over and over that she was nothing to me and that her love was wasted. I laughed in her face, mocked her professionally and personally, and left her there with her pants around her ankles. I wanted her to know who had the power. She got the message."

Grace hissed in a breath and shifted in her seat.

"Good God," Lecoq whispered. "How…cruel." Her expression turned smug. "So you admit you're a villain then?"

"I suppose." Natalya shrugged faintly. "So what? Is the bottle mine?"

"No." Lecoq shook her head. "The actress has something to share."

"I do not," Grace said.

"You do. When the cellist told her story, you went pale. It reminded you of something, didn't it?"

"It was nothing." Grace took a gulp of her tea. She looked as if she were wishing it was something stronger.

Hastings snorted. "Liar. You almost squirmed out of your seat."

"It's not what you think. It's just… I hadn't really thought about what happened before in terms of how my actions might be perceived…on the other side…until I heard her story." Grace fiddled with her watch's gold-link chain. "I concede I mightn't have been my best self, but there were extenuating circumstances. You must understand, I'd just turned"—she lowered her voice—"fifty. Fifty-three, to be exact."

Christ! Genetics were a hell of a thing. Grace barely looked in her early forties, and she was sitting here bitching about her age?

"My roles had dried up. I'd lost my agent, my friends, and my occasional lover. I was feeling…anxious…for my future. I asked my last remaining friend, a woman I had mentored for two decades, to travel with me. I needed a break. She refused because her career mattered more than I did. I knew she was in love with me, so I tried to…sway her, even though I had no interest in her that way. It didn't feel like a bad thing, just a harmless flirtation."

Grace swished a hand about. "I kissed her to make her reconsider, but she became furious. She took it so personally! I never saw her again. Perhaps not my finest hour, but it was harmless enough, or so I thought at the time."

Silence fell.

Lecoq pointed at her. "You played with a woman's feelings for you and threw aside a friendship of twenty years because you didn't want to travel alone? Oh, but it wasn't your fault, because you were desperate and lonely? And it was all so harmless…yet she left you forever?"

"I didn't say I was desperate," Grace snapped. "Or lonely! Merely…anxious. Anyway, she got all huffy and took it the wrong way, so…" She waved her hand. "Life goes on."

"You think it is nothing?" Lecoq pressed her. "Losing this lifelong friend?"

"It *is* nothing." Grace frowned. "We were just in different places. It truly was not much of consequence. Certainly not a patch on this…cellist… carrying out malicious depravities as punishment." Her face twisted in disgust.

Cool fury flooded Natalya. This vain creature who was all neck and cheekbones dared judge her? "No, yours was a more civilised fucking over. I barely knew the woman I crushed. You turned on a close friend."

Grace recoiled. "How dare you compare us? You're a spiteful, punishing creature who abuses power for kicks."

"And you're a gaslighting, manipulative narcissist with the self-awareness of a sock."

Grace turned to Hastings and Lecoq. "You cannot possibly believe my tiny error in judgment is worse than hers?"

"Both deeds are terrible," Lecoq replied. "But the way you minimise what you did is disturbing. I'm honestly not sure which is worse."

"Lovely. Need I remind you what *you* did?" Grace snapped. "Outing that media mogul?"

"Deflection now? You *are* good at manipulation." Lecoq's gaze flitted to Hastings. "Do you have a worse deed than those two? Or do we vote on who wins the bottle now?"

Hastings groaned softly. "Unfortunately for me, I love champagne far more than is sensible. I would give anything to try the '95." She studied the bottle at length, as if deciding whether to participate. "Fine. I cheated on my husband."

"Affairs of the heart are always bad." Lecoq frowned as she picked her words. "But cheating is hardly uncommon. I do not see—"

"I *emotionally* cheated on him," Hastings clarified. "He was okay about the physical side. At first."

They all stared.

With a huff of aggravation, Hastings continued, "I was required to get close to a particular woman for my work. Her power was an aphrodisiac. So was her witty, clever, attractive personality. I slept with her. My husband knew. The more time I spent with her, the more addictive she was. The weeks turned into months. I barely saw my husband; I invented reasons to be near her."

"Are you a prostitute?" Lecoq asked curiously. "One of those high-class callgirls?"

"No!" Hastings folded her arms. "And where I work isn't relevant. Anyway, after we had what could only be termed a real relationship, when I knew she loved me, and…I suppose I felt the same…I carried out the rest of my orders. I fed her false documents that she released publicly as part of her job. It ruined her career in a huge national scandal, got her mocked on every talk show, and shattered her into pieces. I walked away without a word."

"My God," Grace whispered.

Lecoq drew in a deep breath. "That is truly awful."

Natalya stared at Hastings, a chill going through her. She'd thought she knew every kind of cruelty there was. She tried to imagine breaking Alison into emotional pieces like that. Natalya had been hired to kill her and had felt so sick at the thought that she'd abandoned the job. To hurt someone the way Hastings had, someone you actually cared for or…loved? That was monstrous.

Natalya countered Hastings's gaze with a cool look. "So *you're* the villain in first class."

Hastings's mouth tightened at the edges.

Natalya leaned forward and slid the bottle in front of her. "Congratulations. It takes quite a lot to impress me. You win."

Everyone fell silent. And stayed silent.

No one met anyone's eyes. Now exposed, they seemed embarrassed by their admissions.

Grace especially looked as if she couldn't wait to be gone. After a while, she began trying to fill the awkward silence with shallow conversation. Her droll tone did little to hide the rising anxiety in her eyes.

Of course the woman would panic over three strangers having seen her for who she truly was. How…fragile. Probably couldn't wait to get back to her adoring fans.

"Has it occurred to anyone how much lesbian energy there is here?" Grace abruptly asked. She twirled her finger to encompass them all. "Is it something in the drinks?"

Lecoq gave her a hard stare. "I am no lesbian. I'm happily married. To a man. A straight man. Because I am also straight."

"Well, sorry to interrupt your gay panic there, darling," Grace said with a burst of forced laughter, "but so am I. I meant those two." Her wrist flipped in the general direction of Natalya and Hastings.

Hastings sighed. "I'm hardly a lesbian. I've had one…anomalous…attraction to a woman in my whole life. That hardly puts me in the sensible shoes and rainbow glitter crowd. The cellist on the other hand…" Her voice was faintly goading.

All gazes swung Natalya's way.

After a withering look, Natalya said, "Labels are as pointless as this conversation."

That shut them up. Free of further interruptions, Natalya's mind returned to Hastings. She wondered why her cruelty had rattled her so much. It reminded her that she *did* have a line after all. Hurting Alison or those Alison loved was something Natalya couldn't even fathom. Her protectiveness for Alison and Hailey was fierce. Until now, she'd never dwelled on why.

What did it mean?

No. These thoughts were pointless. Natalya had settled things the last time she'd been with Alison. When she'd stopped by, fucked her thoroughly at Alison's request, and then left her with proof of exactly who Natalya was: a recording filled with silence. There was nothing left to say. Natalya was a ghost, passing through.

She'd also given Alison a nudge to move on as Natalya was on the way out the door. By now, the young woman was living life to the fullest, loving, playing her music, and experiencing so much more.

That thought gave Natalya a sudden pang of regret. It would be rather captivating to witness the little mouse transforming.

The urge to go back for her surged again, even stronger this time. For a moment, Natalya tried to picture herself standing before Alison, inviting her to see the world with her. Maybe it wouldn't be humiliating. Maybe her nerve wouldn't fail her.

Maybe I'll kiss her this time.

The thought almost shocked Natalya senseless. It was followed by another: *What would kissing her be like?*

Comfort and warmth and freshly baked bread, Natalya decided. Diary scribbles and lazy smiles and hints of vanilla.

Christ. What *was* this? Natalya didn't do comfort or warmth.

Then again, she'd always thought she didn't crave anything but her music. And yet here she was—contemplating the unthinkable. All because Michelle Hastings, some random first-class stranger, was apparently more vicious than the assassin Requiem.

Hour four

The fog had cleared. One by one, as the various flights started boarding, the women rose and left. First was Grace, who scrambled to her feet and couldn't resist adding, "I'm really not a bad person. You people have me all wrong."

No one bothered answering.

She gave them a glare and swept away.

Next was Lecoq, who eyed the champagne, then shifted her gaze to Hastings and smirked with satisfaction before departing.

Once it was just the two of them, Hastings turned to study Natalya. "You know, you remind me of my ex-husband. The way you look at people…well, *through* them. I knew from the moment you sat down. You're far more than a cellist."

Natalya should have denied it outright. But in that weird moment while sitting in a strange city with a strange woman she'd never meet again, she instead said, "Not anymore."

It was partly true. She still burned sometimes for the hunt. It woke her at night and made her want to chase and punish. But that was all tied up with the alluring mentor who'd made her this way. These days, Natalya tried to bury the memories of her recruitment along with that woman.

"I won't ask what you've done." Hastings's look was speculative. "But perhaps the bottle should have been yours all along." She made to push it Natalya's way.

Natalya stopped its slide. "As bad as I've been, I could never deliberately crush someone I loved." She shot Hastings a mocking smile. "It seems you *are* the worst of us."

Hastings's eyes glinted. She seemed to be forcing a veneer of indifference. "So the narcissist wasn't worse? I did what I had to in order to advance my career. You did what you did for payback. Lecoq was an asshole out of some overwrought sense of entitlement and jealousy. But Grace did it because she *could*. Her friend meant nothing to her. She sees friends in terms of their usefulness. And we at least acknowledge we've behaved badly. Even Lecoq knows she screwed up—that's why she's angry enough to throw away her expensive booze to feel better. Not Grace. Nothing's her fault. She's perfect and misunderstood—hero or victim, nothing in between."

A sly thought slid into Natalya's mind. "Perhaps you should send her the bottle. Inform her we did a recount and she won after all. She'd go ballistic."

Hastings smiled. "I'd do it if I didn't think she'd hurl a five-thousand-dollar bottle of Krug Clos d'Ambonnay against the wall. Sacrilege!"

"True." Natalya considered Grace and the way she'd elegantly slunk off. How similar she was to the woman who'd groomed Natalya to be her pet lethal weapon. So much ugliness hidden behind devastating beauty. "People like her, it's almost a kindness ending their misery. Not for their benefit but for those suffering around them."

Hastings's eyes became half-lidded. "Anyone else, I'd take that as empty rhetoric. You, though…"

"Do you regret what you did?" Natalya cut her off.

"Not often." Hastings studied her. "I'm ambitious; I don't deny it. When I focus on that, I can push my regrets aside." She paused. "Some days, though, I wish I'd kept the girl and tossed the job. On those days, I think about the girl far too often."

Natalya remained silent. Some days, she thought about the girl far too often as well. She'd have the odd, idle thought of maybe sharing with Alison a sight, smell, or taste she'd had on tour. It was becoming more than a distraction.

Hastings regarded Natalya as the departure board changed, announcing Hastings' flight was ready for boarding. "It confuses you that you lost that bet, doesn't it? You assumed you were the worst person in the room, and I just waltzed in and screwed with your world view."

Natalya frowned. "You don't know me."

"I know people like you. I employ people like you—people who reek of danger. I married a man who terrifies people for a living. Although I now suspect you're probably not half as bad as you think you are." Hastings studied Natalya for a beat. "Oh, I don't doubt you've done something dastardly, but…" Hastings paused as if considering the possibilities. "Your accent says you're Australian. What's the worst mischief you could have gotten up to down there anyway?"

Natalya stared. Hastings had no clue.

"Rolling with those underworld gangs in Melbourne perhaps?" Hastings's voice was filled with mirth. "Haven't police virtually cleaned them all up now? I read that somewhere. The only exciting thing your people have going is some crazy female assassin called Req…" She stopped cold. "…uiem." Her gaze flitted to Natalya's cello and back.

Natalya could almost hear her cogs grinding, putting two and two together. *Requiem. Classical music. Cello. Dangerous woman.*

Then Hastings's face paled. "I-I…" She licked her lips. "Oh, shit," she said softly.

Natalya should have been furious Hastings had connected the dots so easily. Instead, amusement rose in the face of the woman's clear panic. Natalya made her tone soft as silk when she replied, "Oh, I doubt she's crazy."

Hastings nodded vigorously. "Please ignore me. I was rambling." She gave a choked laugh. "Besides, mutually assured destruction rules apply anyway." Her voice went up too high.

"I have no idea what you mean." Natalya leaned back. "Anyway, whoever this assassin is sounds like she would retaliate brutally if someone even *hinted* at identifying her. Especially if she'd gotten a glimpse of her betrayer's laptop and knew exactly where she works." It was a bluff, but the widening of Hastings's eyes told her it was an effective one. "Wouldn't you agree?"

Hastings sucked in a breath and nodded abruptly.

Natalya smiled, showing all her teeth. "Now then, let's get back to how bad I'm *not*. You were saying?"

Hastings went paler.

"Nothing?" Natalya goaded her. "You were so sure a minute ago."

Hastings seemed to regather her wits. "You're enjoying this far too much," she muttered. "And I find it interesting that you said earlier you could never destroy someone you loved." Her look became speculative. "Whoever they are must be special."

Natalya's senses shot to high alert. If Hastings was about to make threats against Alison, Natalya would end her where she sat. It wouldn't even be hard. Three different methods came to mind in seconds, two involving the silk curtains. "There's no one," she ground out, her warning clear.

Hastings flinched. "Well, that's a shame," she said lightly. "Obviously there was someone once for you to know with certainty what you'd do."

Was Hastings suicidal? "As I said—"

"No one. Yes, I heard you the first time. It's fine, and for God's sake, stand down. Even your hackles have prickles. I have no interest in you or your love-life." Hastings stood, tugging straight her jacket, and regarded Natalya. Some of her initial intensity returned. "But just so you know, it's not a weakness if you do have someone. To risk your certainty for the uncertainty of love? Well. It takes more strength than I had." Her mouth pulled into a grim line.

Love? Natalya inwardly scoffed. She had no interest in love. Although there was no denying she missed Alison. That didn't mean it was love.

Hastings didn't wait for an answer, just slid the champagne bottle into her shoulder bag, then paused. "You were right. I do have regrets, far more than I like to admit. So don't make my mistake." She held Natalya's gaze. "Go get the girl."

Hastings then turned and strode away without a backward glance.

Natalya watched her go, the words circling her head.

Perhaps she would.

And wasn't that a strangely satisfying thought?

To read more about these villains, check out the following Lee Winter books: *Requiem for Immortals* (Natalya Tsvetnenko), *The Red Files,* and *Under Your Skin* (Michelle Hastings, aka Stephanie), *The Brutal Truth* novel and "The Brutal Lie" short story in the *After Happily Ever After* anthology (Emmanuelle Lecoq), and *Breaking Character* (Grace Christie-Oberon).

Love is Not Nothing

Part One: Masks

Requiem

Natalya Tsvetnenko entered the Wellness-Oase in Spittelberggasse and pushed her sunglasses onto her forehead. Soothing nature sounds filled her ears as she glanced around the foyer. This was one of the most luxurious massage salons in Vienna and, during the past three years Natalya had lived in this city, it had been invaluable for easing the side effects of excessive cello practice and playing with the Vienna Philharmonic Orchestra.

That some of her aches came from injuries sustained in her former career was neither here nor there. Explaining her old war wounds had actually resulted from encounters with underworld assassins was not exactly high on her agenda. Nonetheless, Wellness-Oase's highly trained massage therapists were the model of discretion. And Natalya paid well to have their deep-tissue, full-body, elite athlete's massage that did wonders for her sore points.

She was greeted at the counter by Lotte, an angular, distinguished woman in the white waffle-weave kimono robe and Japanese clog sandals all her staff wore. Lotte raised her hand with an elegant swish. *"Christiane erwartet Sie bereits in ihrem üblichen Zimmer, Fräulein Tsvetnenko."*

So Natalya had Christiane this week, who was waiting in Natalya's usual room. She picked apart German easily these days. Natalya nodded to Lotte and followed her instructions, pleased to have her preferred room, far from the others, which added to her sense of privacy.

She padded softly down the off-white, carpeted hallway, finding room twelve by the usual potted plant on a stand outside it. A sad little *Alocasia sanderiana*.

Natalya leaned forward to inspect it and came away disheartened. Underwatered. Her lips thinned. She would point this oversight out to Christiane. It was always disappointing when the details were overlooked.

Stepping into the cream-coloured room, she smelled vanilla incense and something else with a touch of spice to it. Pleasant enough. In one corner was a crock pot of hot rocks slowly warming. For the next client, most likely, as Natalya had little interest in the latest new-age fads.

Her gaze drifted higher, to the peace symbol mobile dangling from the ceiling, then trailed to the framed prints of bamboo forests and a small bronze Buddha statue on the windowsill under the timber horizontal blinds. She wondered whether Christiane realized the Buddha was about as Japanese as her faux kimono robe was.

The masseuse in question turned at Natalya's arrival and offered a polite greeting, then pointed to the table. Her gelled-back, blonde hair was pulled into a perfect bun that shone under the warm lighting.

"Machen Sie sich bitte frei, Fräulein Tsvetnenko. Ich bin in fünf Minuten wieder da."

Natalya translated that to "Please get ready, I'll be back in five minutes".

She shed her clothes, folding her black linen pants, leather jacket, crisp white shirt, and undergarments into an exacting pile, before lining up her polished, black, ankle boots together under the chair in the corner.

Naked, she arranged herself on the table, placing a towel over her rear to signal her readiness. Natalya had no modesty concerns, especially when it meant Christiane's expert hands could fully access the pressure points and aches in her backside and lower back from too many hours spent sitting.

Natalya had never suffered from modesty anyway. When she examined herself each morning, mapping her scars, she saw power, control, discipline, and beauty in her muscled flanks, strong shoulders, and glossy, straight, black hair. And, sometimes, she also saw delicate hands slipping around her waist and clutching her tightly against an equally naked body, still warm from the shower.

Natalya's lips twitched at the pleasing memory.

It was hard to believe it had been three years since she'd settled here, after a year of touring all over Europe. Four years away from her former life in Australia. A life that was nothing like she'd imagined it would be when, as a teenager, she'd first sought sponsors to allow her to take up a cello scholarship here in Vienna.

The sponsors, associates of her stepmother, Lola, had turned out to be a Melbourne underworld crime family which had sought its pound of flesh, training her as their deadliest of tools. No one would expect a female, especially one so young, and a musical prodigy at that, to be a crime gang's secret assassin. This was what had made her so devastatingly effective, far exceeding expectations.

She'd agreed to only five years. A fair exchange for the investment in her studies. But none of the associates in the crime family had understood why, when her indentured term to them had finished, she'd kept doing their lethal work, freelance. Especially since she still filled the souls of patrons with her music each night.

What those men with empty eyes failed to understand was that each career had its addictions and contained a thrill for Natalya not easily dismissed. Both made her feel like a god who held beating hearts and quivering minds in her hands. The mistake was in ever seeing her as two different people. Assassin or cellist. Requiem or Natalya.

She had always been both. For her it was so simple—the dominant strengths required to face any given situation leapt to the fore, with an attitude to match. No different from choosing different shoes for a change of event. You put them away again when unneeded.

Such philosophical meanderings were usually left in the past these days. Natalya was forty-five and a world away from Victoria's seedy underbelly. Nowadays she only ever stirred the human soul instead of destroying it. She'd made her choice. She had few regrets. It was the price she'd paid to have a little mouse in her life. She'd paid it willingly, once she'd understood.

Natalya closed her eyes, wondering what Alison was doing. She'd said something about going to a farmer's market close to their apartment in Neubau before lunch. She was doing cooking lessons, between taking some violin masterclasses and teaching English as a second language to refugees in a Public Learning Centre in the nearby Fifteenth District. Her enthusiasm for each of these activities was unabated.

It had been unnerving at first, being with someone so different to Natalya. Meshing her existence had been difficult with one so filled with life, love, and empathy, and especially with emotions brimming so close to the surface. Many a time Natalya had questioned her sanity at allowing anyone inside. Not to mention the chaotic way Alison never once lined up her shoes, or always threw her clothes over the back of a chair when a perfectly good hanger was available.

But Alison would smile at her appalled expression and tease her until she decided to overlook the disarray. It turned out the woman had been like the mouse Natalya dubbed her four years ago—she'd curled up, small and soft, close to Natalya's heart, and stubbornly refused to move.

What defense did a world-class assassin have against that?

The massage room's door opened and clicked shut. Natalya felt her back cool as the towel was slid down to her thighs. The slippery noise of massage oil being rubbed into hands filled the air before she felt Christiane's fingers on her back.

The masseuse began slowly, mapping Natalya's contours. As she progressed, Christiane became far more forceful than usual, and twice Natalya swallowed a grunt. She hadn't realised the woman had it in her.

The sound of wet, slapped flesh, and the heat of hands near her neck took Natalya back. It reminded her of the first kill she'd witnessed as a sixteen-year-old. It was an execution for one of the crime family's own, a man caught in the act of betrayal. She could still feel Lola's open hand at the back of her neck, the press of her warm skin against the collar of her school uniform, forcing her to watch.

"Orientation", her stepmother had called it. For what was to come, after Natalya returned from Vienna, once her scholarship was complete and her duties to the crime family began. It was grooming. Ensuring she understood what she was in for.

Natalya had forgotten most of the faces in those lessons. But what she did remember from that first time was the man's eyes. Bleak, black, and terrified, they had made her want to crawl into a hole and hide.

And she also remembered *her* perfume. Sensual, exotic, and arousing.

Natalya's verdict was not unique, judging by the furtive, lust-filled looks the men gave Lola when she wasn't watching.

The accompaniment to the scene was the satisfied grunts of those standing witness when the battered betrayer took his last breath. Their way of saying it was done. Over. The grunts were a ritual to disguise the horror. Natalya understood more than most the need for ritual. Her entire life was ritualistic, from the way she stretched each day, to the way she straightened her possessions, turned on her MP3 player, and held her bow.

After the chilling deed was done, no one had met her eyes. Not even Lola. Natalya had been sent to do her homework.

The wet slap of flesh—pleasure and pain—it all sounded the same. Natalya had learned that lesson often over the years.

Christiane's blows became harder, stronger. Punishing. Like...hatred. Wariness curled through Natalya, her eyes sliding open as she processed the unexpected sensations.

A lone, oiled finger slid up the scar next to her spine and dug in viciously. She gritted her teeth at the pain and stared at the woman's feet. White socks covered them, bisected by the black silk of the sandals.

"The plant outside needs watering," Natalya said softly in German. "It is in terrible condition."

Christiane merely hummed evenly and gave no reply. As if she didn't understand her words. Those telltale toes in the white socks, however, briefly clenched.

Natalya shifted her hands up to sit flat under her chin, lifting her face just a few inches out of the headrest.

"What part of Melbourne are you from?" she said in English, taking a guess. She used her friendliest tone. Her hands slowly edged apart, feeling the roughness of the white towel beneath her fingertips, as she mentally mapped the edges of the massage table.

"Prah..." The word, begun reflexively as a thoughtless reply to small talk, stopped halfway through "Prahran", a distinctively Melbourne suburb.

The masseuse's toes clenched just as the hands on Natalya's back froze. Natalya's narrowed eyes flew open at the confirmation, the knowledge of imminent danger filling her with an electricity she'd not felt in three years, eleven months, twelve days. The numbers came to her without conscious calculation. She knew them each day the moment she woke. The days since she'd hunted as Requiem.

She felt her alter ego slapped from her slumber, unleashed, burning, alive—like molten metal coursing through her veins. In her mind, she could hear the thrumming, primal drum beat of Two Steps From Hell's *Protectors of Earth* shaking her.

Alertness and adrenaline ripped through her with the familiarity of an old friend. She had not felt this sensation since the night she'd ended a corrupt, killer cop—a man she'd choked and drowned in pig swill. Even almost four years on, she could still taste the twisted jubilation mingled with ice-cold rage over what he'd done to the woman Requiem had claimed as hers. And what he'd done to Alison's family.

Without warning, Requiem flung herself from the table, smashing the masseuse to the floor with her bent elbow and snatching up the towel she'd been lying on.

She stood above the groggy woman, bouncing on her heels while she spun the towel into a twisted rope and tested the ends threateningly. Requiem studied the crumpled form on the floor—small, lean, and most definitely not the Austrian woman she knew.

"Unless Christiane's had a lot of work done in the past twenty minutes, you aren't her," Requiem said, voice cold. "Who are you?"

The woman offered her a mutinous look but didn't answer.

Requiem kicked her solidly in the ribs. "Speak up."

The intruder was a short, wiry-looking Asian woman, with brooding, dark eyes, and an appraising stare. She didn't seem alarmed by Natalya's reaction. Rather, she appeared to have been expecting it.

"Where's Christiane?" Requiem demanded.

"Linen cupboard. She'll have a bad headache when she wakes up." The woman's voice and eyes openly taunted Requiem.

"Who are you?" she repeated, menace mixed with danger.

Silence.

Requiem's leg swept out and smacked the side of the woman's nose, snapping her head to the right with the momentum. A satisfying spurt of blood spattered across her white kimono robe.

Still she didn't speak. The woman ran lazy eyes over Requiem's nude form with a hint of appreciation before focusing higher, meeting her furious gaze. Finally her amused lips parted. "I am someone confirming a theory." She wiped her nose and examined the blood on her fingertips. "I see you've lost none of your edge."

"I have no idea what you're talking about." Requiem's tone became low and dark. She tightened the ends of the twisted towel, snapping it straight and relaxing it. Anyone with any self-preservation instincts would have scuttled back.

Her prey did not. Instead she tilted her head back, studying Requiem. "A woman making a garroting cable out of a towel wants me to believe she knows nothing about killing?" came the sceptical response. "That she's not Australia's most infamous assassin, Requiem? A woman who police can't find for years? Not that they're looking too hard. I mean, I found you."

"I'm a cellist," Requiem said with a sneer. She bent down and viciously flicked the woman's bloodied nose. "Vienna." *Flick.* "Philharmonic." *Flick.* "Orchestra." *Flick.* She gave her a withering look. "Anyone around here could tell you that."

"I don't think so." The woman's laugh was light, sounding genuine despite the blood soaking her swelling nose.

Requiem studied her in confusion. Her face had to be hurting like hell, yet she was still smiling.

"Well, you're not *just* that, are you?" the woman continued. "I know you killed dozens of underworld scum before you ran off here."

"Last chance." Requiem yanked the towel in her hands so taut that her sculpted biceps, honed by two-hour workouts every day, stood out in sharp relief. Her voice became terrifyingly soft. "Now—Who. Are. You?"

The smile widened. "A recruiter."

Requiem threw the towel to the floor and squatted in front of her. She wrenched the upper half of the woman's kimono apart with force. Beneath the garment she wore a simple white bra, and Requiem rapidly inspected her for surveillance wires, running her fingers under the bra and around to her back. She felt lower, patting down her groin, thighs, and calves. Finding nothing, she slid her fingers up into the woman's long black hair, pausing behind her ears. Still nothing.

In annoyance, Requiem pushed her away so hard that the woman fell back in a sprawl. Then she pounced.

"Now, let's start again," she said coldly, bracketing the woman's knees with her thighs. "Who the hell are you, and why are you here, invading my space?"

Rather than answer, a slow gaze raked Requiem's body. Something familiar about the way she studied her niggled at Requiem. When the woman finally spoke, her voice was breathless.

"Invading *your* space? Says the naked assassin with her cunt in my lap?" An elegant finger traced across Requiem's muscled stomach, swirling across a small scar above her hip. She arched an eyebrow.

Requiem glanced down at her nude state, then at the finger. "Distracted, are we?"

They both watched the finger drop a little lower, edging towards her neatly trimmed dark hair, and Requiem hissed in a breath of surprise. It had been so long since she'd played with her prey. And even longer still since one of them had the temerity to toy with her back. She'd forgotten how heady it could be.

Arousal shot through her when the dancing digit slid a little lower—merely a fingertip, a fingernail, away from her clit. A prickling sensation shot down Requiem's spine, a warning as sharp as a knife's blade, and Requiem wrenched the hand away and jumped to her feet. She picked up her clothes and said with a growl, "Fine. You have your space. Now talk."

Even with distance from the woman, Requiem's heart thudded in awareness, her body tightly strung. The base, raw emotions were almost overwhelming. This was what she used to do. *This* was the real game. The absolute power. Her body ached to feel it again. Requiem's mounting excitement in her lower gut told her just how close that wandering finger had come. How close the woman would have been to discovering the effect she'd had on Requiem. And that would not do.

The woman sat up casually and leaned back on one arm, a picture of relaxation. Like one of those perfect specimens on the cover of a yoga DVD, all poised class and easy beauty. "I am someone who needs your unique skills, and who understands that you're available and most likely ready for a change."

"Not interested." Requiem slipped on her bra and slid her black boy shorts up her legs.

The woman teasingly began to fiddle with her own robe, widening it. "You haven't even heard my pitch."

"Still not interested." Requiem pulled her pants up with sharp, snapping actions, and almost groaned when the seam hit her groin and shot a bolt of arousal through her. She reached for her shirt, casting her intruder a withering glare. "No pitch can win me over."

"Really? You've been based, or should I say, tied down, in Vienna for three years, I believe. You must be bored by now. Are your little concerts enough? Do you still feel the thrill in your blood, the need to hunt? What if I said the targets were exceptionally vicious and you'd be doing society a favour? These men are the worst of the worst. The challenge of just getting to them would be exciting. Can you honestly tell me what you do now is satisfying enough? Or have they tamed you, Requiem?"

As she spoke, the woman shifted to allow a view of her smooth, flawless legs, all the way up to her white panties. Requiem frowned as she gazed at the ample skin on display. Her heartbeat lifted again, but this time it was not just arousal heightening her senses.

No scars. *At all.* No wounds, nicks, or cuts.

Who the hell was this woman who seemed to have underworld connections and yet skin this flawless?

"You're just an amateur," she said with a dismissive glance. "Playing with fire. What do you know about satisfying me? How could you know? Who have you been talking to?"

"There are stories—more like legends, now—that float around Melbourne, of a female assassin, lethal and sleek as a panther. A predator who hunted, fucked any woman who crossed her, and loved the darkness. Lived it, breathed it. Killed in it."

"Sounds like a tall tale to me."

"Is that so? Shall we test that?" The woman shrugged her robe off her shoulders, dropping it to the floor, fully revealing her sheer white bra. Dark, plump nipples were clearly outlined, erect, straining beneath the silk. "Your needs would be fully catered to, of course. They would be part of the remuneration package. And if I don't meet your requirements, well, we have other women who'd greatly enjoy taking my place."

Requiem studied her, fighting her arousal. She could all too easily imagine having the woman spread before her, crying out for a release that Requiem would take enormous delight in denying her. She *should* be denied—for her presumption in thinking she set the terms. For presuming she could have any place at Requiem's table.

"You think I *need* that?" Requiem reached for her boots to hide the tremble in her fingers at the intoxicating thought. The scent of arousal was in the air, and she was only too well aware it was her own. She hardened her voice in irritation at her own weakness. "How little you know me."

The woman laughed. "You're only human, Requiem. So, back to my offer: Kills, thrills, and unmarked bills. And a pretty perk or two. No one would ever know. Discretion would be absolute on all matters." Her fingers dropped to her own breast and slid across the hard nipple, then slipped her breast out from her bra. It was as smooth, plump, and as perfect and alluring as the rest of her. Her eyes dared Requiem to be interested. Dared her to be tempted. *Dared. Her.*

So presumptuous.

But she was right about one thing—she had been restless lately. She'd never acted on it, but neither had an offer been so tempting. It would be so easy. It wasn't as though Alison would ever know. Requiem could take this job and, while she was at it, take this smug, alluring creature, and make her understand the terrible error she had made in trying to play her. Requiem's smile felt more like a snarl.

It wouldn't even be cheating—it wasn't sexual in the least. It was all about power. It was *always* about power. She was Requiem, damn it. *Requiem.* Once Australia's most feared assassin. She shouldn't have to check herself like some little housewife. Wildness burned inside her, like an animal straining to be let off its leash. Of late, her pulse often quickened at the thought of being out there, being *all* that Requiem was. The darkness was still there. You couldn't turn that off with a pretty penthouse apartment, a classy job, and a sweet woman.

Alison's face floated into mind, fresh-faced, eager, loyal. Loving.

Her lips thinned.

The other woman seemed to sense her hesitation and swayed closer. "It's been three years, Requiem," she said, her voice low and sultry. "Three years of being tied down, playing the meek cellist. And let's not forget you're now being trailed around by that little groupie. You must be tired of both by now."

Requiem froze at the mention of her lover, her breathing compressing into a faint sliver of exhalation. Alarm and rage coursed through her in equal measure.

Had this creature worked out who Alison really was? Who she'd been in Melbourne?

She frowned. They'd known her by a different first name professionally back home. A name she hadn't been interested in reclaiming when she moved here. So how could she have been recognised a world away?

Requiem thought furiously. Since settling into Vienna, Alison had changed her clothing style to sleeker, darker European fashions, and her hair had gone from a messy, brunette ponytail to an auburn pixie cut. Alison's own sister hadn't recognised her at first at the airport during their last reunion. So was it even possible for Alison to have been identified here?

No one alive in the underworld even knew of the connection between them. If this woman had managed to figure out Alison's identity, then that would be it—Requiem would end her. Immediately. Because no one threatened her mouse, or those whom Alison loved.

No one.

Decided, Requiem glanced at the three exits she'd assessed earlier, as she did every time she entered a room: the window, the air vent, the door. She calculated her options. How it could be done efficiently. How it could be done with minimal mess.

"What's her name?" the woman was saying casually, as though she hadn't just signed her own death warrant. "I've seen her. She looks adorable. Where on earth did you find her? The library? At the stage door, clutching an autograph book?" She laughed.

Requiem's nostrils flared. It was the only reaction that betrayed her enormous relief. *She didn't know. She didn't have a damned clue. Alison was safe.* Her heart reduced its manic thudding to a less furious juddering roll of a timpani drum.

"She's sweet, yes, anyone could see that, but where is the challenge?" The women smirked, heedless to the danger that had been coating the air like ash moments before. "You need letting off the domestic leash. *You* were never meant to be a pet."

She stepped right inside Requiem's space, fingers brushing her jaw, and it took every ounce of effort not to crush her for her insult to Alison. Requiem's entire focus and being went into revealing nothing at all of her emotional state.

"So what's it going to be?" the woman asked, sounding bored. "Shall we make a deal? Meet my boss? You're not the only one on my list, you know. Yes, you're at the top, obviously, but I can headhunt someone else. So are you willing? Do you wish to…fill my slot?"

Requiem gave her a stony look, the woman's charm having evaporated the moment she'd dared speak a word about Alison. She could not believe she had weakened briefly in the face of temptation. It wasn't worth it. She *knew* that. The rush that came from a power fuck was just that—hormones, highs, and control, all in a sticky mess. Ultimately meaningless.

For Alison, though, the sexual act was a different thing, entirely one of love. She saw it framed in softness, tenderness, and care. For Alison, it was never about release or power. For her, it was about sweetness, lightness, and surrendering to someone. And while Requiem did none of these things…Alison *did*. She would never brush off sex with someone else as nothing. This deal with the devil would not be nothing to her.

The woman was watching Requiem carefully. She was so close Requiem could feel her breath, smell the faint musk of her arousal. The woman arched herself forward, pressing her breasts into Requiem. Sweetening the deal, she probably thought.

Requiem leaned forward and ran her finger over the erect, bared nipple. It was soft, warm, and oh-so-inviting. Just like old times. Old times that did not have Alison in them. Requiem tapped the nipple pointedly. "I think not," she said with a cool glance and stepped back.

Because it came down to one thing: the mere thought of the crushing disappointment in Alison's eyes if she ever found out Requiem had screwed someone else, even just to teach the cocky creature a lesson, would crush the air from Requiem's lungs.

She could see Alison packing her bags and leaving, because she surely would, given she was that sort of woman. Alison was soft but substantial. Sweet but fierce. She had her pride and Requiem admired her for it, especially after a life of Alison being taught that her needs were nothing and that she was inconsequential. She'd spent most of her adult life believing that her sum worth was that of a nursemaid to her emotionally abusive, narcissistic mother.

When she had broken free, a piece of fire had entered her eyes and never left. It satisfied Requiem beyond words to see it. Women *should* know their worth. Alison knew hers. And her conditions had always been clear in agreeing to throw away her safe, respectable life and follow an unpredictable, dangerous, ex-assassin to Europe. Alison's terms had been simple—they were equals and they now belonged to each other.

The image of Alison's faith and affection flickering and dying…the look of betrayal…it would be like a dagger's stab. If anyone else had inflicted pain like that on Alison, Requiem would have torn them apart. The thought that her own darkness had allowed her to push aside the consequences even for a heartbeat filled her with dismay.

Requiem's voice was cold when she spoke. "Get dressed. You have no idea how to meet my needs. I have no interest in what you offer."

The surprise on the other woman's face was almost comical. "I don't understand. I offered you what you want." Confusion, doubt, and a hint of wariness entered her eyes. "This is what Requiem wants. *This*."

Requiem reached down and handed her back her white robe.

A protest formed on the other woman's lips, then fell, unsaid, as she looked deeper into Requiem's eyes.

The woman pulled the robe on with jerky movements. The confidence of minutes before was evaporating and, as she slid her hand around one ear to curl her hair into place, the familiarity of the gesture hit Natalya in a blinding flash.

"It's Mi Na, isn't it?" she said in surprise, and she ran her eyes over her curiously. "Nabi's sister? You were the one at boarding school while Nabi followed me around like a shadow, watching me as I learned the business. So you took over? In *all* her pursuits?" Her eyebrow lift was deliberately condescending.

How had this slip of a girl thought she could ever be as good as her assassin sister? Requiem studied her unmarked skin and bright eyes. No. There was no way she was an assassin. So what was she?

"Fuck you," Mi Na said flatly, and the intonation was exactly the same as Nabi's had once been when Requiem had shown her in vivid, naked detail the futility of trying to kill her. Worse, of trying to best her.

Mi Na narrowed her eyes and slowly reached for the CD player, turning up the volume on the gushing waterfalls and bird calls, to just short of deafening. Requiem tilted her head, watching her every move. She bounced lightly on her heels, waiting. The woman was an unarmed amateur. There was no threat. But she was curious.

Suddenly Mi Na reached for her foot and flipped her sandal over. Natalya saw the flash of metal too late.

She was fast, terrifyingly so, just like her sister had been, and slid the blade up to Requiem's throat. But Requiem had three times the muscle mass on her, and immediately wrenched her hand away and twisted her arm behind her back. She debated whether to snap it. It would be so damned easy. A nice reminder as to who Mi Na was screwing with.

But Mi Na was as fast as Requiem was powerful. She took three light steps up the wall in front of her and somersaulted over Requiem, freeing her arm the moment her body was higher than her limb. On landing, she kicked the hot-rock crock pot at Requiem, who dodged it—barely.

Scorching rocks flew everywhere, tumbling under the table, towards the walls, and at Requiem, who kicked them away. Mi Na picked up a pair of the stones in her bare hands, seemingly not even noticing their searing heat. She hissed in fury, tossing one at Requiem's head.

Requiem snapped her head away to allow it to whistle by, just as Mi Na hurled the other one. Using her forearm, Requiem smashed that away, too, ignoring the thud of pain. The rock flew straight back, slamming into Mi Na's shoulder, and she grunted.

Mi Na threw her arms out wildly. One hand connected with a small, heavy Buddha statue which she grasped in her fist. She held it up like a club, swooping it viciously back and forth through the air. She hurled it.

Requiem spun out of the way. She didn't move quite fast enough. The bronze weight thudded dully off her back, landing on a sore point. She winced. *Again* with her damn back scar?

She yanked the peace mobile down from the ceiling, just as the woman charged at her. Requiem side stepped her like a bull fighter and wrapped the mess of metal and fishing line around her neck as she rushed by. Mi Na pulled up short and jerked and thrashed as the plastic wire bit savagely into her neck, her face turning hot red.

Requiem yanked hard, as Mi Na, clawing at her throat, desperately tried to free herself. Pulling her close, Requiem leaned into her ear. "One tug and you're dead." She yanked the fishing wire a little to make her point. "You're nowhere near as good as your sister was. If Nabi had wanted it, I'd already be dead. I was aware of her many talents, and she had *so* many. I still think fondly on several of them."

Mi Na growled at the suggestiveness, designed to provoke.

Requiem smiled. The enraged often made mistakes. "So tell me, were you planning to fillet me as we fucked?" Requiem asked. "Or was this seduction routine just to whet my appetite? What you really wanted was for me to agree to meet your fictitious boss somewhere later so you could dispose of my body out of the way? Mm?"

Mi Na cried out as Requiem tightened her hold on the fishing wire. "Answer!"

The woman hissed out a "yes", pain etching her features.

"Well, points for originality. Shame about the execution."

A peace symbol was pressing into the side of Mi Na's face, creating an ironic imprint. Requiem almost laughed. "So why not kill me while I was on the table? Too messy? Harder to hide the stains?"

"With your back turned?" Mi Na said, squeezing out her words with difficulty. "You think I have no honour."

"No honour?" Requiem repeated. "You even sound like her. Who hired you? The dregs of Fleet Crew? Or someone else?"

"No one. This is for myself. For family honour."

Family honour. Requiem's grip eased. She'd been right: this silly girl was no assassin. Great. A civilian on a vengeance kick. Although Mi Na had obviously had some actual training. "Family honour? What does that even mean? Nabi and I were not enemies in the end."

"You broke her heart. She told me. You broke her. Then…I found out later you killed her. You shot her, when she was trying to protect her boss."

Requiem said nothing for a moment, picking apart the anguish in the words, like ligaments from muscles. "I never killed her." She didn't bother denying the rest. The girl's misplaced affections were hardly her fault.

"You used her! Treated her like dirt. And Sal said you killed her. It's my right to avenge her. He trained me to fight you."

Requiem sighed. *Saliya Govi.* The new head of Fleet Crew. Freshly out of jail, if her sources were right. He'd been the smartest gang member left standing when the dust had cleared after Requiem had betrayed the entire Australian underworld. She had wondered how long it would take someone to figure out she'd been the one. Of course Sal didn't know for sure, so he'd manipulated Mi Na and sent her after Requiem. No matter the outcome, his hands were clean.

Slippery little shit.

"I didn't kill your sister," Requiem said in irritation. "Sal has his own agenda. She died of her wounds when police shot her as she was trying to escape."

"Bullshit! And she didn't deserve to die in some dirty alley like she was nothing. She *mattered.* She mattered to *me.*"

A burst of scrambling and twisting resulted in Mi Na wriggling out of Requiem's grip. She let the woman go and sat back on her haunches.

Mi Na did the same and rubbed the red lines at her neck as they eyed each other cautiously, four feet apart.

"I didn't kill her, like I said," Requiem said. "Mi Na, your sister was someone I could no more kill, than she could kill me. That was our relationship. Dysfunctional and complicated, but for assassins, that counts as downright friendly."

There was a strangled, tortured noise and Mi Na brought her hands up to cover her face. Tears slid out from between her fingers as she wept silently.

Requiem stared at the emotional display with distaste, stomach plummeting. She wasn't any good at this. The failings and frailties of humanity were nothing she'd mastered, beyond how to exploit them. The adrenaline was wearing off as the threat passed. She felt the stillness inside herself, and the seeping away of the part of her that was raw, pure, and dangerous, until Requiem faded.

Natalya lowered herself in front of Mi Na and waited until she had her eye.

"I was there. I held Nabi when she died," she said evenly. "I held her when she made her peace with the universe, and made her peace with me. There was too much blood loss to save her. She died well. She was unafraid, she was strong, and I think her family would have been proud of her. I know I was. I told her so."

Tear-filled, suspicious eyes sought the truth.

"I could have killed you just now," Natalya added. "I didn't. So you know I have no reason to lie. You *know* that."

Mi Na became still, dropping her hands to her lap. Natalya could see their tremble.

"I paid top dollar to get Requiem profiled. Dropped out of med school, used all my savings." The words were a whisper, like a long-held secret, and Mi Na stared at her hands as she mumbled them. "I had to find out how to get to you, how to get you vulnerable. To understand who you are. What mattered to you. To work out what you need. What you desire. The profiler interviewed some of the women Requiem…*toyed* with.

"The report I got back said, over and over, you only want power. Power of the hunt. Power over rivals and those who challenge you. *That's* who you are. But you…you're…not her. I don't understand why you said no. What I did wrong. You *should* have said yes. He said you'd say yes."

The plaintive, confused words echoed in Natalya's head. She sighed and rose.

"Go home, Mi Na," she said, injecting menace into her tone. "Challenge me or anyone in my life again and I will be ruthless. We both know that I know where your family lives. I know your father personally. I know which hospital he's in."

Mi Na's brown eyes widened in shock.

Natalya had never let go of her informants' network for this reason. You never knew which tidbit could pay off. For instance, she had been aware that a profiler had been looking into Requiem about six months ago. His subsequent death had been convenient but, for once, unrelated to her. Requiem's were not the only toes the man had stepped on.

"Do not test me," she continued. "You would regret it for the rest of your life. Tell me that you understand that, at least?"

Mi Na swallowed and nodded.

Natalya pursed her lips. She was getting soft. Mi Na's head was bowed again, tears sliding down her cheeks, mingling with the blood from her injured nose, spattering on the floor in an ugly, sopping red mess.

Glancing around at the destruction in the room, and the human carnage on the floor, Natalya shook her head once, and slipped out the door.

Outside, she paused, wondering which way the linen closet was, and how to liberate an unconscious masseuse without anyone knowing…especially the masseuse herself.

She exhaled in annoyance, flexing her shoulders. On top of everything, now she *really* needed a massage.

Part Two: Bare

Natalya

"Hey, you're early!" Alison's voice echoed down the hall as Natalya arrived home at their two-bedroom penthouse apartment. "How come?"

"My masseuse became unwell," Natalya called back. She filed her keys on a hook behind the door and leaned down to give their slumbering, ancient red heeler, Charlotte, a scratch behind her greying ears. "We cut the session short. What's that interesting smell?"

"Come and find out."

Natalya crossed the parquetry floors, glancing at the white walls and precisely placed modern art, musical trinkets, and framed photos of Alison's family.

Pride of place in the hall was a photo of Alison, her sister, Susan, and niece, Hailey, laughing on the couch in their lounge room. It had felt so strange when they'd come to visit. At the time, Natalya had still been adjusting to having more than one voice in her life. And then suddenly there had been wall-to-wall Ryans. Adding to the surrealness, neither of them called Alison by the name she knew her. It was a dead name from a past that she and Alison didn't speak about.

Natalya had taken to hiding out on the roof of their apartment building for the solitude. "A breath of fresh air," she'd told them, as she'd made her daily escape. She'd sat up there, arms around her bent legs, watching over the city like an avenging angel.

She had even caught a burglar one day while she was up there. Natalya smirked at the memory of dangling him over the edge while he'd pissed his pants and swore in three different languages to never trouble her building again. She did miss that—showing vermin the light.

Not that she'd shared that with Alison. Her lover didn't need to know the darkness was still there. What if it frightened her? What if it frightened her *off*?

That didn't bear thinking about.

She headed further along the hall. There was nothing of Natalya here, beyond one photo of her father that gave her pause each time she saw it. It was from before Vadim had migrated to Australia, still wearing his Russian Army uniform. So proud and straight, his eyes direct and cool. She had another photo of him, secreted on the top shelf of her closet, of his wedding day to Lola. But she couldn't bring herself to hang it. The way her former stepmother had died…the way she'd lived…it was all so wrong. Twisted.

Natalya studied her father's bushy brows and lean, long face in this photo. His medals shone. She missed him. He had raised her alone for most of her life, and he had been her only connection with her past. She had been on her tour of Europe just seven months when the nursing home had called her. It had rocked her to her core, hearing of his death, even though it wasn't unexpected.

His funeral had not felt safe enough to attend. The reason lay only a few steps away. Natalya and Alison didn't discuss it, then or now. They didn't discuss a lot of things. What was the point of scraping over the past? It wasn't necessary. They had the present. They had this.

But the ache was there as she studied her father's gentle face.

"I'm making a new recipe I learned in cooking class. Here, come try it." Alison's disembodied voice sounded so excited.

Natalya smiled in spite of herself and headed to the kitchen.

Every pot and pan in existence had been pressed into service in the steam-filled room. Tomato spatters were everywhere, along with eggshells and vegetable offcuts. But all Natalya could see was one thing—the delight in Alison's shining blue eyes. Her hair was sticking up at random angles, and her nose wrinkled as she focused.

Alison held out a wooden spoon to her. Natalya inspected the tomatoey goop on it and her nostrils twitched. Didn't smell half bad. Her tongue inched out to taste it. Bold, primary flavours hit her, as onion, tomato, and garlic punched in. Then the aftertaste hit.

"How much booze did you put in this?" Her eyebrows lifted in surprise.

"Enough to give it a kick. I might have improvised that bit. Why? Did I overdo it?"

Natalya's lips twitched. "I think that could kick a donkey. It's tasty, though, aside from that."

"Damn. I wanted it to be perfect. For our anniversary."

Natalya paused and her brows knitted together. It wasn't quite two years since Alison had moved to Vienna. She remembered the date distinctively, as she did all dates, times, and places. Details were important.

"October 16," Alison supplied. "It's five years to the day that you first met me outside that experimental music club."

Ah.

"*Met*' is not quite how I remembered it," Natalya said. "I'm fairly certain breath-freshener-as-mace was used as a threat on my life."

Alison gave her a sly grin. "Well, sure, but calling it the anniversary of your stalking me because you wanted to kill me has some unsavoury connotations."

"Well, when you put it like that…" Natalya smiled and decided if Alison could whitewash those days, so could she. She winced as she shrugged out of her jacket and slid it on the back of a wooden chair at the kitchen table.

"Did you hurt yourself?"

Natalya glanced up. Alison's eyes never missed much.

"My masseuse found that scar on my back today, and decided it needed a special kind of pummeling." She wriggled and straightened her back, stretching a little. "Actually, I think she used her entire body weight on it at one point."

"Ouch," Alison said in sympathy, putting the lid on the pot and then turning the heat way down.

Natalya ran her eyes over her lover, taking in the tight jeans and blue shirt rolled up at the sleeves. She felt a familiar tightening of arousal, something she'd never stopped having for this woman. Any thoughts she might become bored with her, or of this life, were fears that had yet to come to pass.

Alison came closer and the smell of her freshly washed hair and scrubbed skin, mingled with tomato aromas, made Natalya want her even more. More than anyone she'd ever known.

What had Mi Na called Alison? A sweet little thing? Actually, she was a woman who had stopped an assassin in her tracks by just being herself.

Alison's keen, interested gaze took her measure. Something of Natalya's desire must have shown in her eyes, because Alison's cheeks warmed. "In the mood, are we?" she asked.

Always in the mood. For this, and for you.

Natalya had never used to *want* like this. But everything was different with this unassuming woman. She had redefined what Natalya's body craved. Natalya allowed a seductive smile to curl her lips, making her interest known.

Alison's lips captured hers immediately, and her tongue sought out Natalya's with enthusiasm. Alison pressed hard against her, pushing her into a wall and grasping fistfuls of clothing as she eliminated all space between them.

Natalya groaned in surprise and delight. She loved it when Alison took the initiative. Oh, Natalya always loved flinging Alison down and taking her until her body was a series of shaking, whimpering trembles. But this, this burning need, was something else. It undid her every time.

She was propelled into their bedroom, *their bedroom*—even after all this time, the shock of that still took adjustment. Natalya had been alone for so long that negotiating things like shared beds, bathrooms, and kitchens still sometimes made her itch with discomfort.

When Alison nudged open the door to their bedroom, Natalya pulled away, her eyes widening.

Red petals. On the floor. On the sheets. The music, playing on an iPod in the corner, was a string duet. Two instruments seemed to be dancing around each other, feeling each other out, flirting, seducing. Philip Glass's *Double Concerto for Violin, Cello and Orchestra*, she noted. *Duet No. 2.* How apt: a cellist and a violinist. She glanced at Alison who gave her a cheeky grin.

Alison's lips were back on Natalya's, claiming her. That magical tongue was doing things to her that were positively obscene. An approving gasp worked its way from her throat. Natalya's eyes fluttered closed and she felt her outer clothes wrenched down her body with desperation. There was little skill; it was pure need.

It brought her back to *that* day.

Their first time together. The *real* first time. Not the earlier time she'd allowed Alison to have a taste of her, a small piece as a farewell because the woman's soft eyes had pleaded for it and Natalya couldn't deny her, despite knowing it was a terrible idea. Risky. She'd held back to protect herself, but it hadn't entirely worked. She'd still given far more than she'd intended. Not all, but more. And she'd thought of little else since.

Natalya had held out for a year. Finally she had returned one night and, heart hammering in her chest, had asked Alison to return with her to Europe. It was a pivotal moment. For the first time in her entire life—a life spent toying with and controlling others—she'd kissed someone. On the lips.

It had been terrifying. And intoxicating.

Afterwards, they'd barely gotten back to Alison's apartment before they'd begun tearing clothes off each other. And then… She swallowed at the memory of a time that had left her so vulnerable she could scarcely breathe.

Alison, hair still wet from the light rain that night, had pushed her down, eyes intense and dark, and smoothed her hands all over her, mapping her naked body with a joy that seemed to come from knowing Natalya was hers. She'd touched her. All of her. For an eternity. Because she could. Because Natalya had allowed her to, as her equal.

Natalya had watched the swaying of her pale, bare breasts, revelled in the softness of her skin, as Alison's burning fingertips teased and touched all around where she most wanted it.

Natalya hadn't asked for more, or for anything, because she'd wanted Alison to take her any way she wanted. It was the most profound and hardest gift she had ever given anyone. Natalya's fingers had curled and retracted, fighting her fierce need to have control, to reclaim her power on that confronting, thrilling, terrifying first night.

Her jaw had tightened each time her body quivered—betraying its weaknesses at desiring to bend to the will of another. The apex predator side of her didn't want to want this. But, as she'd discovered after roaming Europe alone, not having this was far worse than admitting to needing it.

Natalya's skin and muscles had shone from perspiration in her efforts not to show how hard it was to be so laid bare. Beneath Alison's fervent explorations, and in those eyes watching her so intently, lay a well of desire. *This* was all Alison had wanted in order to be happy.

Even if the fight to surrender killed her, Natalya wanted to give her this night.

Alison's fingers had stroked her muscles, explored her dips and lines, teased her nipples and skidded over her ribs, before worshipping the planes from her hips down. She had laid heated lips upon her most intimate flesh, tasting her with relish. She'd brought Natalya to the edge over and over but never let her cross. Instead, those taunting lips had rushed back up to Natalya's and murmured against her mouth how much she loved this. How often she had fantasised about doing this, *exactly this*, for so long. How much having Natalya, this way, having the power, meant so much. How it had meant everything.

And then, finally, when Natalya had been gasping, on the edge again, voice and nerves raw with want, Alison had entered her for the first time. She had nudged her way between her swollen, wet lower lips with a single, long finger. Slow and gentle, with a tiny, sweet smile on her face, she'd pushed in as far and as deep as she could. And in so doing, she'd discovered Natalya's darkest secret.

Natalya had tensed because, like the kissing earlier that evening, this was not something she'd done before. Even when alone, she'd never explored much beyond the surface. Without the thrill of power, there had never seemed much point before.

Thanks to her highly active life, Natalya had no idea whether she even still had an intact "virgin's veil" as they used to call it. So she had lain there, frozen, expecting something—pain, blood maybe… Not everyone experienced these things, but still, she'd tensed, waiting for it.

Alison's shocked eyes had told Natalya the moment she'd worked it out. Because while Requiem had claimed dozens of women over the years—aggressively, powerfully, confidently—no one had ever taken Natalya.

Nabi had come closest; Requiem had indulged her more than most. But it had still meant nothing and hadn't crossed her strictest of lines—she'd never allowed such a liberty as kissing or this particular intimacy.

No one had crossed that line until Alison.

Alison had withdrawn her finger and whispered "Oh," her eyes bright with emotion.

Natalya had found no words sufficient to tell her to stop whatever that look was. How could you put a concept so big into sliced up, rearranged spreads of letters? How could you explain the threats to her body and soul that she'd experienced so young? That in order to feel strong and protected, she'd allowed no one to touch her beyond the superficial?

The act of touching others was nothing to her. Getting people off meant the power was hers, the control hers, and her invincibility was assured. But to allow someone *inside* you—in every sense—that meant something.

Alison's hand had cupped Natalya's reddening face, eyes filled with questions.

Natalya hadn't been able to explain the heat in her own cheeks. It wasn't shame. Not embarrassment. Whatever it was, it had burned across her skin, and she'd wrenched her head away. She hadn't the words for any of this.

But Alison hadn't wanted her words. Instead she had laid herself across Natalya's body, pressing her belly, breasts, and thighs against Natalya's; she'd threaded herself under and through her arms, merging with her. She'd kissed her once more. Thoroughly. Because she now could. Then she'd rocked against her.

Under those delicious, intoxicating, soft kisses that had felt like a fever to Natalya, and against the sweetness of Alison's body, rhythmically sliding against hers, Natalya had burned from the inside out. She had gradually come apart, gasping in a shuddering orgasm that, for the first time in her life, had absolutely nothing to do with power. It had to do with something else entirely. Something she hadn't been ready to think about.

*

"Where were you just now?"

Alison's voice broke into Natalya's memories, and she blinked back to the present. Her fingers drifted through the rose petals on the sheets and she glanced up. "That night together. After your concert. When I came back for you."

There was a nod, like she already knew. Maybe Natalya always had the same distant look on her face each time she thought of that experience.

Alison pushed her flat onto her back, pressing their bodies together. The weight and warmth was reassuring in its familiarity. "I've been thinking of you all day," she said against her throat between feverish kisses, "thinking of all the ways I'm going to have you. All the ways you'll *know* you're mine."

The words took a moment to penetrate the fog of Natalya's overheated brain. Her breasts were seized by hot, frantic fingers, and then a tongue and teeth asserted their claim on her.

But Natalya was still stunned. How had she known?

"They can look at you," Alison was murmuring. "All your fans, outside the Musikverein every night. All those women, all those men who want you. I see their eyes. I'm not blind. I recognise the look. I see it in the mirror every day."

Alison sucked hard on her nipple, causing Natalya's back to arch. "I see *your* eyes too," she said. There was a pause and only cold air, as her soft lips lifted off Natalya's breast.

Alison's knowing gaze met Natalya's surprised one. Her small hands were suddenly tugging at Natalya's boy shorts, pulling them down, but Natalya did not, could not, break the gaze. Alison's fingers gave one final, sharp tug, and Natalya was naked, exposed. Her arousal on display.

"I see your eyes too," Alison repeated quietly.

Natalya watched her uncertainly, even as she felt a hand dusting her source, tracing her quivers. Finding the telltale, wetness betraying her sharp need.

"And I remind myself that your fans can want you all they like, and you can appreciate them admiring you, but they're not who you chose, are they?" Alison studied her.

"No." Natalya looked at her directly.

With a nod of approval, Alison made her way down Natalya's body. She breathed hotly over her intimate flesh that was trembling to be touched, straining for attention.

Natalya closed her eyes, waiting, her breathing harsh and fast.

She felt Alison pause her inspection and heard her almost idle question. "Did you kill her? The masseuse who hurt your scar today? Because I know masseuses. Especially the expensive kind at that fancy salon you like. Unless specifically asked, they leave scars well alone. So I'm guessing that was no masseuse. I'm almost afraid to ask who she really was."

Natalya's eyes sprang open. She glanced down to find Alison watching her closely, her look hard to decipher. Natalya should have known better. It was something they both had in common—a sharp eye for details. She usually appreciated that quality in her lover.

"It was touch and go. But no. Still alive." Natalya left her tone deliberately light. Alison could take it any way she liked.

"Did you have her then?" Again there was the strange expression.

The harsh, unspoken awareness hung between them—that *this* was what Requiem did. Requiem fucked anyone who fucked with her, one way or another. Of course Alison knew that better than anyone. But in some twisted way, this topic usually fell under the category of things from Requiem's past they never discussed.

But today the past was the present. It was a reasonable question.

Natalya licked her lips. "No." She added conviction to her voice. "*No.*"

Alison's eyes glowed, and their faint glint of possessiveness, fear, and tension slipped away. Desire and warmth took their place. "Good," she said lightly, as though Natalya had merely confirmed she'd picked up milk on the way home. "And now I'm going to make you forget anyone but me."

Natalya shivered. Alison's tongue was suddenly driving between her legs, and Natalya cried out at the sensation. Her fingers spasmed and clutched at the sheets as her body was plundered by Alison's nimble tongue.

Natalya hovered between states of being as those demanding lips blew on her, pulled, licked, nibbled and claimed her. Natalya gasped as the wetness flowed from her. Inside, it felt like a wolf was howling, as though Requiem was crying out in abandonment, as Natalya twisted, moaned, shuddered, and finally came hard against the feverish mouth of the woman she had claimed as hers.

Hers.

"I feel." Natalya exhaled the words so softly, unaware she'd even said them until the blue eyes halfway down the bed blinked up at her.

"Mmm," Alison whispered against her flesh. "I know that. You pretend it's only ever with a cello in your hands, but I know better. I've seen it. Especially fear."

An objection flew to Natalya's lips at this outrage. It died at Alison's next words.

"When I told you my sister was coming for a visit." Alison's eyes danced with mirth. "Who knew even the scariest assassins have in-law anxieties?" Her look dared Natalya to deny it.

Natalya felt no desire to confirm that unsavoury little factoid. Her breath was still unsteady when she replied, "I meant that I feel love."

It was something else they never talked about. Not since that night, two years ago in the rain, when she'd gone back for her and explained she was terrible at this, that she didn't do love, but they should be together anyway.

She might not do love, but she'd felt it that night. A hint of it, a wisp, swirling around her senses, edging in, like a whisper demanding to be heard. The feeling had almost swallowed her whole when they'd kissed. The knowledge of what this thing between them might be had scared the daylights out of her. Not enough to run, though. She was no coward.

Natalya waited for Alison's reaction, a lip caught between her teeth.

The stillness between them seemed to swallow all the oxygen. The intensity stripped any amusement from Alison's eyes.

Natalya wondered if she'd made a terrible tactical error. A coldness filtered into her veins at the thought that this thing might actually be more one-sided than she'd thought. She'd foolishly exposed herself, stripped herself bare and now…

Alison's eyes softened and lit up with delight. Every emotion in her heart chased across her face. Relief surged through Natalya as Alison smiled and slithered her way up Natalya's body.

"Hey," she whispered. "I thought maybe you did. Hoped you did the way I do. But it's everything hearing it from someone who always says she doesn't do love."

Natalya's eyes fluttered closed and her lips twitched. "Well, I *don't* do love. As a rule. But apparently the rules don't apply to you. God knows, no rule in existence has ever worked in the past."

She felt the weight of Alison, solid and steady, slide across her torso. An arm slipped around her ribs, claiming her. Natalya cracked an eyelid and saw within Alison's blinding smile that addictive essence that she knew she could never give up, no matter what.

Natalya had been right, the night under that soft rain, when she'd gone back for this unexpected woman. Her little mouse. She'd sensed then what she understood now as the truth.

Love is not nothing.

To discover the story in which Alison and Natalya first met, read *Requiem for Immortals* by Lee Winter.

Other Books from Ylva Publishing

www.ylva-publishing.com

The Red Files

Lee Winter

ISBN: 978-3-96324-534-3
Length: 304 pages (103,000 words)

Ambitious journalist Lauren King is stuck reporting on the vapid LA social scene's gala events while sparring with her rival—icy ex-Washington correspondent Catherine Ayers. Then a curious story unfolds before their eyes, involving a business launch, thirty-four prostitutes, and a pallet of missing pink champagne. Can the warring pair join together to unravel an incredible story?

Under Your Skin

Lee Winter

ISBN: 978-3-96324-026-3
Length: 332 pages (111,000 words)

What do a food-delivery robot, a face from the past, and plans to microchip veterans have in common? Caustic DC bureau chief Catherine Ayers would love to know but she and Lauren King are busy wedding planning in Iowa. That means a lot of beefy brothers, a haughty cat, and a sharp-tongued Meemaw. But she's sure she can play nice. Well, pretty sure.

A twisty lesbian romance sequel to *The Red Files.*

The Brutal Truth

Lee Winter

ISBN: 978-3-95533-898-5
Length: 339 pages (108,000 words)

Aussie crime reporter Maddie Grey is out of her depth in New York and secretly drawn to her twice-married, powerful media mogul boss, Elena Bartell, who eats failing newspapers for breakfast. As work takes them to Australia, Maddie is goaded into a brief bet—that they will say only the truth to each other. It backfires catastrophically.

A lesbian romance about the lies we tell ourselves.

Breaking Character

Lee Winter

ISBN: 978-3-96324-113-0
Length: 315 pages (106,000 words)

Life becomes a farcical mess when icy British A-lister Elizabeth and bright LA star Summer try to persuade an eccentric director they're in love to win Elizabeth her dream role—while convincing a gossiping Hollywood they're not. Worse, they're closeted lesbians who don't even know the other is gay.

A lesbian celebrity romance about gaining love, losing masks, and trying to stick to the script.

Hotel Queens

Lee Winter

ISBN: 978-3-96324-457-5
Length: 319 pages (104,000 words)

At a Vegas bar, two powerful hotel execs meet, flirt, and challenge each other—with no clue they're rivals after the same dream deal. What happens now they've met their match?

An opposites-attract lesbian romance as layered, sassy, and smart as its characters.

Requiem for Immortals

Lee Winter

ISBN: 978-3-95533-710-0
Length: 263 pages (86,000 words)

Requiem is a brilliant cellist with a secret. The dispassionate assassin has made an art form out of killing Australia's underworld figures without a thought. One day she's hired to kill a sweet and unassuming innocent. Requiem can't work out why anyone would want her dead—and why she should even care.

About Lee Winter

Lee Winter is an award-winning veteran newspaper journalist who has lived in almost every Australian state, covering courts, crime, news, features, and humour writing. Now a full-time author and part-time editor, Lee is also a 2015 and 2016 Lambda Literary Award finalist and has won several Golden Crown Literary Awards. She lives in Western Australia with her long-time girlfriend, where she spends much time ruminating on her garden, US politics, and shiny, new gadgets.

CONNECT WITH LEE

Website: www.leewinterauthor.com

Sliced Ice

"Five Times Felicity Met Elena" (2021)
"Aliens of New York" (2021)
"The Brutal Lie" has been previously published in the anthology *After Happily Ever After* (2020) by Ylva Verlag e.Kfr., Germany
"Skye Storm's Invite Absolutely Everyone Ultimate Pool Party" (2021)
"The Friend" has been previously published in the anthology *Language of Love* (2018) by Ylva Verlag e.Kfr., Germany
"Number Five" (2021)
"Flashbang" (2015)
"When DC Met Iowa" (2021)
"First-Class Villains" has been previously published in the anthology *Glimpses* (2020)
"Love is Not Nothing" (2017)

ISBN: 978-3-96324-530-5

Available in e-book and paperback formats.

Published by Ylva Publishing, legal entity of Ylva Verlag, e.Kfr.

Ylva Verlag, e.Kfr.
Owner: Astrid Ohletz
Am Kirschgarten 2
65830 Kriftel
Germany

www.ylva-publishing.com

First edition: 2021

Credits
Cover Design by Adam Lloyd

www.ingramcontent.com/pod-product-compliance
Ingram Content Group UK Ltd.
Pitfield, Milton Keynes, MK11 3LW, UK
UKHW041855190726
13854UKWH00002B/918